I0674042

NEANDERTHAL DREAMS

A Stone Age Nightmare
by
Koos Verkaik

Outer Banks Publishing Group
Raleigh/Outer Banks

Neanderthal Dreams. Copyright © 2021 by Koos Verkaik. All rights reserved. Published in the United States of America by Outer Banks Publishing Group – Raleigh/Outer Banks.

www.outerbankspublishing.com

No part of this book may be reproduced in any manner whatsoever without written permission except in the case of brief quotations embodied in critical articles and reviews.
For information contact Outer Banks Publishing Group at

info@outerbankspublishing.com

This book is a work of fiction. All the characters and events in this book are not real, and any resemblance to actual events organizations or actual persons living or dead is unintentional.

FIRST EDITION – May 2021

Library of Congress Control Number: 2021935256

ISBN - 978-1-7367218-0-3
eISBN - 9780463823644

The Forgotten Melody of the Neanderthal Man

The Neanderthals—Mysteries from Our Past!

Often taken for primitive, on their broad shoulders stood a head containing a larger brain than ours.

How much Neanderthal blood runs through our veins? That's very hard to tell—but if it's there, it might influence the nature of our dreams...

It is said that the first modern men crossed with other human species—including Neanderthals—which should have had a least one positive result: a strengthening of their immune systems. Neanderthal genes were supposed to increase the chances to survive and be conducive to the success story of modern men, who swarmed to the farthest corners of our planet and even started to explore the universe beyond it.

Mysterious, sturdy, strong, magical, elusive, intelligent Neanderthal man!

Homo neanderthalensis. Named for the first-place identifiable specimens were found, in Germany, in 1856 in a limestone quarry in the Neandertal valley where the Düssel river flows.

Extinct.

Disappeared from Asia fifty thousand years ago and from Europe thirty thousand years ago. What was the reason? Different possibilities are suggested.

Food: They may have served as food for modern man. *Homo sapiens* could have hunted Neanderthals in order to eat them.

Cannibalism: They may have eaten each other, for ritual reasons or forced by hunger. This could have caused the spread of deadly diseases.

Weapons: *Homo sapiens* could have ousted them with better weapons.

Feminism: Women may have joined in the hunt and been wounded or killed in disproportionate numbers, lowering opportunities for breeding.

Numbers: Modern men were in the majority. They appeared in large numbers in the Neanderthal territories. It was an unequal fight!

Mix: It is also possible that modern men and the remaining Neanderthals merged...Skeletons have been found that appear to be hybrids of Neanderthals and Cro-Magnons, the earliest modern humans. If this crossbreeding of both types of mankind should prove to be real, there's no saying that they themselves shouldn't have been fertile as well and could have descendants.

The size of the Neanderthal brain surpassed ours. No doubt they made use of language. The Neanderthal larynx is identical to that of modern man.

It is asserted that Neanderthals had red hair and freckles.

They were social and took good care of the weaklings, wounded, and deformed members of their tribe.

Just like modern men, they made use of different kinds of makeup.

Neanderthals invented countless tools and weapons without getting the ideas for them from *Homo sapiens*.

Neanderthals grew up more quickly than *Homo*

sapiens. They lived fast and died young. Forty years was a very high age for a Neanderthal, but there are indications that some Neanderthals lived to be significantly older.

Three hundred thousand years ago, Neanderthal men already used flint drills. Little or nothing is known about their clothes, but the drills might very well have been used to work with animal skins.

They were excellent hunters, and recently scientists have discovered that they also had corn, fruits, and vegetables on their menu. This wipes the floor with the theory that they could have become extinct because of an imbalanced diet.

They buried their dead and covered the graves with flowers.

They were significantly stronger than *Homo sapiens.*

An incredible finding in Slovenia was a part of a bone flute that has to be between forty thousand and eighty thousand years old. The instrument maker was most likely a Neanderthal. The holes in the flute were drilled at the correct distances to assure harmonic tones. Maybe the flute's maker hit upon the idea when he heard the wind whistle in a hollow, broken bone that stood upright in the ground to support a tent of skin.

Neanderthal men managed to survive severe ice ages. Fire was an important ally. They warmed themselves at the fire and used it for the preparation of their food. Two hundred thousand years ago, Neanderthals inhabited an enormous territory that stretched from England to Iraq! But as *Homo sapiens* revealed himself as the stronger band leader, the Neanderthal flutist disappeared into the background, and finally his playing was no longer audible.

This book is about Neanderthal dreams, which are more special, spectacular, and interesting than ours!

Their flutes fell silent, the tones have faded away, the Neanderthals are like a forgotten melody...

Prologue

Death struck several times that day among the snow-covered limestone rocks.

A blizzard blocked the view of a Cro-Magnon man, who tried to keep his balance, leaning on his spear, when he stopped for a while to take a rest.

Dressed in fur and leather from top to toe, he looked like a battered cave bear. He peered through the small opening between his cap and the stand-up collar of his long coat. All he saw was a moving wall of snow.

Then, for a short moment only, the weather gods held their breath.

The man stared in surprise and full of disbelief into the wild eyes of a huge stag. The animal, just as scared, wanted to shrink back but couldn't get away; its left foreleg was stuck in a rock crack under the layer of snow. Its nostrils opened wide. A panicky gasp of breath crystallized in the frost. Then it lowered its head and waved its enormous, sharply pointed antlers to and fro.

Man and animal vanished from each other's field of vision as the weather gods started blowing again and restored the wall of snow. The Cro-Magnon, an experienced hunter, jumped behind the stag. The animal started to kick backwards with its hind legs. A loud roaring sounded as the stag tried to turn around and broke the jammed leg.

The spear ran through the neck, right under the jaw.

The Cro-Magnon finished off the stag and drank from the warm blood.

Then he left his prey behind and vanished into the white.

He experienced the icy cold in a pleasant way—this morning he had retired to a cave, where he had eaten from a mixture of mushrooms and plant extracts.

Now he had to go back to his tribe as soon as possible, in order to get help. It would take five or six strong men to skin the stag and cut it into pieces with sharp stone knives.

The killing of the animal had brought on a stream of adrenaline that had invigorated the hallucinating effect of the mixture. He found himself in a state of euphoria and ran, with the storm at his back, as hard as he could.

Not much later a group of Neanderthals encountered the dead stag. They understood what had happened and knew that the Cro-Magnon soon would return with fellow tribesmen. Using their knives, they appeased their hunger with huge pieces of meat. The group moved on, leaving two strong men behind to hew the bones. They wanted to take as much of the stag with them as they could carry. Making use of their enormous strength they pulled the animal's tendons apart. There was a grim expression on their almost chinless faces.

The storm lessened. It stopped snowing. Cro-Magnon hunters loomed up in the distance, starting to howl when they caught sight of the thieves.

The Neanderthal men rose to their feet immediately. They snatched lumps of meat and took flight.

But they had to drop their catch as their attackers

came closer and closer. They sank down deep into the snow, fell down, scrambled to their feet, ran along...Spears whizzed through the air and hit them. The Cro-Magnons, delirious with anger, fell on the wounded Neanderthal men and stabbed them with their stone knives. They knew themselves to be in the majority and experienced no fear. But the Neanderthals, stronger than the Cro-Magnons, didn't give up. Bleeding from different wounds they were already doomed, but still they fought back. They were of squat stature, and with their heavy bones they were massive fighting machines. One of them crushed a Cro-Magnon skull with a big bludgeon. Then a spear went deep into his heart and he fell down. The second Neanderthal man went under a short time later, covered with stab wounds.

The double murder hadn't satisfied the Cro-Magnons; they started to follow the group's tracks. One of them stayed behind to gather the discarded lumps of meat and drag their dead companion back to the place where the remnants of the stag lay.

The Neanderthal group had found shelter under an overhanging cliff. There they waited for the two men. They sat down close to each other around a small fire. With their eyes closed they tried to catch sleep and find rest in a common dream.

But at the moment they found themselves ready to enter their dream world, they became aware of the approaching danger. They jumped up and tried to escape. There were elder men and women with children in the group. Three young Neanderthal boys, no matter how strong and brave, were no match for the Cro-Magnons. Then they found the entrance to a cave and jumped inside. The last of them to reach the cave, one of the young men, was caught by a sharp knife that hit him right under the prominent brow ridge over the eye.

Moments later, the Cro-Magnons entered the cave. It was a big room, and in the semidarkness, they spotted a narrow tunnel. A short investigation told them that the tunnel went steeply down. It was too dangerous to go on. The Neanderthals had disappeared into the tunnel, and it was obvious that they were in lying in wait for them there.

They decided to go back and bring the stag to the tribe before carrion eaters got air of it.

But before they left, they rolled big pieces of rock into the cave and threw them into the tunnel. When they heard how the rocks collided with one another in the depth, they knew that they had blocked the entrance.

The Neanderthal group would never see their snow-covered territory again...

1

"It is impossible to put into words exactly what you want to say. You cannot even read between the lines. Some feelings are beyond description. Sometimes the words are on the tip of your tongue, and at the same time they are further than the mind can reach. You want to catch them, but they remain hidden forever behind the horizon. There is no such thing as perfection."

Lying on his bed in his hotel room in Las Vegas, Vic Emmett looked at the huge screen of the monitor. He saw himself and heard himself.

His head swelled into a grotesque close-up until he could only see his nose and lips and the vague contours of his eyes hid behind his sunglasses.

"That is the life of a songwriter. It is an endless quest. It is said that the ancient Egyptians learned how to summarize the words of their gods in hieroglyphics. He who was able to translate them in the right way would conjure up revelations of unknown beauty."

He was alone in his room on the twentieth story. On the ground floor, in the biggest hall of the hotel, hundreds of people from the music and film industry had gathered, and everyone there was watching the same documentary as he. That was the way it had been arranged. First a filmed impression of his life, then a show with all the artists who had made hits with his songs, and finally his own appearance on the stage.

Vic Emmett was in his late twenties and was not in the least enthusiastic about a tribute that normally was only accorded to old heroes. He felt like a puppet at his own party, dancing as Greg Albin from the record company pulled the strings. He hated it that Greg had forced him into a role in which he had to act himself:

"You are the loner who stays in his room while we are having a ball with all our guests. Only after all your hits have been sung by others will you come on. You wear your sunglasses and act indifferent, as if it isn't all about you at all. You don't make a speech; you only mutter a word of thanks. And then the best musicians, who know all your songs by heart, are ready for you."

"Which makes me into a Vic Emmett who imitates Vic Emmett."

"What do you want, then?"

"That you cancel everything. I don't like to be on stage, I prefer to keep in the background."

"Which will explain your late arrival, your indifference, and your muttering. We have taken care of the rest. We tickle the press and make a beautiful recording of the entire happening."

The Vic Emmett on the monitor pulled off his sunglasses to wipe the tears from his eyes. He was six years younger there. His hair was longer, and he was even leaner than now. For the first time since the unexpected death of his girlfriend he was talking to the press, and he couldn't keep his emotions under control any longer. Then the black glasses covered his light-brown eyes again.

"Rita had never used drugs before," he heard himself say. "We had such beautiful plans for the future. It will always remain a mystery to me why she went out that evening with Ken Canning. They cannot tell me any more. My God, an overdose...She had met him because I had written a song for him. How I wish I never wrote that song."

"And that song was to become a hit, largely due to the tragic circumstances surrounding it," a voice sounded, while the song in question sounded in the background. "The text was gloomy, almost sinister. From that day on, Emmett wrote more and more intensively about the dark sides of life."

There were shots of him and his girlfriend, of Canning and his band, and then, all of a sudden, there were trembling fragments from a film that showed his father and mother during a holiday in France long ago.

"Death also struck in an earlier stadium of Vic Emmett's life," the voice continued. "He was only fifteen years of age when his parents ..."

Vic switched off the monitor and sprawled in his easy chair. He couldn't stand it, that the death of his dear ones was used over and over again to give him the image of a songwriter who took strength from misfortune and managed to carry on in a pool of misery. He considered his life as a flash in the darkness, and like countless other creative spirits he intended to use that short period to erect a monument for himself that stood there long after he was dead and gone; his song texts were the stones of his imaginary structure.

Only a few moments ago he had heard himself say:

"Some feelings are beyond description. They remain hidden forever beyond the horizon."

It was his biggest wish to put the ultimate song text on paper and so make the impossible possible.

Up to now he hadn't been successful in that at all, and therefore he asked himself time after time why he was honored today as if he had achieved something special.

After some time he switched on the monitor again. The documentary had finished, and he saw a live impression of what was going on in the big hall of the hotel. While he watched the performances of different artists and listened to the music, he wondered why so much money had been put into this event. He was not a star of such a caliber that he deserved a tribute of this magnitude. That knowledge made him uncertain. From the moment that Greg Albin had submitted his plans for this day to him, he'd had the feeling that the man was trifling with him.

In the big hall, top musicians raised his compositions to a high level, but the music sounded stale to his ears. These were no masterpieces.

There was a knock on the door. A bodyguard opened the door from the outside and let in a waiter, who entered bearing a number of snacks. Vic already had an extensive meal laid out in his room. Then Greg Albin appeared in the company of a journalist and a camera crew. All of a sudden the room was packed with people from his management and others milling around whom he had never seen before.

Greg was a big, stout man with bristly sideburns and stiff, short curls.

"The atmosphere there is perfect," he said, pointing at the monitor. "When you throw money about in Las Vegas, everything becomes possible. What do you do with a couple of hundred guests after a turbulent party? No one has to leave the building—everyone sleeps right here in the hotel!"

Nobody could see Vic's eyes grow big behind the dark glasses.

After some time everyone disappeared again and Vic was taken along to a cloakroom on the ground floor. Jack Hamilton, his manager, introduced him to some special guests who had been promised they would get the chance to have a talk with him and get photographed together with him.

"This is Alice Wilkerson from Canada. Mallory Lee from Kentucky, Joe and Silvia Keller ..."

Vic shook hands, exchanged brief politenesses, and posed for the photographers.

Not much later he let himself be carried along like a boxer on his way to the ring, through a labyrinth of corridors. He began to feel anxious. Mike Brewer came walking next to him. Mike was one of his few friends, a kind-hearted man who had produced most of his records.

"Good luck, Vic," he said.

They went around a corner and came into a broad corridor where a camera team was waiting to accompany them to the hall.

"What a waste of money," said Vic in a soft tone, so that only Mike could hear him.

Mike remained walking next to him and shrugged his shoulders. He turned his head and came so close to him that Vic could feel his beard prickle in his ear.

"What does it matter? Don't think about it. I heard that everything was paid for by Jacques Poiron, so that will be all right, won't it?"

Vic stopped abruptly and almost immediately everyone around him stood still as well; only Greg Albin and a bodyguard, who led the way, walked on with large strides. Vic's world began to spin. Jacques Poiron was his grandfather; Vic's real name was Victor Poiron, but he had adopted his mother's surname deliberately to avoid being associated with old Jacques, the fabulously rich French businessman.

He managed to control himself and started to walk again.

"I don't believe I was supposed to tell you that," sounded the voice of Mike Brewer. "I'm sorry, Vic. I should have kept my big mouth shut. I can imagine how you feel right now."

"So how do I feel?" asked Vic, his lips hardly moving.

There was a cameraman right in front of him who walked backwards with long strides.

"Rotten. Don't let it worry you. This is Las Vegas. The false jewels sparkle here, and the only rough diamond is you!"

Another corner, another corridor. At the end of it high doors opened. Excited voices sounded, and cheers went up. The band of gifted musicians began to play. It was, of all numbers, an instrumental version of the first song he had written after the deaths of Rita Cianello and Ken Canning.

The corridor seemed endlessly long. To Vic Emmett, the searching poet, it was as if time slowed down.

Every step he took brought on a new stream of thoughts.

A new future for his parents in America. A heavy quarrel over the telephone between his father and his grandfather. The wild ride after that in an old Chevy. His father behind the wheel; his mother next to him in front; he, their only child, on the backseat. The fatal accident. He was the only one who survived.

Another step.

He could guess what Greg Albin was going to say.

"You're the only one who's making a fuss about it. For what purpose? An outsider gives money to make your star shine. That's good for you, and that's good for me. Money is money, and a fat lot I care about who's the generous giver."

The next step.

The music stopped. A muttering rose. He thought about his manager Jack Hamilton's remark:

"What the hell is the matter with you? Make the most of your opportunities. It was your own choice to become an artist, and now you have to give the people what they are asking for. Just be grateful for the fact that there is someone out there who's willing to put money into your career."

"The true song hasn't been written yet," he thought, and compressed his lips into a grim stripe.

Then he entered the hall and climbed the steep stairs to the stage. He was welcomed with a burst of cheering, and even his dark sunglasses could not protect his eyes against the countless spotlights that followed him.

A loud and clear voice announced him as the composer and songwriter who preferred to stay in the background and only rarely performed his own songs himself; this was one of those unique opportunities to hear the young master sing and play. The words that followed were drowned in the cheers of the wild audience.

And he stood there wishing he was somewhere else.

Someone gave him a guitar. Musicians slapped him on the back. He walked up to a microphone and muttered a word of thanks.

He started to play an intro that immediately was recognized by everyone.

The band joined in.

Introvert as he was, he paid no attention to his surroundings and concentrated on the music.

That evening Vic Emmett played and sang nine numbers.

They were almost perfect.

* * *

Vic woke up in the big hotel bed and looked at his watch. It was half past nine in the morning. To the left of him lay a girl of about twenty. She pushed herself against him, and her hand rested on his chest. Her long blond hair hung down across her face. The woman at his right was a couple of years older than himself. She had short brown hair and lay on her side with her buns against his thigh. Last night Greg Albin had sent them both to his room.

When there was a knock on the door for the second time, he realized that he had woken up from the first knock. He carefully moved to the edge of the bed, stood up, and walked to the door. He turned the key to the left and opened it. Mike Brewer, a head taller than himself, looked down on him. He'd perceptibly had little sleep. His screwed-up eyes were red. Nervously, he stroked his beard.

"Can I have a talk with you, Vic?"

"Come in," said Vic, stepping aside.

Usually Mike would have made fun of Vic's nudity or made remarks about the two sleeping women on the bed. Now, however, he took a seat, heaved a sigh, and stared in front of him while Vic went to the bathroom to brush his teeth and shower. Vic wore a white bathrobe when he entered the room again. He sat down on a chair opposite to Mike.

"I believe I'm a servant of the devil himself," sighed Mike. "I am the messenger of evil. No doubt you remember what I told you yesterday, right before you went on stage..."

"Of course. Jacques Poiron paid for it all."

"I picked the wrong moment to tell you. Well, I guess every other moment would have been wrong as well, but still . . . right before your appearance . . . there was no way out for you, and you had to climb that stage and sing. First of all I will give you my compliments for the fact that you took it so well and did such a fantastic show."

"The devil. Messenger of evil."

Mike plucked at his beard with ten fingers.

"Greg instructed me to tell you. I kept putting it off and then, all of a sudden, I blurted it out. Greg wanted to know how you would react when you heard that your grandfather had put down so much money to make your star rise. The documentary about your life was broadcast yesterday by a bunch of different stations."

"I didn't know about that."

"I tell it to you now. In friendship. Please, don't stop believing in my implicit affection for you, Vic. The commercial stations have received money for the broadcasting. It has been in all the newspapers that have always been kept away from you. You know that the entire show was filmed as well, yesterday. As soon as it is edited, it will be broadcast as well by the same stations."

Vic shrugged his shoulders.

"All right. I thought it strange from the beginning that something that grand was organized for me. Now I know who's behind it. I don't think I will trouble myself about it. It has already happened, it is already a thing of the past. Greg Albin and Jack Hamilton will repeat that I will only gain from it."

"There is more. It doesn't end here. This time Greg sent me to you to tell you something else."

Vic looked at him with a frown.

"I've known you quite some time, Mike. Never ever worry about our friendship. Are you really that nervous?"

"Well, yes!" he cried out in despair.

The two women on the bed woke up with a start. Leaning on their elbows, they stared around the room. Then they sank back, turned to each other, embraced each other, and closed their eyes again.

"I know you are not exactly commercially minded, Vic," said Mike. "Try to understand what I am going to say. There is a certain proviso in your contract with Jack Hamilton. Being your manager, he is qualified to make you change record companies if this will be evidently to your advantage. In a case like that you have no right of veto."

"I am well off with Greg Albin's MultiRec, aren't I?"

Mike stared at the ceiling and took a deep breath through his mouth.

"You are sold, Vic. There is nothing you can do about it. It has already happened."

"Why? To whom?"

"I will tell you. To start with your second question: to the French Disque Dragon. A brand new company. And I wouldn't be surprised if it had been set up especially for you. Your grandfather has everything to do with it. He must be very fond of you, or perhaps he needs you badly for something, for if I have to answer your first question..."

"Why..."

"Yes. I know nothing about your grandfather's motives. But Greg and Jack are only doing this for the money. None of you ever had to complain about money, but now you can all consider yourself to be rich."

Vic said nothing and frowned for the second time.

"All three of you get the same amount. Thirty million dollars for the record company, thirty million dollars for the management, thirty million dollars for you ..."

Mike added a long row of curses to it.

"It's only you who are being transferred. All the artists who were present to pay homage to you yesterday will remain under contract with MultiRec. Your grandfather has pulled ninety million dollars out of his hat, and I was given the doubtful honor of being the one to tell you. Of course I will proceed with my work as a producer for MultiRec, so this will also be the end of our cooperation..."

He stood up. His tired eyes had become moist.

"Tonight there will be a gathering in a restaurant somewhere here in Vegas. Greg and Jack will be there, and then someone from Disque Dragon, and you, of course. You will hear more about it soon. Well, I don't know if I have to congratulate you now or not..."

"Me neither," reacted Vic. "In all fairness I have to admit that I don't know what is happening to me."

Mike walked to the door.

"Of all artists, I preferred to work with you, Vic. I think you know that. I was always very happy to help you on your search for perfection."

"Yes, I know that very well, Mike." He tried to smile. "Don't you think you can get rid of me that easily."

As soon as Mike had closed the door behind him, Vic rose to his feet and took off his bathrobe. With big steps he went to the bed, with the firm intention to do what he'd been too tired for last night. They welcomed him with open arms. The blond girl looked at him with sparkling eyes.

"I thought I was still dreaming when I heard about all that money," she said. "I think it will be just terrific to lay someone who has become thirty million richer at one go!"

"This is Las Vegas," said Vic. "If you only stay here long enough, you will see that happen again to someone else—no doubt about that."

They both laughed.

As he started to caress her, he felt the dark haired woman press herself against his back. Not much later the blond girl really thought he did it so well because Fortuna, the goddess of luck, had given him strength. The truth was, however, that Vic Emmett had grim thoughts with every push.

"Everything happened unknown to me!"

"Too cowardly to inform me!"

"They sent Mike to tell it to me."

"Jacques Poiron! I don't even know him."

"Thirty million—thirty million—thirty—"

She came earlier than him. He turned on his other side and looked into the dark eyes of the second woman.

2

That afternoon he gave interviews in his hotel room and received several artists who wanted to see him before they left Las Vegas. He made music with them and ordered food and drinks for everyone. Greg Albin and Jack Hamilton didn't show themselves. Someone from the management called to say that there would be a limousine ready for him at eight to drive him to the restaurant where the gathering would take place.

Two hours before eight he asked his last guests to leave and he himself went out searching for Mike. Mike was not in his room. Vic found him in the casino, feeding coin after coin into a slot machine. It was crowded in the casino, and most of the visitors had been present at last night's show. Everyone wanted to have a talk with Vic, and he had hardly any time to say something to Mike, but he managed to make clear to him that he wanted him to come along to the meeting.

Right after eight they were sitting together in the back seat of the promised limousine. Mike was still looking tired. He hadn't only gambled that afternoon, he'd also drunk a lot.

"Why do you want me to be there?" he asked, looking

around in surprise as if he only now realized that he was on the road.

Mike was at his best when he sat at the controls in a studio, where he drank coffee instead of whiskey and made artists rise above themselves. He was a terrific producer and earned a reasonable salary working at MultiRec.

Vic looked outside through his sunglasses and the dark side window. It was still broad daylight, but to him it looked as if the lights had gone out in late-night Vegas.

"I don't know yet where this new situation will lead to and where I will end up," he said. "Together we've come quite some way. Perhaps it would be better to go on together."

Mike began to swear.

"That would be great, Vic. Simply great.'

There was a silence. Mike opened the little bar of the limousine and took out a small bottle of whiskey. He unscrewed it and placed the small neck between moustache and beard.

"Your grandfather," he said then, musing. "What kind of a man is he?"

Vic shrugged his shoulders.

"I never met him, so there are no personal memories. It seems that he has been an inconspicuous man for a long time, with a huge interest in history, anthropology, archaeology, and paleontology. Fascinated by our distant ancestors, the Cro-Magnon people. A quirk that went from father to son. My father bought and read countless books about it, and now I have them all. I even bought more piles of books to keep informed about the latest developments. My grandfather worked hard, and as an amateur archaeologist he put all his money in excavations. Then something happened that completely changed him. He abandoned his family. There was a divorce. My father stayed with my grandmother till he married and emigrated to America. In the meantime Jacques Poiron became a man of consequence in the business world. In a short while he managed to gather fabulous riches. The only two things connecting us are the French language that my father taught me and our common interest in prehistory. It seems as if it's in our genes; my father was a professor of archaeology in various universities. For the rest my grandfather is a mystery to me."

"Suddenly he is interested in you."

"That is a fact, yes. I have no idea what he means to do with me."

Just as on the day before, he thought back now to the fatal accident with the Chevrolet in which his parents were killed.

"Anyway," he continued, "it's a crying shame that Greg Albin and Jack Hamilton allowed themselves to be bribed behind my back and have yielded to the temptation of big money. I have learned their true nature, and we will all go our own ways. As far as that is concerned, I can be reconciled to it. After tonight I will never see them again. If you are going to get yourself another little bottle of whiskey, give me one as well."

Mike nodded and opened the little bar.

"Let's drink on the future, Vic!"

At the restaurant, a waiter led them to a separated area. Greg Albin and Jack Hamilton were already there and sat at a table in the company of a very pretty young woman. She had sky-blue eyes. She had put up her hair. As soon as she noticed Vic, she stood and walked up to him. He could look her straight in the eye, for she was almost as tall as he. After having introduced herself as Régine Moret, she said in French:

"They don't understand a single word of French. I am sorry that everything went so quickly and that things were arranged without your knowledge. Don't blame anyone for that. I promise you everything will turn out just fine. From now on you shall want for nothing. Always keep in mind that I'm on your side."

She made a gesture to the table and continued in English:

"Please join us. I am managing director of Disque Dragon. The money in question has already been deposited into your account."

She led Vic to a seat at the head of the table and seated herself to his right. To his left sat Greg and Jack, and Mike took the empty seat next to her. For a moment she put a hand on Mike's the shoulder and said, looking at Vic:

"You heard the news from your best friend..."

"After the matter was already settled," said Vic.

Jack Hamilton nervously rubbed his bald head.

"I'm very sorry, Vic. I would have loved to go on with you for years on end. But this was an offer I simply couldn't refuse."

Greg Albin backed him up.

"We let you go with pain in our heart, you may rest assured of that."

Vic decided not to react to that and ignored both men. He leaned back in his chair and waited till the waiters had filled the glasses with red wine.

Then he said:

"Since so much money has been thrown about, Régine, I propose that we round up the amount to a hundred million dollars. I want Mike Brewer to leave MultiRec without the slightest problem. See to it that he gets ten million dollars to go on as a independent producer."

Mike made a grab at his glass and lifted it to take a good swig. Then he decided that it was impolite to drink first, and he put it back on the table.

"Are you willing to let Mike go?" Régine asked Greg.

"If that is what Vic wants, yes . . . yes, then Mike is free to leave our company."

"Good. That is settled then," said Régine. "Mike gets his ten million."

Now she raised her glass.

"There's noting you can't get here in Vegas," she said. "Especially for this gathering I have ordered a wine from the region where Vic's grandfather and father were born. A very tasteful Bergerac from the department Dordogne. I drink to a golden future for everyone here, including myself, and especially for Vic."

She pursed her lips. It was almost as if she kissed the glass. For a moment she closed her eyes.

"A taste full of promise, if you ask me," she said with a

sigh.

Mike's hand was trembling so much that the wine dripped into his beard as he raised the glass to his lips.

"Ten million!" he said, slowly shaking his head. "And it was arranged in a few seconds."

"We'll keep on working together, Mike," said Vic. "No matter what happens." Then he turned to Régine and asked, in French: "Is it proposed that I come to live in France? Don't let yourself be misled by my behavior. I'm only checking myself because I don't know at whom I should be the most angry. My grandfather is behind all this, and at this point I don't understand a thing about his intentions. He's understood very well that money can buy everything. Those two men here are the living examples. What am I expected to do? Why is Jacques Poiron flinging that much money about?"

"It is true that you are expected in France," Régine answered in French. "It is up to you to decide if you want to stay there or not. All I can say here and now is that your grandfather needs you. The old Mr. Poiron can permit himself quite a lot. What you call flinging money about is no more than small change to him. By the way, he urged me to bring over his kind regards to you. He knows much about your career and says that you will find the ultimate, perfect text you are looking for so eagerly. Thanks to him ..."

"But . . . could you please be a little more specific?"

"I prefer to continue in English," she said, looking at him with a smile, and then looking around the table. "Let's order something special. After dinner we could try our luck in a casino. I will pay for everything for all of you, so actually you cannot lose anything at all..."

Mike Brewer didn't feel like eating. The others enjoyed a good meal. Greg Albin and Jack Hamilton did their utmost to make clear to Vic that they were his best friends and longed to continue the friendship forever.

"When someone puts so much money on the table for a relative," said Greg, "who are we to not make the deal?"

"I wasn't associated with it at all," Vic remarked. "To you I was nothing but merchandise, like a load of scrap iron or a secondhand car. Let's not mention it anymore. When we go out gambling in a little while, my dear friends, I propose that you'll go another casino than I..."

He went on eating, mulling over Régine Moret's last remark about his search for the ultimate text. Suddenly he wondered why he was no longer hearing the voice of Mike Brewer. He looked up from his now empty plate and saw that Mike had sunk down against the back of his chair and had closed his eyes.

Tiredness and booze had taken its toll.

He had fallen asleep.

"Ten million for his dream," grinned Vic.

"Dreams are worth much more than that," responded Régine, and then she covered her mouth with her hand as if her own words had frightened her.

Vic didn't notice it and wouldn't remember it either when he actually had met his grandfather and had more to do with dreams than he ever could have expected.

During dessert Mike sank forward, crossed his arms on the tabletop, and rested his head on them. When it was time to leave the restaurant, he was awakened and taken back to the hotel in a limousine.

Vic and Régine went outside. It was late. There was artificial light in a thousand colors with a dark sky above it.

"Do you know you way around here?" asked Régine.

"What for?" said Vic. "If you want to get rid of your money here, it doesn't matter which door you open..."

3

From the outside, Castle Ricard still looked like the ruin it had become after its destruction at the beginning of the seventeenth century. The round, white-plastered main tower had been preserved the best and stood there like a huge candle inside the crumbled walls. The foundation, made of enormous square pieces of rock, had been laid hundreds of years earlier to the order of a long-forgotten nobleman.

On the inside, Ricard had been totally rebuilt to the ideas of its present owner, Jacques Poiron. It counted more than forty rooms. It stood on a bend of a river in the French department of Dordogne and was surrounded by rocks.

Time laughed at a building of medieval origin; in this region the history of mankind went back tens of thousands of years further; Neanderthal and Cro-Magnon men had left behind traces of their existence in countless places. Here the rivers had ground deep clefts in the porous limestone, and fissures and caves had come into being that had been ideal hiding places for humans and animals.

One day, two months before Vic Emmett's gig in Las

Vegas, Jacques Poiron opened a door of the castle and stepped outside. He had enjoyed a light lunch of bread and different kinds of cheese, and as always he had drunk a glass of red Bergerac. With his hands behind his back he walked through the park that surrounded Ricard and went down a steep path to the river.

He was slender, with hazel-brown eyes and a narrow forehead. Photos from the time he was still a young man showed the spitting image of his grandson Vic Emmett in old-fashioned clothes. And one day Vic would look exactly like the old man who walked here along the river.

Jacques remained standing for a while at the edge of the river and looked over his shoulder to the castle. He wondered where his two dogs Roc and Arnoud were; they usually came running up to him with wagging tails when he went for a walk. They'd probably had their meal recently, too, and now lay sleeping in the shadow somewhere. It was a hot day.

He went on and reached a part of the park where old oaks stood and then continued along a sloping ridge overgrown with juniper bushes.

No one could see him from the castle.

Here the old man suddenly started to hop.

The leather soles of his shoes softly ticked on the stone path, and every now and then he turned around elegantly or made long leaps. Light-footed as an elf, he moved on. His slender fingers stroked the thick, moss-grown roots of an oak that grew on the ridge. He made a bow to a big stone and waved to the left and to the right as if he greeted creatures that were only visible to himself.

Old Jacques Poiron laughed without a sound, jumped, and turned around and around. A moist glitter came into his eyes. He pulled up his knees high and spread his arms. Every now and then he took a few steps backward and then turned around and around again before going on. There was a certain pattern in his movements, and his flexibility made it clear that he had practiced them many times. It looked as if he were performing a ritual dance.

Not far from the river stood a wooden bench. He hopped toward it, sat down, leaned backward, crossed his arms, and stretched his legs. This was the destination of his short walk. He sat here as often as he could, after twelve, after lunch.

As he stared out over the water, the glitter quickly disappeared from his eyes. Their light brown irises grew dim. He barely moved—only his breast rose and sank, hardly visible under the jacket of his dark suit.

It looked as if he had gone into a trance.

Behind him a figure moved in the shadows of the high ridge. A man in a black rubber wetsuit came up to the bench. The tight rubber cap and the big diving goggles made his face unrecognizable. Hidden under a bush at the foot of the ridge lay a small harpoon gun with which he had shot and killed the watchdogs when he had come out of the water and they ran up to him barking. There was a sharp knife in his hand. As soon as he had reached the old man he stooped behind him, flung an arm around his neck and pushed the knife under his jaw and against his Adam's apple.

"Keep quiet," he whispered. "Before long you'll get plenty of time to talk. If you start to scream, I'll cut your throat. I have a serrated knife. Make me angry and your head will fall to the ground..."

Jacques did not move.

He continued to stare straight out in front of him.

"All right," said the man in the wetsuit after a pause. "I think you understand me. You sit here every day. I have been watching you. You perform a strange dance and then you sit down here. Jacques Poiron, one of the richest men in France, behaves like a little child when he fancies himself unobserved. What are you actually? A childish genius? Well, make no answer to that. I have more important questions."

The grip around Jacques's neck slackened. The knife remained pricking his Adam's apple.

"I thought that the lord of a castle would have blue blood, but what I see trickling down your neck is red. Listen to me, you old fool. You can save your skin by telling me what I want to know. You have built yourself an empire by making choices. The right choices, time after time. You work magic with shares, with purchases and sales, you sell good advice for lots of money, you pile up millions on millions, you're a magician who's able to make gold out of old iron. No one knows how you manage to do it every time, again and again. Tell me your secret, and I will spare your life."

The sharp serrations of the blade slid along the neck of the old man and left a dark stripe behind on the white skin.

"Now let me hear your voice. Your secret, Poiron! You have a formula that never fails. It is as if you always knows what the future will bring. Now that knowledge is worth a life. Yours. Or is it such a big secret that you are wiling to die for it? You didn't lose your voice, did you?"

Jacques remained silent.

The knife slid up and down and opened the skin.

"I already acquired a taste for killing when I shot down your dogs. They will never bark again. Your predictions always come true. You seem to know beforehand which shares will come up and which will go down. But you couldn't foretell your own death...Still not going to speak? Very well. There are other ways to make you talk."

The knife was taken away. The man caught hold of him, lifted him from the bench, and dragged him to the river. Jacques did not struggle. He was pushed into the water and forced to sit down on his knees. Two strong hands pushed him forward and held his head under water. Only after fifteen seconds was he pulled up again. The attacker did not notice that Jacques did not spit out water nor gasp for breath.

"That was not long enough, I guess. There is a big chance that you will choke the next time. Or is there something you want to tell me? You snap your fingers and it starts to rain money. Pass on your knowledge, old man! Even if I should let you live today, you never know at your age if you will still be here tomorrow..."

Still Jacques did not react.

For the second time his head was pushed under the water.

The man in the wetsuit slowly counted to thirty. Then he pulled up the head of Jacques Poiron by the gray hair, and this time he was frightened because there still was no reaction at all. He leaned forward and turned the head of the old man to one side. Through the glasses of the diving goggles he looked into the dim eyes of his victim.

"My God, man, you're not dead, are you?" he whispered.

Now he started to shake Jacques vigorously.

"Say something to me! Let me hear your voice!"

For a second time he looked into the eyes of the old man. Seized by panic, he let go of him, waded further into the river until his feet no longer touched the bottom, and dived under.

The stream had already taken him along quite some way when he came above the surface again. With long strokes he swam to the other side, clambered onto the rocky bank, and disappeared, without looking back, between a group of trees.

In the meantime Jacques Poiron's eyes had gotten back their luster.

He was still sitting in the water, and it looked as if it only dawned on him now what had happened to him. Then he stood up and staggered back to the wooden bench, where he found the knife.

Later that day the police would also find the harpoon gun.

In his soaked suit the old man began to climb the path along the ridge.

"My dogs!" he muttered. "Roc! Arnoud!"

He touched his neck. His fingertips became red with blood.

While he had been hopping and dancing around just a while ago, he was walking slow now and panted with every step. Tobias Dupont, his chauffeur, had just come back from a drive to Les Eyzies and was walking to a side door of the castle with a cardboard box in his hands when he saw Jacques stumbling along. Immediately he put the box on the ground and ran up to his employer.

"Mr. Poiron! What happened to you?"

"Tobias, go and look for the dogs," responded Jacques.

"I think I'd better bring you inside first," said the chauffeur and then repeated his question: "What happened?"

Ten minutes later the doctor was present and after a quarter of an hour the police had arrived, starting an extensive investigation. The scratch on Jacques's throat wasn't anything serious and after he had taken a bath and changed clothes, he was looking fine again. He received police inspector Martin Legrand in one of the period rooms of the castle and offered him a glass of wine.

Legrand, a big man in his early forties, sat down gingerly on the edge of an antique chair and hardly dared to move when he heard the wood crack. The men raised their glasses and before the inspector was able to ask a first question, Jacques had already begun to talk.

"I have already spoken to one of your colleagues, who made notes. A man in a wetsuit seriously threatened me. He completely surprised me. I did not recognize him, and I never heard his voice before. I was most upset. I loved my dogs so dearly..."

"Someone like you should protect himself better," said Legrand. "Think about buying yourself some well-trained watchdogs as soon as possible...Seriously threatened...Could you tell me more about that, please?"

"The man said that I was able to read the future and know exactly what has to be done to make lots of money. He demanded that I tell him my secret—otherwise he would cut my throat. Later he dragged me into the river and pushed me under. Being almost choked to death for a couple of times should make me talk. He expected that I would tell him then what he wanted to know so badly..."

Legrand did not only feel uneasy because his chair cracked with every move he made. He was sitting face to face with one of the most powerful men of France, who owned large parts of this region. The big villas right outside the grounds of Ricard were occupied by Poiron's business partners. He had landed estates and woods, owned hotels, houses, and companies. Never before had he set foot in this imposing castle, never before he had spoken with Poiron or even shook hands with him. To him he had always been a living legend, and now he was here to find out how it had been possible for someone to make an attempt on his life. There was something he didn't understand, and he had to ask a strange question.

"You did not tell him what he wanted to know," he carefully remarked.

Jacques shrugged his shoulders. "What should I have told him?" He gave the policeman an inquiring look.

"That is only for you to know . . . or for nobody," responded Legrand, and then he came up with his important question.

"How did you manage to escape from your attacker?"

A shiver ran down the inspector's spine. Rumors were going the rounds in the little towns and villages making Poiron out to be an eccentric, a mystical fool who performed complicated dances and greeted creatures that remained unseen to everybody else, who talked to stones and trees.

The men drank from their wine. Then Jacques said:

"How could I remain silent and escape from death at the same time? I simply don't know. It will always remain a mystery, Legrand, till you find the offender and ask him the same question. It looked very much as if something scared him. All of a sudden he let go of me, ran further into the river, and dived under. Believe me, I find this just as odd as you do, but it is a fact that his sudden flight has saved my life."

Legrand nodded.

"We will do our utmost to find the offender. All we know for now is that he is tall and slender. That is what you have told my colleague. And then we have the knife and the harpoon rifle. Perhaps we can find out where these weapons were bought and by whom. Was it a one-man action by someone who thought he could make money quickly, or was the man instructed by someone else? Do you have enemies, Mr. Poiron?"

"I don't think so. I hope not...In the business world they say that money attracts money. Maybe in the underworld they say that money attracts criminals."

"We policemen say exactly the same," said Legrand, and for the first time since he had sat down he managed to produce a smile.

Then he rose to his feet, emptied his glass, and put it on a table.

"It will take some time till my men have combed the park thoroughly. If one of them has some questions, I hope you are willing to answer them..."

"Yes, of course."

"I will occupy myself with this case, and I will inform you immediately when there is any news. I am relieved to see that you have escaped with only a few scratches, and I hope you will be able to sleep quietly tonight. I really meant it when I mentioned well-trained watchdogs—and you should get yourself a bodyguard."

Jacques stood up too and shook hands with the police inspector.

"You are right. Ricard is burglarproof and I have always counted on the protection of my chauffeur, Tobias Dupont. No one ever stopped to think that I could come into danger in the park. From now on we will keep that in mind. Goodbye for the present, and thanks very much for your help so far."

"Don't mention it, Mr. Poiron. The police are always at your service."

The inspector made a light bow and walked to the door. He went through a long corridor, and the front door was held open for him by Tobias Dupont.

Jacques Dupont was an old man who kept a big secret. When he stood at the grave of his dogs the next day, in a corner of the park, he decided to get something organized about which he had already been thinking for a long time.

He wanted to see his grandson Vic Emmett.

4

Inspector Martin Legrand wondered how it could be that the old man had behaved in such a calm way when he talked to him just a moment ago. He had expected Poiron to be in panic or in any case nervous and frightened. There had been an attempt on his life; someone had attacked him on his own territory, put a knife on his throat, almost drowned him, killed his dogs with arrows...And Poiron had told him about the events calmly, short and to the point, over a glass of good wine.

He drove his old police car, a Citroën, slowly over the drive that cut through the grounds, waving at some policemen who were still at work there. The wrought-iron fences at the entrance were opened by a police officer. Legrand waved at him and drove along.

Here, at both sides of the road, stood the villas of Poiron's business partners. In popular speech this area of the little town of Saint-Milles was called the Golden Street. So many curious people had gathered here that he was forced to stop. Nadine Aron, editor in chief of the local newspaper, knocked on the side window and he rolled it down. Next to her appeared Armand and Claire Laurin, who lived in one of the villas.

"What exactly happened, Martin?" asked Nadine. She leaned with her hands on the door. She had short, bleached hair and the sunburnt skin of her face showed wrinkles at the eyes and the corners of her mouth. "I saw the doctor leave, and I know that there are still policemen in the park."

"Has something happened to Jacques?" Claire Laurin wanted to know.

"Everything will be all right. Why don't you come to the office later, Nadine?"

Before she was able to answer, Armand Laurin knocked on the roof of the Citroën.

"If the both of you want to come inside with us for a while, you can tell us what's the matter. If something serious has happened, I don't feel like waiting for the newspaper to get the details."

Martin nodded, accelerated again, and then parked in front of the Laurins' big villa. When he had stepped out of the car, he immediately asked Armand:

"Doesn't everyone here work with Mr. Poiron? Didn't you call the castle, or did nobody who come to give you any information?"

Armand smiled and led Martin to the door.

"Mr. Poiron will answer the phone to nobody, and his staff never gives any information. I thought you knew that."

"That's new to me," said Martin.

A few moments later Martin was telling his story to a large group of people from the Golden Street, while Nadine Aron made notes for an article in *Le Journal de Saint-Milles*.

* * *

The kernel of Jacques Poiron's secret was the way the ability to experience his special dreams had come to him. He had learned to deal with this ability, and next he had built his dream world. He began to live two lives. Everything he did after he had woken up was of less importance than what he went through during his afternoon naps on the bench at the riverbank and during the night.

That night he went to bed early.

In the rooms of the white main tower his privacy was guaranteed. A hallway led from the main building to the tower, where a door provided the only access to it. The door opened into a big, round space that functioned as a reception hall. A steep spiral staircase in the center of the hall pierced the tower like a corkscrew, allowing access to the floors above. There was no elevator. The only man other than Jacques who had a key was his help and stay Tobias Dupont, who lived with his wife in another part of Ricard.

Jacques had prepared himself for the night.

Before he went to bed, he carried out a special ritual. He entered the hall and locked the door behind him. The wall of the ground-floor room was encrusted from floor to ceiling with different sorts of stone. Marble, quartz, granite, agate, jade, basalt, turquoise, emerald. and even rare meteoric stones formed fantastic patterns in all their specific colors and forms. He walked along the wall and stroked the stones with both hands. To him they were all animated, just as he felt specific vibrations of stones, trees, and plants when he danced at the bank of the river around noon.

In his magical world there was no such thing as dead matter. It was not that he, being a philosophical man, had become an adherent of animism who assigned a soul to everything he saw around him. He actually was able to see the divine spark in all things.

As he touched different stones, he quickened his pace until finally he was dancing along the wall, in a trance. He went around and around, faster and faster, and then went to the center of the room and climbed the winding stairs. Waving with his arms, jumping from step to step, he reached his bedroom on the upper story. He did not pant. Jacques lay down on his bed and reached for the cord above his pillow. He gave it a pull, and the lights went out in all rooms of the tower.

In the darkness he stepped into a miraculous dimension.

For a moment he touched his wounded throat. Slowly he rolled onto his side and pulled up his knees.

There was smoke. The smell of burning wood. Howling wind. Piercing cold.

He had the feeling as if he was covered by fur.

Icy thoughts whirled like snowflakes through his head and filled the depths of his mind and froze the rational thinking part of his mind. His emotions appeared like icicles and pierced the darkness.

Then there was light. Dead matter had come alive and beamed an impressive feast of colors, clearly perceptible to his mind's eye.

Jacques found himself in a world he knew only too

well. Everything here had been built by himself, dream after dream. This was the town of his dreams, where the pavement vibrated softly under his feet, where the air crackled with his own energy. It was a town full of palaces, where all doors and gates stood wide open for him. A forest of towers reached up high in the sky; arched bridges connected the palaces; and domed roofs of gold, silver, and jade shone everywhere. Whimsical as human thoughts, the streets and lanes twisted together and rivers streamed along high walls. There were numerous canals and deep, dark pools.

Stone after stone, he had built up his dream world. This town was alive; it breathed with his lungs, beat to the rhythm of his heart, and bared the soul of its builder. Yet it was far from being completed.

The gardens and parks were covered with flowers. The trees bore fruit like giant diamonds. There were sculptures of stone and wood. Some rooms were decorated with beautiful hangings and murals and were lit by candles that spontaneously began to burn when he entered. Other rooms were dark and empty.

The only inhabitants of the town were birds. They varied in size but were all colorful, and many had tails of long, pliable feathers.

There were no human beings.

Jacques had never met anyone during his wanderings.

With measured steps he went through the streets. He held his hands behind his back and looked, as always, at the results of his hard work. Every now and then he stopped and looked over his shoulder nervously.

Here he had piled up one dream on another and he felt at home.

Home—that was the right word. As soon as he had fallen asleep he had started to dream, and when he dreamt, he was at home.

Yet the beauty of this town was superficial. It was a chain of similar thoughts that had produced identical structures, and the sculptures and paintings were mostly unimaginative and lacked the passion of a true artist. All the domes were alike, just as most of the towers and arched bridges. The plumage of the birds was too glaring to be beautiful. His fantasy was limited, and he could not summon enough courage to complete his town. Along all the edges unfinished palaces waited for the creative power of his mind.

All this did not bother Jacques in the least. For this was his home! He had only made use of his special capacity that formed the kernel of his secret.

What did bother him were the shadows that moved around in his town.

Not so long ago, he had noticed them for the first time. He knew that they were not materialized figments of the imagination. They were elongated shadows of creatures that carefully and anxiously kept themselves hidden from him. The feeling of not being alone any more in his own city began to make him nervous. Often, when he suddenly turned around, he glimpsed a shadow disappearing around a corner or through a gate. On those occasions he was convinced that he also heard shuffling sounds, or even footsteps. Obviously someone had managed to enter his dream world.

But this time not a shadow had shown itself so far, and he felt more at ease now than in other visits.

Jacques used his stays in his city for materialistic purposes. Here he could put out his feelers to dimensions that remained unreachable to him when he was awake. Events from out of the future and the past were whispered in his ear, and he only had to concentrate to hear all kinds of interesting things.

He went through the gate of his favorite palace. It was the first building he had planned, and it was situated in the center of his city. He'd had to pile up countless stones that were all animated and sent out impulses to each other. All the buildings together formed something that might be compared with a colossal brain, of which the rivers, canals, streets, and lanes formed the veins and the nervous system. He had cut the stones himself from dream rocks.

Entering a huge hall, he felt an unpleasant pressure on his head and shoulders. Here the energy the building radiated was clearly perceptible. Jacques began to float. Right under the high dome of the hall he turned a somersault. The he dived down, slid through a corridor, and whirled along stone staircases up to the upper story. There he came into a room wherein a wooden desk stood. The outer wall counted twenty high, arched windows. He sat down on a chair behind the desk and leaned with his elbows on the surface.

"Let's start with the purchase and sale of shares," he said aloud. "After that I want to consider taking over and hiving off. I want the figures of tomorrow and the day after tomorrow, a statement of the situation after a month, a year ..."

He leaned backward, stared outside through one of the windows and began to rattle off the names of different companies.

"Alamans Automatique, Heros Enterprise, Computer Commotion, Triple International, Freihals, McCulloch, Section Triomphe, C. Martel, Modi Electronics ..."

Altogether he called out more than forty names. Then he repeated them, but this time at long intervals.

"Alamans Automatique ..."

He held his head obliquely and screwed up his eyes, as if he were listening to something carefully.

"Heros Enterprise ..."

Every now and then he nodded, sometimes he shook his head.

Every now and then he smiled, and sometimes he shrugged his shoulders indifferently.

Every now and then his mouth fell open with surprise, and sometimes he raised his hands in despair.

"Modi Electronics ..."

Jacques Poiron did business with the future.

After a long period of deliberation and decision making he floated away from the desk with a smile and left the room through a window. With a light heart he tumbled through the air. He reached out his hands to the streets beneath him and colored the walls as variegated as the plumage of the birds that skimmed past him.

Floating around gave him a feeling of relaxation.

His spirit was big enough to contain a city wherein he himself was able to roam about.

He glided slowly down to a park and landed softly with his feet on the grass. He had darkened the sky, and now lamps were hanging in the trees. Silver fish swam in a round pond. As he walked up to it, he looked over the water to a palace with dark windows. He thought he'd seen an ink-black figure sneaking through the gate. Now he wanted light shining behind all the windows, which happened immediately. He could clearly see a dark figure dive away from the window in a room on the third story.

"Who's there?" he shouted.

It was not necessary to start running; he did not have to go past the pond and through the gate and climb the stairs in order to reach the third story. He found himself immediately in the room, where a thousand candles burnt. It was a big, bare room. There was no one there. He went to a window and looked outside. He lightened the darkness so that he could see more. In another building something was moving. It was one of those shadows he had seen so often lately. He pointed at the building, and immediately it collapsed. With the power of his will, he destroyed the buildings behind it.

"Who's there?" he shouted again.

The figure and the shadow frightened him. Suddenly he realized that he was busy breaking down his own, carefully built up world, and he almost panicked.

"I have to get out of here," flashed through his mind.

He opened his eyes, rolled onto his back, and stared at the dark ceiling of his bedroom in Castle Ricard. His forehead and breast felt sweaty. For the first time he felt the stinging pain in his neck where his attacker had cut him with the big knife.

And the next day, when he was standing at the grave of Roc and Arnoud and decided that he wanted to see his grandson, he felt weak and nervous. He felt old. He sank down on his knees and stroked the friable soil with his fingertips.

"You must buy a stone of shining black marble," he said to Tobias Dupont, who was standing not far away from him. "How I will miss these dogs."

He rose to his feet and staggered. Tobias was with him in a second and supported him.

"Are you all right, Mr. Poiron?"

"Yes. I'm just a bit tired. Let's go on. Everyone is waiting for me."

They went through the park to the drive and down the drive through the wrought-iron gates. They walked to the big house of Armand and Claire Laurin. Someone let them in and led them to a side wing, where the doors to a meeting room stood open. Tobias stopped there. The door was closed behind Jacques.

At a long, oval table sat the business partners, waiting for his valuable advice.

Normally everyone would have greeted him briefly, after which he would have sat down quickly in order to start the meeting. Now everyone got up to shake hands with him and to ask what exactly had happened the other day.

"Armand and Claire have told us one thing and another, Jacques, but now we will hear the whole story from you yourself," said Bertrand Collin, whose house was built right next to the Laurins. He was a tall man with a bald head and strikingly white eyebrows. "If you only knew how shocked we all were."

"Please, please," said Jacques, while he made averting gestures. "Please sit down, all of you. "It might have been worse."

But everyone noticed that he looked old and fragile.

He told them what he had also said to inspector Martin Legrand. Short and to the point. Claire wanted to know if he suspected anyone in particular.

"The man in the diving suit could have operated all by himself or have acted under orders. I can suspect everyone or nobody. Nevertheless, I will see to it that I will be better protected from now on."

Taking his seat, he proceeded to the order of the day. The partners reached for their notepads; Jacques himself needed no more than his memory.

"The Freihals shares don't seem to be very high, but they will not go any higher. Never again. If we sell today, we make a small profit. Soon the company will not no longer exist."

A muttering went up. Jacques still knew how to surprise his partners. No one doubted his words. When he said that a big company like Freihals was going bankrupt, then that was considered to be an established fact.

"Someone could make a bid for C. Martel in Paris. This year it will remain a small, unspectacular business. Next year extra men will be engaged and they will need another, much bigger office building."

After he had said all the things he had on his mind,

the partners informed each other about what they had done after yesterday's meeting. Soon after that they left the meeting room to go to work with the new facts. Jacques stood up, walked up to a corner of the room, and beckoned to Régine Moret.

"I need your help, Régine," he said.

She looked at him with her sky-blue eyes.

"Always at your service, Jacques."

"Come to the castle this afternoon, at three o'clock. I must have a word with you. Keep in mind that you'll have to leave for the USA very soon."

She nodded.

"Three o'clock," she said.

He thought Régine one of the most sympathetic partners and knew he could entirely trust her. Together they left the meeting room. Tobias Dupont had waited for him and came walking up to him to escort him back to the castle.

5

Vic and Mike sat down on high leather armchairs in a studio in Nashville. It was late at night. Two weeks ago they had traveled from Las Vegas to here by air. Vic had worked with the best musicians, and Mike had sat at the controls of the most expensive equipment with a happy smile on his face. They had played songs Vic had never recorded before. Texts and tunes flew together, hazy thoughts became clear, new ideas came up spontaneously, and Vic had surpassed himself.

Régine Moret had arranged the studio for them, and the bill was paid by Disque Dragon. It was agreed that before Vic left for France he would record all the songs he had in his head, and that was done now. Mike had switched off the equipment, and now he leaned back in his chair.

"Satisfied?" he asked Vic, and without waiting for his answer, he continued with a grin: "Well, I am! It is terrific to be independent and to have time to make something beautiful. We take a wealth of recordings with us to France. Régine has promised me a complete, brand-new studio there. I will mix all songs there, and then we can decide which ones we will release. We'll have a wide choice, won't we?"

He rose to his feet and left the studio humming. He came back with a bottle of mineral water and a bunch of bananas. Since he had come to Nashville he had drunk no alcohol.

"I drink to the health of your grandfather," he said. "The man who has made me happy. And I don't even know him."

"Memories come back to me," said Vic. "Odd things my father told me about him."

"Odd? How do you mean?"

Vic started to laugh and pointed at the bananas.

"Mental manipulation. Pay attention. The banana is nutritious and rich in vitamins. There is no seed or nut from which a banana tree grows. You need the offshoot for that. So where did the very first banana trees come from? Aliens brought them to earth from their faraway worlds. It is suggested time after time that they did so. The banana is an extraterrestrial fruit..."

"Utter nonsense," reacted Mike. "What are you trying to say?"

"Mental manipulation," repeated Vic. "From now on you will never eat a banana again without thinking of aliens."

Mike pulled a fruit from the bunch and started to peel it. He wanted to take a bite, but all of a sudden he burst out laughing.

"Damn!" he said. "It works! So that's a game your grandfather likes to play. I really look forward to meeting him."

"So do I," said Vic.

Mike ate his banana, then shoved his chair behind the mixer and turned it on. A few moments later the two friends were listening in silence to the last recorded songs.

Via interviews in different magazines Vic announced the coming release of his new album and that he was going to France. He flew from Nashville to New York, where he owned an apartment in Brooklyn. There he arranged everything for his departure. A week later he met Mike again at Kennedy Airport, and together they took a plane to Paris.

Régine Moret had gone back to France earlier. She would see to it that they were picked up from their hotel in Paris by a chauffeur, who would bring them to Castle Ricard in Saint-Milles.

It was Tobias Dupont who turned up in front of the hotel one early morning, in an extended Mercedes. The luggage was put in the trunk and Vic and Mike, who'd just had breakfast, stepped in. They leaned backward, stretched their legs, and listened to Tobias, who told much more about his employer than Régine Moret had done during her stay in the US. He sat relaxed at the wheel and drove the car slowly through the busy streets of the city.

"You look exactly like your grandfather," he said in French, looking in the mirror. "Believe me, it is just as if I have taken a huge step back in time and bring home a young Jacques Poiron. He has told me time after time to give you his kind regards. I really believe that it makes him happy that you are coming to the castle. Despite the fact that something happened that really threw him off his balance."

Vic gave a short version of the monologue in English and then asked Tobias:

"What has happened?"

"Someone as fabulously wealthy as he attracts danger," said Tobias. "I should have been aware of that. I am not only his chauffeur, I am also his bodyguard. As far as that is concerned you will see me often, for my wife Julia and I live in the castle. Well, I just came back from Les Eyzies when I saw your grandfather stumbling through the park. Some fool had threatened to kill him with a knife or to drown him in the river if he wouldn't divulge his secret."

This frightened Vic. Again he translated for his friend and then asked the most obvious question:

"What secret?"

"His way to make money. Very much money. Success makes enemies."

Vic kept on asking questions. Outside it began to get warm. Inside the big Mercedes it remained cool.

"Who is protecting him now?" Vic wanted to know.

"I came to Paris yesterday and spent the night in a house owned by Mr. Poiron," said the chauffeur. "That is why I was able to show up at the hotel so early. But before I left the castle I saw to it that men were present to keep an eye on your grandfather."

Now the car drove over the highway from Paris to Orléans. The chauffeur told about Poiron, about the partners, about quotations and all kinds of enterprises Jacques had bought or sold. He talked in detail about the business Poiron did, and suddenly Mike remarked, in English:

"He is well informed for a chauffeur, isn't he?"

Tobias nodded with enthusiasm and responded, also in English but with a heavy accent:

"You must understand that Mr. Poiron takes care of everybody very well. Yes, I am only the chauffeur and his bodyguard, but I have a splendid block of shares and a nice sum in the bank. I am very open about that. I do not think there is anyone in Saint-Milles who has not been rewarded by him. He is the generous giver and now someone has got the crazy idea to threaten him with death and get a secret out of him."

Tobias Dupont was a stocky, broad-shouldered man with short, brown hair. He acted with great self-assurance and constantly let go of the wheel with both hands to make gestures.

"Saint-Milles is blessed with her lord of the castle," he continued. "I am very pleased to be able to bring you to him. It will do him a world of good to see his grandson. I have heard that you are famous in America."

Vic did not respond to the last remark.

"In fairness I have to say that I have never met my grandfather before. It will be a strange experience to be able to shake hands with him today."

"That will not happen today," the chauffeur hastened to say. "Mr. Poiron has arranged it in a different way. He feels that it is better that you first let yourself be informed about him by others, and in the meantime get used to your new surroundings. First you will meet other people. And of course I will always be there to answer all your questions."

"That sounds as if he expects me to stay for a very long time," grinned Vic. "I count on it that I can leave any time on my own sweet will."

"Without a doubt," said the chauffeur. "Without a doubt ..."

When they drew near their destination late in the afternoon, Vic opened the side window and took off his sunglasses. With mixed feelings he looked at the beautiful landscape of the Dordogne. This was the native region of his ancestors; if his father hadn't gone to America, he would have grown up here himself as well. He could not recognize what he had never seen, but his heart beat fiercely when the car drove past a river running through a valley worn deep in the limestone, through little towns and quiet villages. He saw deep clefts and fantastic masses of rocks. The car went up along a steep road. Then a twisting road over a rock plateau led him along fields, meadows, and extensive woods. The air was cloudless blue. He began to worry more and more about the fact that he was not able to explain to himself why he was here right now and not in America. The car smoothly took some sharp bends and then began to climb down again.

"Down there is Saint-Milles," said Tobias. "Wait, I will stop on a spot from where you can look down on the little town and the castle. Further up Ricard will vanish from sight again behind the rocks."

The car reduced speed and finally came to a standstill on a narrow parking lane at the edge of a cleft. All three of them got out. Tobias began to point enthusiastically.

"The church, the square . . . the bridges. The river splits Saint-Milles into two districts. There live your grandfather's partners. Behind the villas is the park— and look, there's the proud white tower of Ricard. The castle, the villas, and most houses of Saint-Milles are owned by Jacques Poiron, just as almost all the land you can see here around you."

"Don't the partners prefer to live in a their own houses?" asked Mike in his best French.

Tobias started to laugh.

"Well, they live there for free, that's a fact," he said. "No, the truth is that they are all extremely wealthy and own houses all over the world. Mr. Poiron prefers to keep everything in the neighborhood of the castle for himself."

"He was born here in Saint-Milles," said Vic. "My father was born here, too. My mother lived in Les Eyzies. How strange it is to stand here now."

"I can imagine that," said Mike. "A grandfather who throws millions about might spring a surprise. Who knows, maybe you'll be standing here again after a couple of years and then everything you see will belong to you..."

They got back in the limo. The road went down steep, straight across the rocks. Tobias had to step on the brakes constantly. The center of Saint-Milles was a big square, split in two by the river; the two sides were connected by three arched bridges. There were shops and houses, little hotels and sidewalk cafes. At one of these cafes Régine Moret was waiting for them. As soon as the three men had sat down with her at a table, a waiter appeared with a bottle of Bergerac. Vic had put on his sunglasses again and pushed his chair back into the shadow of a thick walnut tree.

"Did the journey tire you?" asked Régine.

"I'm all right," he answered.

"I suggest that we have dinner here outside," she said. "This is an excellent restaurant. After that Tobias will bring you to the Castle Ricard."

Thereupon she bent aside to Tobias, who was sitting next to her. She whispered something, and he nodded. There was an anxious look on his face when he turned to Vic.

"Régine just told me that your grandfather had another bad night. He didn't sleep well again. I thought you should know that, and she agreed and gave me permission to inform you."

"From this I gather that he doesn't sleep well often. Is he sick?"

"That is difficult to say. My wife and I are the first ones who see him in the morning. We have much contact with him during the day. If you ask me, he has been going downhill fast since the day he was attacked. He himself says that has nothing to do with it. The doctor visited him that day and said that he was healthy. The scratch on his neck has almost vanished. But it is very well possible that the man with the knife has hurt him mentally. On my request the doctor came around one more time, but he couldn't find anything. He says that your grandfather probably is overtired. And that could become fatal at his age."

"What do you yourself see?" Vic wanted to know.

"In the morning I see a jaded ghost appear. During the day I see him get better again. He eats and drinks as usual, does business as usual, and by the evening he is visibly recuperated. The next morning he is depressed again and looks as if he hasn't had a wink of sleep. Maybe it's not good that he retires to his tower. It is because of this that I am so very happy with your arrival."

"But why am I not allowed to see him today?"

Régine cut in:

"Mr. Poiron has stated explicitly that he wants to put off the meeting for a while. He has drawn up a little program for you. A conducted tour. Through the residential area, through the neighborhood...I'll be showing you around everywhere."

"The reason is not exactly clear to me."

"I think he first wants to hear from us if you like it here and how you are...He's already asked me a thousand questions about our encounter in Las Vegas. Keep in mind that you will be meeting each other for the very first time, and that can make an old man very nervous.

Vic nodded and leaned over to the table to get his glass. The others followed his example.

"Welcome to Saint-Milles," said Régine.

"My first glass in France," sighed Mike. "If it tastes good, many more will follow...Cheers!"

Vic laughed and pulled his chair back into the sunlight.

"Cheers, all of you. I'll just wait and see what will

happen in the next couple days. I think it best to consider this a well-deserved holiday. By the way, I'm beginning to get hungry."

"We'll do something about that right away," promised Régine.

The meal that was served not much later was very good. As Vic enjoyed it, he looked at the people on the square and listened with a smile to Régine and Tobias, who tried to teach Mike as many French words as possible in a short time. All of a sudden he that a man and a woman had stopped in front of the pavement and stared at him. The man was long and lean, with a moustache and a bald head, and held a camera in his hands. She had short, bleached hair.

"Vic Emmett, the celebrity from America!" she said, stepping forward and reaching out her hand. "Would you allow us to take a picture of you?"

Vic looked over his sunglasses to Régine.

"Nadine Aron from *Le Journal de Saint-Milles*," she said. "Together with her husband, Maurice. He is a photographer."

Vic rose to his feet, shook hands with both of them, and then posed near the walnut tree to get photographed.

"No doubt we'll see each other frequently," said Nadine. "Saint-Milles is just a small town, as you will have noticed already. Régine told me about you. I didn't even know that Mr. Poiron had a grandson. Tomorrow, on behalf of everybody, I will welcome you on the front page of the paper, and later I hope to be able to have an interview with you. Enjoy your meal. See you later..."

"See you later," said Vic.

He sat down again and picked up his fork and knife.

"She is not just the general editor of the paper," said Tobias. "Together with Maurice she owns it, and they also have a print shop. It was your grandfather who set them in the saddle. He owns the building where they have their offices."

Vic pointed with his fork to the restaurant, and his eyebrows appeared above his sunglasses. Régine understood him and said with a smile:

"Oh yes, restaurant Chez Marcus is owned by your grandfather as well. He likes to sit here on the pavement or, when the weather is bad, inside at the window. Jacques Poiron knows all about good cooking."

6

Vic was used to luxury and to a strange bed. That night he slept like a top in one of Ricard's most beautiful rooms. The next morning he got up early and took a shower in the adjacent bathroom. After having dressed, he went out into the corridor and blinked against the glaring sunlight shining inside through high windows. Tobias had told him the night before that he could find a kitchen at the end of the corridor.

Halfway down the hallway, he passed a door that had been left ajar and looked inside. His mouth fell open when he saw the furnishings. Along all four walls were six-foot-high bookcases. Above the walls rose a mighty, irregular dome made of plaster, creating the impression that the library was built in a cave. Vic entered the room and looked up. The dome was covered with beautiful paintings after the fashion of the old Cro-Magnon artists. There were woolly-haired rhinos, deer, horses, mammoths, aurochs, and bison. A lamp shone down from the highest point of the dome. In a corner of the room, right in front of the books, stood a life-sized dummy. Vic immediately recognized the sorcerer from the cave of Les Trois Frères; he had seen countless pictures of it in his father's books, which he kept in his apartment in New York now. Only rarely had the Cro-Magnons created human images, and therefore the sorcerer was a curiosity. The original was only 2.5 feet tall, a figure drawn in black on the stone wall of the cave. It was a man dressed in animal skin. His face remained hidden behind a mask with erect ears and a huge antlers. The eyes were as big and round as those of an owl. Vic walked up to it and touched the beard. He supposed it was made of the long-haired fur of an animal. Then he walked along the bookcases and stopped here and there to pull a book out. There were books with photos from cave art, bound reports containing detailed descriptions of caves, studies of Cro-Magnon people and Neanderthal men, encyclopedias, reference books, essays about prehistoric France. Vic became enthusiastic. He would like to sit here for days on end and study all these books closely. In the middle of the room stood a wooden desk and a chair. The desktop was empty, except for a wooden picture frame. He was surprised to see that it contained a photograph of himself. He could not remember where it had been made; there were thousands of pictures of him wearing sunglasses and standing in front of a mike. He had a feeling that the photo had been placed there on purpose. It was as if someone whispered to him: "Welcome. This is where you belong. Right here, in this room..."

He nodded.

"I will come back here soon," he said in a soft voice.

He went back to the corridor and walked on to the

kitchen. Mike, dressed in a long bathrobe, was sitting at a round table and enjoying an extensive breakfast.

"Vic!" he said cheerfully. "Come and join me. No way can I eat this all by myself."

For the time being Vic stuck to coffee and watched in amusement as his friend stuffed himself with food.

Tobias and his wife Julia entered. He introduced her to Vic, and she immediately asked him if everything was to his liking:

"If you need anything, all you have to do is ask."

"Thank you," he said. "There is more than enough."

They both nodded and left the room again.

"We've got a little time till Régine arrives to pick us up," said Mike. "I'm going to dress, and then I'll come back to the kitchen."

"Better come to the library, halfway down the corridor," responded Vic. "You'll find me there."

Vic sat at the table reading when Mike entered in the company of Régine.

Just the way Vic himself had reacted, Mike stood still and looked around with his mouth open.

"Vic . . . this is art! Are these replicas from, uh ..."

"The Cro-Magnon people," said Vic his voice full of enthusiasm. "*Homo sapiens,* just like us. Our direct ancestors, you might say. My family always had a special interest in the Cro-Magnons. First my grandfather, then my father, and finally me myself."

"Your father even became a professor of archaeology. You have told me about that."

"Yes. Only now I realize that many of his principles originally came from old Jacques. I'm reading an old book here right now in which Jacques used the margin to write his comments. Here and there I see his well-known three O's."

He showed them a certain page of the book.

"What does it mean?" Régine wanted to know. Her face was radiant with curiosity. "I really would like to know."

"It's very easy. Old, older, oldest. Grandfather is a suspicious man, if I am not mistaken. Anyway, he has his doubts about everything. When dates turn up in books about prehistoric times, he always comes up with the three O's. Let me explain it."

He placed the book back on a shelf and pointed at the painted animals.

"It is said that the first Cro-Magnon men arrived in this area between thirty thousand and thirty-five thousand years ago. They brought all their knowledge with them. Many things had to be arranged before a man was able to go to work in a dark cave. There had to be light—cups filled with animal fat in which a wick was burning, for instance. Everything had to be there with which to make a painting. Blowpipes to spit colored powder on the wall. Brushes made of hair and moss. Coloring matter of red and yellow ochre. Black manganese oxide. Solid scaffoldings to be able to work high above the ground. Oh, their culture is old, older, oldest..."

He looked at Régine and Mike and after he had reassured himself that they were listening attentively, he went on:

"My father also made use of the three O's, and they can be found in many of the books I inherited from him. When human fossils were found and scientists suspected they were about one and a half million years old, he would say that the species in question had existed much, much longer. The world is old. Humans are old, and ape men are even older."

He walked to the sorcerer. Carefully he put his hand on the shoulder of the dummy.

"Here we have an extensive library, focused on one and the same subject," he said. "Hundreds of thousands of pages filled with information. Still, there is no one on earth who can tell you if this wizard from the cave of Les Trois Frères actually existed. And if he really was a real person of flesh and blood, then no one is able to tell us which rituals he executed, not to mention what he said or thought. Anyway, I want to devour all these books. Oh, Régine, I am so happy to be here! I can find so incredibly much information here!"

"If you only knew how glad I am to hear you say that," said Régine. "For almost everything that's on the program for today has to do with this. We will be making a tour of the most important find spots and museums. Now I know for sure that you will enjoy that. As far as I am concerned we can leave right now."

Vic was enthusiastic. But he could not help asking, "Why are we going there? Is that the wish of my grandfather?"

"Yes."

"I don't quite understand it."

"Patience," smiled Régine. "Give him time to recover.

This morning I heard from Tobias that he is feeling a bit better now. But he prefers to stay in his rooms in the tower for the time being, and besides Tobias he doesn't want to speak to anyone."

Now Vic became suspicious.

"Did something happen to him? First there is that story about a man with a knife..."

"Don't you worry. Let's make the most of this day."

And it became a beautiful day. It became a beautiful week! Vic was impressed by the beauty and rich history of the surrounding area. He went to Les Eyzies, the town often called the capital of prehistory, and visited several museums, saw caves in the neighborhood that once accommodated Cro-Magnons, traveled through the valley of the Vézère river, and all the time he had a feeling as if he had gone back in time many thousands of years. On the first day Tobias drove the little company around in a luxury van. On the second day Vic sat next to Régine in an Italian sports car. Tobias stayed behind at the castle and Mike was busy setting up a new studio in an office building behind the Golden Street. Someone from Paris who was able to supply the necessary equipment had arrived especially for him. The person who was going to be Vic's new manager had already moved into an office there. Vic had asked if the man from Paris could bring a guitar with him, and soon an expensive Gibson appeared in the castle library.

One day he was introduced to his grandfather's most important partners and was taken around some villas in the Golden Street. For the first time in years he wasn't thinking of his former lover Rita Cianello all the time; seldom had he been in a better mood. He was laughing all the time, and time after time he put his dark sunglasses away in the inside pocket of his jacket. He was moved when he entered painted caves and listened attentively to the stories of the guides. He didn't wonder any longer why Jacques Poiron wanted him to see this all. Life was good. The sun tanned his skin. At night he sat down by himself in the library, reading books and playing guitar. Slowly new compositions began to take shape in his head.

Then, one early afternoon, he went to Saint-Milles all by himself for the first time. He walked out through the park of the castle and went down the Golden Street, and after a quarter of an hour he reached the center of the little town. On the pavement of restaurant Chez Marcus he waited for Nadine Aron from *Le Journal de Saint-Milles*; he had made an appointment with her. She appeared right on time and drank a glass of Bergerac with him, after which she took him with her on a walk through another part of the town, until they reached the building where the editorial staff and the print shop were established.

"Let me show you the pictures my husband took of you in front of the walnut tree," she said. "After that he will, if you agree, take a number of new pictures of you. In the studio, but also in town. Worldwide there's great demand for news about you, and I really look forward to firing lots of questions at you. As a matter of fact I am the only journalist at the moment who can tell something new about you, and Maurice is the only photographer who can send out recent pictures of you. Which is quite a unique situation, and to speak honestly, I am very pleased with that."

Vic shrugged his shoulders. It had never bothered him that press people made international deals with exclusive material and made a lot of money from it.

From the outside the office building looked old-fashioned. It was entirely made of heavy, roughly cut out blocks of stone. Inside, everything was ultramodern. Nadine showed him around and then took him with her to the big office she shared with her husband. In the middle of the room stood two desks. The wall behind her desk was hung with paintings—mostly landscapes from the area. He recognized Castle Ricard, and there was also a portrait of his grandfather. The wall behind her husband's desk was filled from floor to ceiling with photographs taken by himself.

"Maurice used to do a lot of traveling for the big magazines," Nadine explained, when she saw that he was looking at the pictures with interest. "Flora and fauna have always been his specialty. In the jungles of South America and Africa, in the oceans, you see elephants, lions, and numberless fishes of all possible colors. Coral reefs, deep lakes, but also the highest mountains . . . you name it, and he has been there, from Australia and New Zealand to China and Japan—till he came to Saint-Milles and met me!"

She perched on the desk top with a notepad on her lap. A ballpoint sat behind her left ear. Her short, bleached hair stood up in spikes. Vic liked her and felt at ease in her company. She started to ask questions, and he took his time to answer them. Maurice came in and took some pictures of him. Later Vic posed in the studio, while Nadine went on with the interview. A stroll through the town led them back to Chez Marcus, and he invited the couple to have dinner with him. They went inside.

"I really have enjoyed everything I've seen the last days," he said, when they sat down to dinner. "In America I prefer to withdraw into myself and try to avoid company as much as possible. When I have to tour, I travel from town to town and retire to my room at night. All I see are halls filled with unknown faces. Everyone claims that they know how I am. But that is an illusion."

He heaved a sigh.

"Now I have spent some days in the country. Long walks, wonderful views. The caves and the museums. It all made a deep impression on me. I feel comfortable here. And it is pleasant to sit down here and have a talk with you."

"Then you should stay here forever; in a couple of years you might be calling yourself lord of the castle," grinned Maurice.

"I cannot make myself believe that..." he said.

Nadine, who sat opposite to him, put down her fork and knife. She leaned forward with her elbows on the tabletop and said in a soft voice:

"Yes, let's talk about that, about living in Castle Ricard. Trust me, Vic, this stays between us and will not be written in any newspaper. Régine has told me that Jacques would love it if you decided to settle down here."

Suddenly Vic had to laugh.

"Isn't that strange for a man who did not even show up to greet me when I arrived here, and who I still haven't even met?"

"You will meet him soon enough," she said.

"How do you know?" he wanted to know.

"This is the first day that you are not in the company of Régine Moret."

"That's right."

"Was she with you all the time when you were still in America?"

"Yes. As my grandfather's acting manager."

"You still do not know very much about the partners from the Golden Street. Régine is his confidante. She is a very intelligent psychologist. Your grandfather has asked her to fathom your character. Now she obviously knows enough, so she did not feel she needed to come with you to be present while you had a conversation with us."

"A psychologist," said Vic. "I did not expect that at all. Do you really think that she had to observe my behavior?"

"I am very sure of that. She has seen how you are in America, and now she also knows how you are here in France."

"What's the use of it?"

"Well, I have no answer to that. All I know is that Régine often acts as an industrial psychologist; she talks with all people who want to do business with Jacques Poiron."

"That happens everywhere in the business world,"

said Vic. "But when it is something between a grandfather and a grandson, I have my objections."

As a matter of fact he was baffled. His hand slid under his jacket, and his fingers touched his sunglasses in the inside pocket. Finally he decided not to put them on.

"You know so much about his doings," he remarked.

"Of course," said Nadine. "I can be honest about that. Saint-Milles is a small community, and I am the one who reports the news. I know everybody by name and am well informed about everything. And everything here revolves around your grandfather. He is the owner of this restaurant, he has given Maurice and me the chance to start our business here, he—"

"I know all that. I heard it from Tobias Dupont, when we were sitting outside here."

"You see?" laughed Maurice. "Even you are well informed about things like that, and you've only just arrived..."

Vic walked back to the castle by himself. It was getting dark. At the gate he pushed on the button of the intercom and looked up to a camera. A guard, engaged recently, appeared and opened the gate for him. The man held a dog on a short leash; two trained watchdogs had been brought in the day before.

Once inside Vic went to the library, where he picked up his guitar and sat down on the chair. He touched the strings and started to hum a melody. Every now and then he sung a few words or a half line. His cell phone started to ring, and he took it out of his pocket. It was Régine Moret: she wanted to know about his meeting with the journalist.

"Listen, Régine," he said, "I am trying to make a song right now."

"Then I won't bother you any longer," she responded in a cheerful voice. "It will take some time till Mike's studio is ready, but as far as I know the necessary equipment is already there. Mike's working hard, and he plans to sleep in the studio tonight. I'll see you tomorrow, Vic."

"Maybe," he said.

"Maybe?" she repeated, and he knew by the way she pronounced that single word that she was on the alert.

"If I don't meet my grandfather tomorrow morning, I will pack my things and go to Paris, where I will catch the first plane to New York."

Without waiting for her reaction he broke the connection.

Softly he played on. Now he didn't sing any more. Mike had never come to keep him company when he was here in the library, but one way or another he had always found it pleasant to know he was somewhere in the castle. Now, all alone, he did not feel at ease. He looked up at the paintings. Suddenly he went cold all over. He had the feeling someone was watching him. The sorcerer stood there in the corner and stared at him. Vic put away his guitar. He picked up his cell phone and called Mike.

"I hear you are very busy."

"You bet," the familiar voice sounded in his ear. "It is unbelievable, Vic. This is going to be a perfect studio with everything I need. I only have to ask for something, and they order it for me. Today I really had the feeling that I have found paradise."

"Are you planning to stay there?"

"Yes. There's an empty apartment right above the studio. I'm allowed to move in there. Please come and take a look around here tomorrow."

"Promised. See you."

It was no use telling Mike he was toying with the idea of going back to America. Vic got up and walked slowly along the shelves of books, stroking the spines with the middle finger of his right hand. He felt restless. He had the inspiration to write a song, but he was too distracted by the circumstances.

It was impossible to summarize the meaning of a thousand books into one short, brilliant line.

It was impossible to make a comprehensive song.

Making the ultimate text was a superhuman effort.

Now he left the library and walked through the corridor in the opposite direction of the kitchen. In a room where he had never been before he saw a black piano. There were also a number of benches and low tables and a marble fireplace. The walls were bare. As soon as he had taken place on the piano stool and had touched some keys, he knew this was the ideal room to compose in. The sound of the piano was wonderful. Soon he was in deep concentration. He played and sang and strung a new pearl onto the long chain of impressive compositions.

After the final chord had faded out, he straightened his back and turned around on the stool.

His mouth fell open as he took in the figure standing in front of him

As in a nightmare he saw himself as a man of old age, balancing on the edge of death.

"Vic ..." said the man.

Vic took a deep breath, rose to his feet, and walked up to him with unsteady steps.

"Grandfather...Is that you?"

He embraced the old man. Through his clothes, his grandfather felt as lean as a rake.

"Welcome," said Jacques Poiron. "Welcome home!"

7

Vic would have asked Jacques a thousand questions. Fast, without a pause. And the answers would have been short and to the point. Yet he was not even able to finish the first question that came to his mind:

"How come you ..."

After he had let go of the old man and taken a step backward, he remained standing there undecidedly.

"This is not the right place for a conversation," said Jacques. "There's that hollow sound. Come, let's go to the kitchen. By the way, what you played a minute ago sounded beautiful. The acoustic qualities here are perfect for the sounds of all kinds of instruments."

He stepped up to Vic, put a hand on his back, and pushed him in the direction of the door.

"My grandson," sighed Jacques, when they were walking down the corridor. "You look so much like me. I have seen so many pictures of you and so many movies. I am sure that I have heard all the songs you ever wrote. That is why I dare to say that I know for certain that what you just played and sang is brand new. Did you compose it here, between the walls of the castle? How proud that would make me."

In the kitchen they sat down at a table, face to face with each other. Jacques kept on talking. He told about Saint-Milles and its surroundings and about the history of the Dordogne. Twice he rose to his feet, first to get himself a bottle of wine, an opener, and two glasses, and then to close the kitchen door.

"Well," he said, "I have only spoken about things that came to my mind spontaneously. In the meantime we have been able to take a look at each other and to get used to each other. No doubt you have noticed that I have mentioned nothing at all about myself. That is what I would like to do right now. Or do you want to know first why I have asked Régine to invite you to Ricard?"

"You have given me an awful lot of money."

It was the first time he had opened his mouth from the moment they had left the other room.

Jacques shrugged his skinny shoulders.

"I could have given you tenfold that amount. Or a hundredfold. Actually it is not important. You know, Vic, I am happy to see you. You are family. But while you look like me from the outside, from the inside you are different. Where our characters are concerned, we are not cast in the same mold. You are such a sensitive young man. My mind was always set to money. Now I want to work on your talents. Please allow me the time to explain everything to you. The ultimate song text you are searching for . . . there is a big chance you will finally be able to write it."

"I do not understand..."

"Of course you don't! You haven't the faintest idea

what I am going to tell you. That is why I ask you one more time, Vic—allow me the time."

"The ultimate song text. You know even that about me."

"It intrigues me."

"Millions of dollars in my bank account, Grandfather. A psychologist to test me. Visits to museums, drives through the landscape. Suddenly life has become a big mystery to me. And let us not forget about the past. We never had contact with each other. My parents died. No word or sign from you! Now please don't expect me to think all of a sudden that you are such a nice man. Besides, I am not for sale. Maybe I will give you your money back someday and go back to America to pick up the thread."

"I certainly hope not," said Jacques, and it seemed that Vic's words had frightened him.

Only now did Vic notice a dark stripe on the white neck of his grandfather and remember about the man who had used a knife.

"I shouldn't have said that, Grandfather. All right, I will give you the time to make certain things clear to me."

"Thank you. That is a great relief to me. Do you have any idea yourself why I let you come to Ricard? I mean . . . besides the fact that I looked forward to meeting my grandson..."

"Of course I have thought a great deal about that. Although you have thrown your money about, I don't believe it has to do with financial affairs. I think that was just a generous gesture to show your good will. But in fact, I think, it is finally all about my good will..."

He looked at Jacques. The old man looked back at him frankly, and Vic realized he was sitting face to face with a man of unprecedented power; the owner of this castle, the owner of half of Saint-Milles, the owner of so very much more.

"Three things occupy my mind," Vic went on. "I already mentioned the psychologist, Régine Moret. And then you talked about the finding of the ultimate song. Third, there is something which has always occupied you, my father, and myself and which obviously is an important part of a game that is about to start. I am talking about the past that can be found everywhere in this area. The life of the Cro-Magnons, the Neanderthal men . . . I am not able to combine this all yet, but I do believe I'm on the right track. Does that make sense to you?"

"Yes it does, Vic. Régine told me that you are a dreamer. Besides that, you have a firm character with drive and courage. You're not easy to be put off, and you dare to go your own way. If I succeed in making you enthusiastic about my plans, I know I can count on you. There is much to win for the both of us—for you, besides immense richness, the ultimate song."

"Which brings us to point three."

"The fascinating past!" The eyes of Jacques brightened, and he smiled. "That's right, that's what it's all about. This is not the right time to tell you all about it. But I will tell you something that has to do with this as well. Vic, I know that I have done things that made us all drift away from each other. I divorced, lost all contact with my wife and with your father. You were born in the USA, your parents were lost . . . and I was engaged with other things that demanded all my attention. Looking back, I know I acted wrongly. On the other hand, it brought me to where I am now. It is useless to say now that I am sorry."

"That is never useless..."

"Then I will tell you that I am really sorry."

Again they looked at each other. Jacques's lips trembled. The stripe on his neck moved when he swallowed. Tears welled up in his eyes.

"I will repeat it, I'm truly sorry. I have built up an empire where money rules. Now I am nearing the end of my life, and all that money begins to become less important to me. You have met my partners. They worship me, for I am the man who has made them all rich. In fact they have enough to enjoy their money for generations on end. I will spend my remaining time on other things. Together with you I will make some investigations."

He wiped his face with the sleeve of his jacket.

"I know I can be honest to you. I'm scared, Vic. Scared to death! I need your help. Please, stay with me and help me. Your efforts will be amply rewarded. Unknown richness for you, Vic. Although I know you are not after money at all. I am sick and tired of all my materialistic partners and I hope to achieve something together with you which will bring us both to a higher spiritual level. Yes, yes, I am well aware that this all sounds puzzling. Give me your confidence, and then we can start the most special undertaking you can imagine."

He refilled the glasses.

"Will you stay? Can I count on you?"

"Well—yes. For the time being I will stay here."

"This calls for a toast, Vic. We drink to everything you can wish for. Wine is the crown of civilization..."

"And raises man above animal," said Vic.

Jacques was pleasantly surprised.

"You know that expression?"

"From my father. He has told me so much about you. Many of your pithy sayings became winged words to me."

"Is that so? Do you still remember them?"

"The three O's, for instance."

"Ah, yes. The history of us, *Homo sapiens,* goes further back than we thought. We have been here for many, many millions of years. I've always said so, and I still do."

"No mouse has ever become a rat."

"That's a fact, Vic. It is predetermined. It is very well possible that in a hundred million years or more there will be mice as big as cats. Still, they will not be rats, but just very big mice. Evolution is a complicated process. Later I will tell you much more about that. Now it is time for me to go to sleep. I want to dream. Do you dream often?"

"Almost every night."

"Do you remember what you dream?"

"Sometimes. Well, most of the times not..."

Jacques rose to his feet, walked up to him, put a hand on his shoulder, and said:

"We will have long talks about dreams as well. I wish I'd already let you in on all my secrets. Then you might be able to help me chase away all the demons from my dreams and lighten my dark nights."

He saw Vic giving him a questioning look.

"Later, Vic, later. Sleep well. We'll meet again tomorrow, right here, for a big breakfast."

"Sleep well, Grandfather," said Vic.

The old man turned around and shuffled to the door. It became quiet in the kitchen after Jacques had closed the door behind him. Vic remained sitting at the table for a couple of hours and emptied the bottle of wine. Then he went to his big bedroom. He was happy that he finally had met his grandfather.

Jacques was already present when Vic entered the kitchen the next morning. Julia Dupont had made coffee and now was busy frying eggs. There was fresh bread on the table. Vic noticed immediately that his grandfather looked tired. Yesterday the wine had colored his cheeks. Now his skin was pale. But his eyes sparkled when he saw Vic.

"You are an early riser, just like me. Did you have a good night?"

"Without dreams," grinned Vic, as he sat down.

"That's not true. One dreams every night. It is just that you don't remember. Do you have special plans for this morning?"

"I promised to visit Mike Brewer in the new studio."

"Good. Then I will join you. I suggest that you first come with me to the house of Armand and Claire Laurin. It gives you the opportunity to attend a meeting."

"Good," said Vic.

They ate and talked, and then they went on their way. They walked through the park to the Golden Street and entered the Laurins' house. In spite of the early hour it was crowded in the meeting room. Régine avoided Vic's look. He knew she had called his grandfather last night and told him he had threatened to go back home. He was introduced to some partners he had not met before, and then he was asked to take a seat next to Jacques. A few moment later he witnessed the miraculous ritual that took place here almost every morning.

Jacques rattled off names and figures, talked about buying and selling, and gave his current vision on the developing of international operating businesses.

On Vic's right sat a man by the name of Felix Baudin. He was of a small stature, had straight hair, and wore a bow tie. He took notes. Suddenly he wrote something down on a new sheet of his notebook, tore it out, and shoved it at Vic.

"Jacques Poiron is our prophet," the note said. "Be proud of him."

Vic did not know how to react to this. Finally he gave Felix a short nod, folded up the sheet, and put it in his pocket.

Jacques continued. His hands rested with spread fingers on the tabletop, and he gazed at the ceiling.

"Dunning International will go up by leaps and bounds in the coming months. It is wise to buy shares now. Later I will fix the point of time to sell again. Wait for my instructions. Bankruptcy is imminent for Erik

Kosakov Limited. I suggest that our partner Bertrand Collin deal with the matter today."

"Understood," said Collin, who sat opposite to Vic.

Like an oracle in trance, Jacques rattled on for half an hour. Then he fell silent, shoved back his chair, and stood up. Someone gave him a cup of coffee. The partners were busy talking; they took counsel together and made use of their telephones to pass information through to their own offices.

"We're always here together with the same group," said Tessa Collin to Vic. She was the wife of Bertrand. "It is such a pleasant change to see a new face. Money, that's what it's all about here. You have no idea how much is traded here every day. And all the profit ..."

Together with him she went to the coffee machine. Régine Moret was standing there, and this time she smiled at him.

"You will stare your eyes out when you see the new studio presently," she said. "But if there is something missing, all you have to do is mention it."

Vic felt uncomfortable. He was no judge of the way business was done here. At the moment he had finished his coffee and intended to walk out of the door, his grandfather popped up behind him.

"Come along, Vic," said Jacques. "I am done here. Now you've seen yourself how I handle these things."

Together they left the Laurin house and went through the Golden Street to the studio. Tobias Dupont followed them at a short distance.

"No one knows how I manage to plan this all out, over and over again," said Jacques in a soft voice that only Vic could hear. "I will never tell them. Everything I come up with is the plain truth, and my words lay the foundation of new earnings. Soon you will know the ins and outs of it. You are the only one I will tell all my secrets to."

Vic put his hand in his pocket and found the folded note from Felix Baudin. He took it out, tore it up, and threw it in a trash can at the side of the road.

"I'm not interested in money at all," he said. "Of course I'm just as curious as everyone else about the secret behind your fabulous successes, but money ..."

"Other things are important to you and I know that only too well. Together with you I want to change course. You are a sensitive personality and soon, when you are able to go where I have already been, you will experience it all in a totally different way. That is what makes it so very interesting."

"So there is a way to learn this?"

"That's a way to describe it, yes."

As they walked they passed the huge villas of the partners. Jacques kept up a stiff pace.

"Did you prefer to go by car?" asked Vic.

"I like to take a good walk. Most of the day I spent retired in my tower. When I'm outside, I want to enjoy the beautiful weather and feel the sun on my skin."

Just before they entered the building where the studio was situated, Jacques said:

"Don't forget, Vic, that everything we discuss remains between you and me. Don't discuss the things I tell you with anyone."

"I understand that, and you can count on that."

They found Mike Brewer in the studio, where he was busy mixing the songs Vic had recorded in Nashville. The music blasted from the loudspeakers, and Mike banged his head to the rhythm. He looked up from the new mixer and smiled when he saw Vic. Immediately he turned down the music and stood up.

"How about it?" he shouted. "The newest equipment, the best! This is an eldorado for any producer!"

The bearded giant walked up to Vic and reached out to embrace him. Only then did he see Jacques Poiron standing there.

"Mr. Poiron?" he asked hesitatingly. "I can see the resemblance. Your grandson looks like you. And I, uh ..."

He extended his hand.

"I mean, you are Mr. Poiron, aren't you?"

"Oh yes, I am," answered Jacques with amusement. He grasped Mike's hand and shook it.

"Mike Brewer. Vic's producer. I really don't know how to thank you for the money. I feel so relieved, I've become a different person. This studio really is phenomenal!"

"Pleased to meet you," said Jacques. "I only have the best intentions towards Vic's friends. Are you happy here?"

"I've already forgotten to think about America, and there's a big chance that soon I will not even remember that it exists at all," grinned Mike.

"Feel free to turn up the sound again. I really love everything my grandson creates."

Mike went back to his big leather chair behind the mixer. For half an hour the three men listened to different songs. Vic was enthusiastic about the way they sounded now.

Then Mike showed his both guests around. There was a room full of brand-new instruments—the best quality and most expensive guitars, keyboards, and drums on the market. The studio counted several different recording rooms, and technicians were still busy connecting the different pieces of apparatus. Mike's private rooms had already been fixed up.

"I just ordered furniture, and it's already been delivered," said Mike.

In the corridor hung a framed photograph of Vic. He stood there with his arms crossed, leaning against a walnut tree.

"A little present from *Le Journal de Saint-Milles*," said Mike. "Maurice Aron took the picture when Vic had just arrived and was sitting outside at Chez Marcus. Remember? It appears that everything here can be arranged quickly. The day before yesterday I ordered myself a new car, and yesterday morning it was parked right in front of the studio."

"And still there are people who think that a small town like Saint-Milles is fast asleep," said Jacques. He gave both Americans a contented look and continued: "You can call me by my first name, if you wish. No formalities between us. I consider Vic as my equal, and his friends are my friends."

"That's all right with me, Jacques," said the giant.

Vic seemed to find it difficult to join in. He remained silent. When they went back to the studio, they ran across Régine Moret. She looked worried.

"Nadine Aron was attacked," she said, without greeting them first. Not waiting for their reaction, she continued: "She was coming back from an interview. There was a car parked at the side of the road, and a man gestured at her. He said he needed help. Her husband Maurice called me. When she pulled over, the man grabbed her and made her answer questions about you, Mr. Poiron. She did not know the answers. Then ..."

The words stuck in her throat. The others waited silently. She took some deep breaths and recovered her voice.

"Then he hit her feet several times. With a golf club. Some of the toes are broken. Maurice called me from the hospital. She's there right now. Fortunately I had the presence of mind to ask him to keep this out of the newspaper. Even under these circumstances Maurice hasn't lost his sense of humor. He said that his wife did not feel fit enough to write an article for *Le Journal de Saint-Milles...*"

8

The little hospital at the side of the access road to Saint-Milles was a luxury for the inhabitants of the town and the neighboring villages. Everyone knew it was fully paid for by Jacques Poiron. He had appointed a matron who had gathered a perfect staff around her. The eccentric rich man had done so from interested motives. Now he had his own hospital close by.

Curious about what had happened to the Saint-Milles journalist, Jacques sent for Matron Charlotte Laffont; she received a call and was asked to come to the castle.

He had gone back to the park by himself and sat down on his bench at the bank of the river to dream. When he had awakened and entered the castle, Tobias Dupont told him that Charlotte was already waiting for him in the Louis XIV period room. In the meantime Vic had returned to Ricard, too. His grandfather wanted him to join the conversation.

Charlotte was a middle-aged woman, tall in stature, with short gray hair.

"Inspector Legrand will also inform me later about what exactly happened," said Jacques, "but first I want to hear it from you."

Charlotte was obviously not a person who would take orders from anybody; she would never give information to outsiders about a patient's situation. For a powerful man like Jacques Poiron, however, she had to make an exception.

"The big toe of Mrs. Aron's left foot and two toes of her right foot are broken," she said. "Fortunately, the bone is not crushed. Both feet are in a cast, and it will take quite some time before she will be able to walk again. Only after she calmed down a bit and received some medication, was she able to talk about what had happened to her. It is simply horrible that something like this could take place in our neighborhood. In broad daylight! Someone hit her feet with a blunt instrument till the bones broke."

"What do you think yourself? Could it have been a golf club?"

"That is very well possible."

"There are many golf links in this area," said Jacques meditatively. "Legrand should access the membership rolls. I want to see them myself. Someone wanted to get something from her about me. I am very curious to hear what Nadine has to tell me about that."

Vic listened in silence. It struck him how vigorously his fragile grandfather acted.

"How did she manage to reach the hospital, Charlotte? It seems unlikely to me that she was able to drive a car with broken feet."

"She had done an interview in Les Eyzies. Her husband was on his way to the same address to shoot pictures. That's the way they're used to operating. It's useless for Maurice to be present during an interview, so he takes his pictures afterwards. On his way back he saw his wife's car at the side of the road and stopped. By that time her attacker had already disappeared."

Jacques kept on asking question after question, and Charlotte answered them all amply and patiently. After half an hour she said goodbye and went back to the hospital.

"I want to have a talk with Nadine Aron herself as soon as possible, and with Inspector Legrand as well," said Jacques. "I will take new measures. Someone knows I set Nadine and Maurice Aron in the saddle and made the foundation of *Le Journal de Saint-Milles* possible. This same person seems to believe that Nadine, being the most important representative of the press in this region, knows a lot about me. Next time one of the partners will get abused. I want to have a number of guards present in the area all day and night."

Now, suddenly, he looked tired. But he showed that he was made of the right stuff when he suddenly stuck out his chin and gave Vic a firm look.

"If you are ready for it, I will share my secrets with you now."

Vic nodded yes.

"I'm ready, Grandfather."

Jacques rose to his feet and began to walk up and down the room.

"Now the time has come to take you into my confidence, I almost don't know where to begin. You have to realize that you could be confronted, too, with an insane attacker who puts a knife to your throat, crushes your toes, or does even more terrible things to you. That poor Nadine Aron could not give answers to his questions, simply because she did not know them. In my case that was different. And soon the same will go for you. I will see to it that you will be the best-protected person of us all. Still, there will always be the risk of running up against someone who wants to squeeze the truth out of you. In a case like that there must be someone in your neighborhood who can rescue you."

The room was filled with pieces of furniture from the time of Louis XIV. The ceiling was decorated with gold-winged angels. There were tapestries depicting hunts. Jacques walked past them and looked at them as of he was seeing them for the very first time. Vic sat on a couch, bent forward, his elbows resting on his knees, waiting patiently for the moment his grandfather would begin his story.

"Did you understand that, Vic? There is always a chance what happened to Nadine and me happens to you. You will have to be constantly on the alert."

"Understood," said Vic curtly.

"All right then. Let me start to tell you something about magic..."

Vic sat up straight and frowned.

"Yes, you will ask yourself why I begin on this. What I will explain to you is not very easy, Vic. But perhaps you will agree with me that we humans are odd creatures. We have gone far by thinking rationally. We look around us and want to find an explanation for everything we see. We are constantly busy with materialistic things.

Everything turns on money and power and the ways to survive. But there is more that we need. The mind is also searching for the fantastic, the divine, the magical, the unexplainable. Why can't we be content with the reality of the day, with what we know and see, what we are able to touch and feel? There are so many things we would like to believe in, ideas that enter our heads that we can never ever forget again. Our brains are filled with things we know are impossible, and still we never succeed in getting rid of them. No one has an explanation for that strange quality of us mortals, except for me."

He stood still with his back to a wall tapestry and looked at Vic triumphantly.

"You could suggest that the solution can be found in the word I just used: *mortals*. Afraid as we are of an unavoidable death, of that black hole of infinite silence, we search for something to cling to. An idea, a religion, magic, sorcery. But there is more. We impute qualities to ourselves that actually are not ours at all and that we never had at our disposal in the past. Allow me to give you some examples."

He walked over to the chair opposite to the couch on which Vic sat.

"Take something like levitation. A man sits on the floor, closes his eyes, and concentrates. Suddenly he comes loose from the ground. Very slowly he begins to rise. Then he floats through the room, slips through an open window, and comes back in through another window. A moment later he sits there in his place again and opens his eyes. I think you have heard about things like this."

"Yes," said Vic. "Many stories are told about levitation."

Jacques nodded.

"And they all have something in common. They are all wrong. No human being is able to neutralize gravitation. There is no such thing as levitation. Actually we all know this, but it would be so beautiful if someone really was able to ascend just like that and float round."

He pointed to the ceiling, where the painted angels flew on their golden wings.

"No one ever was able to shoot a picture of an angel, but that does not alter the fact that many people believe that they exist. The same goes for elves, trolls, ghosts, and other apparitions. Who is actually able to move objects only by using the powers of his mind? Who only has to close his eyes to be able to see things that happened in the past or to receive information from the future? How we wish this were all possible, but unfortunately it is not so. Can you transmit thoughts or make your spirit travel while your body is in a state of deep rest? Which value must we assign to oracles and devils or demons, to gods and demigods, to vampires, witchcraft, the evil eye, black and white magic, spiritualism, and who knows what else? These are subjects that give us the creeps when we merely think about them. We already shiver with all these mysteries, and we know that superstition is something that is stored deep in our genes. There is magic in every man, while no one seems to be able to actually do something with it. Magic is as unreal and elusive as a dream."

He stared ahead of himself, and there was a dull expression in his eyes.

"A dream, yes..." he said, this time more to himself than to Vic. "But I don't mean our dreams, not the dreams of common people."

It took some time before he went on. Now his eyes were bright again.

"I'm glad you did not interrupt me. For it is not my intention to have a discussion with you. There is so very much I wish to tell you. Let me do the talking. Slowly but surely the truth will dawn on you, and then you will come to the same conclusion as I—namely that I have discovered something too fantastic to be true. And still it is true...

"Well, so much about magic for now. I want to bring on something else: the history of man. I have been interested in that from my youth up, and of course it was simply terrific that I was born in the Dordogne, where I could experience directly who our far ancestors were. Fortunately my passion was understood by your father, who even became a professor of archaeology. And now you are here and with you I can talk about all these things, for this fire is also burning inside of you. Régine has told me how enthusiastic you were when you visited the museums with her, when you looked at the cave paintings and took walks to the old shelters of the Cro-Magnons."

"It was a stunning experience to be able to see what I had read so much about," said Vic. "Are you trying to tell me that you have discovered something about their magic? Is that the reason why the sorcerer of Les Trois Frères is standing there in the library?"

A smile passed over the face of the old man.

"There is much more going on, boy. True enough, you are thinking in the right direction, but there are things you simply cannot know about. You cannot even guess about them. Everything is much bigger than you think. Just as the library where the sorcerer stands sinks into insignificance beside the collection of books I keep in my tower. What you have seen is a number of books about one and the same subject. I paid a small fortune to an artist who made the sorcerer for me, and it is the only one in the world. He studied photographs from the cave and made a splendid dummy. The director of a museum once made a bid for it, but I did not respond. Oh—I do have to come back to magic. Remember well that magic does not bring us humans any further! We are, as I already mentioned, rational thinking beings. We went through astounding technical developments, and we occupy ourselves with exact sciences. Magic is a sidetrack and is just as elusive as ..."

He paused and smiled again.

"Like your final song text! You will have to deal with magic, and only then will you be able to write that text. Now pay attention, Vic. I am going to tell you a big secret. I never told it to anyone before."

Vic sprawled on the couch and relaxed. The old man began to talk.

"In my young days Ricard was a ruin. The community of Saint-Milles did not have enough money to restore it and make a tourist attraction out of it. The foundation was overgrown. The park was a wilderness. The river had formed a swamp where countless mosquitos hatched out every year. No one ventured to go there. Except for myself. Being an amateur archaeologist, I turned every stone there. All I found were vipers and lizards, bugs and spiders. The tower of the castle, in which I would build my own chambers later, stood proudly upright and was a refuge to bats. Many times other investigators, older than I and much more experienced, had told me there was nothing more to discover in this neighborhood. They had found that Cro-Magnons had lived here and had built shelters under the protruding rock behind what was later the site of the castle. Different objects had been found there—arrowheads, hand axes, a fine tooled piece of a horn, and the image of a horse scratched in stone. One day I decided to go there again. It was my intention to enter the ruin this time. It had been a long time since anyone had been there. It was a Sunday. The rest of the week I had to work. It was chilly and damp in the large rooms of the castle. I walked here, where we are sitting right now, and almost slipped on the smooth floor. Many of the inner walls had collapsed. With my flashlight I shone out in front of me, and carefully I went on. I reached a stone staircase and soon found out that it had been cut out of the rocky bottom on which Ricard was built. After ten steps I could not go further because the passage was filled with heavy rocks weighing anywhere from ten to seventy pounds. Obviously no one had ever taken the trouble to move them away. I remembered a historian who had told me there was a small cellar in

Ricard, cut out in the rock, that had been used to store wine casks and food. This had to be that cellar. I began to clear out the staircase. I picked up stone after stone and threw them up behind me, where they landed on the floor. Only when the battery in my flashlight had almost died did I go back outside. I told nobody what I was doing, not even your grandmother.

"The next Sunday I was back there, and this time I had brought a couple of oil lamps with me. I had a good reason to work myself into a sweat this way. Something had struck me that escaped the notice of others. It had been taken for granted that the cellar had been cut out in the Middle Ages to create a cool storage space. After the castle was destroyed at the beginning of the seventeenth century the cellar was, one assumed, emptied and then filled with boulders. The stairs were all of the same length and breadth. The walls were smooth up to breast height. Above that was a rough vaulting. There I didn't see any marks of cutting. That had made me think, and I had come to the conclusion that this was the entrance to a natural cave that had been widened and wherein the staircase was cut out. It was impossible to determine the original state of the entrance; the rocky ground on which Ricard was built had been leveled. I supposed that the cellar once had been locked by a wooden latch. That Sunday I managed to go ten steps deeper.

"Seven days later I was back again. The work became more difficult now, for I had to get back upstairs with every stone I removed. Then back down all the steps to pick up the next stone. I was so deep under the ground now that I knew for certain this was not just a storage area. I bared the twenty-fifth step and lifted a boulder that was heavier than the others. I had to use all my strength for it. Carefully I stepped back with it, upstairs. Suddenly the stone slipped through my sweaty hands and bounced down the steps. It landed on some other boulders, and then something happened. With a thundering noise all the boulders disappeared into the depths, like grains of rice down a giant's throat. I remained standing there in fright. After I had calmed down a bit, I went to get an oil lamp and carefully descended again.

"Soon I reached the floor of the cellar. The mass of stones had disappeared down a passage in a direct line with the staircase. I held out the lamp in front of me and looked around. The cellar was not big, as the historians had already told me. In fact it was a part of the cave itself and the floor had been leveled, while the ceiling was still rough and unprocessed. The dark passage had been closed with a stone plate, which had been broken into pieces now by the tumbling boulders. I stepped into the cave and went down the steep passage—every now and then I had to stoop or even go on all fours. The walls were damp. I still remember how I touched them with my fingers and considered it had been a long time since another human being had gone the same way. And then a strange thought entered my mind. I had a feeling that I was not alone here. It was an alarming experience. you cannot give an explanation for the fact that you feel the presence of someone else. My stream of thoughts narrowed like the tunnel I went through, and as I wriggled myself through a hole, I could only think about an entity that could not be far away from me. There was an unpleasant feeling between my eyes. Something tried to enter my mind. A headache came up, and I began gasping for breath. The lamp began to flicker, and that scared me so much that I suddenly was able to think clearly again. The frightful thought that the lamp could go out brought me to the edge of a panic. I turned around and rubbed my shoulder against the wall of the tunnel. Crawling, shuffling, and running, I reached the cellar again. There I managed to calm down a bit. I sat down on the stone stairs and put down the lamp. The wick was still burning. For over an hour I remained sitting there with my feet on a step of the stairs and stared into the darkness beneath me. Then I rose to my feet and started to rummage through different rooms of the castle. Somewhere I found some large stone plates, and I dragged them to the staircase. It was a tiring activity. I covered the hole with the plates and then put a great number of stones on it. No one could easily find the cellar now. But I already told you, Vic, that actually no one came here anymore anyway."

Vic had not interrupt his grandfather a single time. Even now he only nodded. Jacques stroked his chin, and his eyes narrowed.

"I went home. I was so confused! And that night I discovered that something inside of me had changed. I had a small workroom where I kept my books and notes about historical finds in the neighborhood. I sat there and took two dice from the drawer. I started to play a certain game. You probably don't know it. You throw the first die and remember the number of points that came up. The trick is to throw the same number of points with the second die. You keep throwing long till you succeed. Try it once yourself. It seldom happens in one throw, and it almost never can be done twice in a row. Most of the times you have to throw over and over again to get the same numbers you got the first time. Now I managed to do it with every throw. Soon I began to wonder if I could predict the number of points with a single throw of the dice. I threw the dice twenty times and made no mistakes. Later I could not remember what had made me take the dice from the drawer. Anyway, from that moment on I knew I was dealing with a special gift. This was only the beginning of a long line of peculiarities. Now come along with me..."

Jacques stood up and left the room. Vic followed him through a long corridor to the library. There Jacques pushed against the shoulder of the sorcerer of Les Trois Frères. The dummy rolled aside, moving easily on wheels concealed in the pedestal. Jacques took a number of books from a shelf. There was a little panel with push buttons built into the wooden wall at the back of the shelf. Jacques touched a number of them. A part of the wall came forward with a soft humming noise and then shoved to the right. Vic looked through the opening that had come into existence and discerned the flat rock bottom on which Ricard was built. Right in front of him was a hole. A stone staircase went down steeply. After the tenth step he could see only darkness.

"The cave ..." he whispered.

"The cave," repeated his grandfather. "I suppose you have understood that I went back here later. With better lamps. With more courage. Later I will tell you about that journey of exploration."

"When?" Vic wanted to know.

"This evening. We will have dinner together. After that you will know everything..."

Vic kept on staring into the darkness until his grandfather moved the wall back again. Then he blinked his eyes as if he had suddenly awakened from a dream.

9

That evening Vic had dinner in a room of the castle where he had never been before. Julia had put silver dishes on the table; her husband Tobias had taken care of the wine and lit the fireplace. Thereupon they had left Vic and his grandfather alone. They sat opposite to each other at the table. Along the walls stood tens of life-size dummies in armor. Steel hands clutched maces, swords, and lances.

"Enjoy your meal," said Jacques. "Serve yourself. Before I tell you about my experiences when I went into the cave for the second time, I want to bring up something else briefly. When the Cro-Magnon tribes arrived in this region, thirty-five thousand years ago or probably even earlier, they knew that they were not alone here. Already about one hundred thousand years before them other human beings had showed up..."

While he dished up his food, he looked at Vic with raised eyebrows.

"The Neanderthal," said Vic, assuming his grandfather wanted to hear this. "Their tracks go back even a quarter of a million years."

Jacques nodded.

"Old, older, oldest . . . remember? We can consider the Cro-Magnons to be our ancestors. We stem from them. We are not descendants of the Neanderthal. I think you already know all that, too."

"When the DNA of Neanderthal was first analyzed, it was concluded that it differed too much from our DNA to consider a mix of them with modern humans possible. New research was done, and it turned out that modern man mated with more primitive sorts, including the Neanderthal. A special exchange of genes ..."

Jacques put his knife and fork back on his plate and enthusiastically clapped his hands.

"Great! You really know something about it. We may consider the Neanderthal man, just like ourselves, to be a *Homo sapiens,* a man of sense. He came to a bad end. His track led nowhere. Among all those billions of sensible human beings on earth we'll find not a single Neanderthal. Much has been speculated about the extinction of the Neanderthal. I think you and I can come up with a great number of explanations given by scientists and dreamers about the mysterious disappearance of these special humans. They could have been driven away by the Cro-Magnons or even have been eaten by them. It could be that the Cro-Magnons brought a disease with them from which they were immune themselves but which killed the Neanderthal."

"The Cro-Magnons were more creative and had better weapons," Vic added to the list.

"How strange it is that no one ever has wondered what would have become of our world if the Neanderthal finally had the best of it," remarked Jacques.

Vic looked up in surprise.

"That has never crossed my mind. What an interesting thought!"

A big smile passed over the face of the old man.

"We can imagine a little bit how a Cro-Magnon was thinking. But there is nothing we know about the thoughts, feelings, and ideas of a Neanderthal. For now we will let this subject rest. I will continue my story about the cave."

Jacques took a bite; Vic drank from the wine.

"It was Sunday again. A rainy, gloomy day. This time I had brought a helmet with me with a lamp on top of it, and I was wearing good mountaineering boots. I had a rope and even a small pickaxe. I had told your grandmother that I would be out all day. She had shrugged her shoulders indifferently. Our marriage wasn't up to much. It was chilly and damp in the castle. After I had opened the entrance to the cave again, I lit the lamp and went downstairs. I remained standing in the cellar for a while to muster up courage. I don't mind telling you that I was afraid. But my curiosity was much bigger than my fear. Carefully I went down into the darkness. Again I had to stoop every now and then and go on all fours. The feeling that I was not alone there also came over me again. It was useless to try to shake myself free of that. The deeper I went, the more I came under the spell of a coercive power that began to rule my mind. I began to search for something to concentrate on. Moving my head from left to right, I lighted the walls with the lamp on my helmet, looking for paintings or carved pictures. You know that artists in former times chose the most strange places to create eternal evidence of their existence."

"Yes," said Vic. "Imprints of hands have been found in places that can only be reached with the most effort. Deep down in caves, in narrow, small rooms where any torch would extinguish, men pushed their hands against the ceiling and spit paint round wrist and fingers, so that a silhouette came into being."

"That was exactly what I was looking for," continued Jacques. "A hand, a little drawing, no matter what; it deflected me from that unknown power that obtruded itself on me. In the meantime I went farther, deeper and deeper into the cave. Every now and then I lay flat on my belly, and then the fear grew that I would get stuck there and would not be able to turn back. I felt an unexplainable pressure on my ears, as if I were in the depth of the sea. Suddenly I noticed that I was gasping, and then the panic struck. How can I explain to you that I thought I was going to drown in the dry tunnel of a cave? With stretched arms I shoved through the narrow space. Unexpectedly the tunnel went down sheerly, and I started to glide. Fortunately the pressure on my ears had gone now, and I was able to take deep breaths again. I had the sensation as if I were riding a bobsled. The bottom was smooth, but my clothes tore on pointed protuberances in the walls."

He fell silent for a while. Staring on his plate, he searched for words.

"I slid towards a bright white light, Vic—a mystic would interrupt me now and say that I had a divine experience; that way one could also mention a feeling of rebirth when I finally managed to return from that narrow cave and suddenly, as by magic, had these enormous powers at my disposal—but this was different. I began gliding more slowly, and finally I lay still in a blaze of light. I had to close my eyes against it. My body turned cold. I rolled on my side and pulled up my knees. Slowly I came loose from the ground. Floating in this room, with my eyes still closed, I began to see things! I saw images in my mind's eye. Figures of men loomed up. Bent over, they ploughed through a thick layer of snow. An icy wind was blowing. They wore clothes of fur. In their right hands each held a stick on which he could lean, and with their left hands they pulled a fur hood over their heads and with screwed-up eyes looked our from under the brim. Weapons hung down from their belts. It was freezing hard. After some time they reached a small cave and went inside. The entrance was closed by animal skins. Inside a fire was burning. It was smoky and dim. People were lying on the ground next to the fire. Slowly they sat up. Short words were uttered. Fingers, numb with cold, peeped out of snow-covered sleeves, and gestures were made. I knew what was going on, I was even able to understand the jabbering: "No food. No catch." Someone raised a sad howling. The newcomers lay down as well. Dry wood was thrown in the fire. Then everyone curled up, and it became quiet. All that was heard was the crackling of the burning wood. The people lay against each other and were asleep. Still I had the sensation that I was floating. I went up to the ceiling of the cave and looked down at the sleeping figures at the fire. A woman shoved the hood from her head. I was lost in wonder when I saw that she did not have the face of a Cro-Magnon woman. In this cave Neanderthals were sleeping...And then it flashed on me how these people had managed to survive the hard circumstances of ice ages. Suddenly I knew, Vic, what it was that made them so different from us..."

"Neanderthal ..." said Vic. "What a peculiar experience! Go on, please, go on!"

"I name a word. *Bar-er*. It means something like 'the sleep of the bear.' What does a bear dream about, when he hibernates? The Neanderthal slept like cave bears, deep and long. Then they were free from the hardship of reality. Gone were the hunger and the extreme cold. There we find the difference between us and them, Vic. The most important part of our life takes place when we are awake. Neanderthals experienced their most beautiful moments during their sleep. In their dreams they led a happy life and they built up their own dream world. There they met with each other—in a world they could keep entirely under control. Now you see, Vic, how two different *Homines sapientes* with their enormous brain capacity reacted to their environment. We took possession of the earth and now are even able to storm the universe, while the Neanderthals took possession of the huge kingdom of dreams."

"Incredible! But how do you know all this?" said Vic. "You were there, deep under the ground in the cave, and you were confused. Where did that white light come from, and how was it possible that you began to see people who lived such a long time ago? You talk about things no one else knows about."

"But do you believe me?"

"You are able to put things together that other people don't even dare to begin with. Yes, I believe you."

"Later I will give you more details. Yes, you have to know how I found out about all this. First you must imagine the two forms of *Homo sapiens* who had to share their territory. The Cro-Magnons developed quickly. They worked together and were always making better weapons. They built shelters and guarded their possessions. Among them were true artists, and they learned to communicate better and better all the time. Many useful inventions were made. These people were bound to change the world and have it all their own way. Countless years earlier the Neanderthals had managed to face the cold and developed the habit of collecting sufficient food in a short period of time to get them through the night. Tough as they were, they did not need so very much. Water and an adequate meal had to do. They only did the most necessary things and then curled up near the fire to travel to the land of dreams. Now that I have told you this, you will understand they hadn't a ghost of a chance against the javelins, axes, and knifes of the Cro-Magnons who took them by surprise in their sleep. That is the main reason for the fact that there are no more Neanderthals left ..."

Jacques gave his grandson time to come to grips with all this. Julia and Tobias Dupont came in to clear the table. As soon as they had left again, the old man continued his story.

"The end was near for the Neanderthals. We will never know exactly how their brains worked. Anyhow, they experienced their dreams in quite another way than we do. To them it was all real. At night they were able to fly, work magic, make the impossible possible. Only the fact that our ancestors lived next to them, Vic, explains our craving for magic!"

"Were they able to communicate?"

"Not really. The language of the Neanderthals was limited, that of the Cro-Magnons still in development. Our ancestors learned to know magic by the enormous power of the Neanderthal minds. Where Neanderthals slept, there was more crackling than just the fire—the sky above them was full of flashing energy! Listen, Vic. As I already said, their end was nearing, their numbers lessened and lessened. A group of frightened, hunted Neanderthals found the cave. They wanted to hide from the members of a Cro-Magnon tribe who were on their trail. Deeper and deeper they went inside. And right at the moment they thought they were safe, big boulders came down through the tunnel with a thundering noise. The entrance had been blocked by their archenemies, and the group found themselves sitting in a small room, packed in complete darkness. Now they were doomed to death. They knew that. First they slipped away into the safety of their dreams. Hunger and thirst woke them up again. Physically weakened, they were mentally still strong. They had met in their dreams and taken the time to comfort each other. Bravely they decided not to await their horrible death, but instead to precipitate it. They ran out of oxygen, and the air was slowly poisoned. They searched for each other's hands in the darkness. Sitting together in a circle, they began their final trip to the land of dreams. There they combined their mental powers. It became light in the small room. They admitted death in their familiar dream world and welcomed it with a powerful counteroffensive. It was a collective suicide in a way unknown to us. They did not want to suffer any longer, and with combined effort they pushed the life out of their bodies and the spirit out of their brains. There was a crackling and flashing in the cave. There was no outlet for the freed energy, and so it ate its way into the cold walls of the cave.

"Once, in the long ago, someone took the stones out of the tunnel. The bottom of the cave was empty. I have no idea who it could have been, but I do know what he experienced. For I have been down to the bottom of the cave as well. The primordial power of Neanderthal brains still crackles like electricity through the close air of the cave and spatters from the walls. I had the sensation that my body was floating when I was there and was flooded with light. For a moment I got a sight of the inner life of the Neanderthals who had died there, and that is why I am able now to tell you so much about them; my own brain was filled with information. It was not a vision, caused by claustrophobia or other kinds of fears, Vic—it was a real experience. I know that no one will believe me where this is concerned, except—"

Vic reacted immediately.

"Except me." And he continued: "After I have gone

down into the cave myself ..."

Jacques raised his glass. He was visibly affected. Tears welled in his old eyes.

"We drink to that, son."

"Yes, Grandfather, we drink to that."

They both took a sip.

"Thank you, Vic. You understand, and you do not immediately rise against it. It is not the time yet to ask you if you are prepared to go down into the cave. Soon we will discuss that. But first I will give you some more information. The blaze of light disappeared. Something had filled my brain with marvelous thoughts—and also, as I would find out later, with marvelous powers. I was exhausted, and it cost me hours to get back above the ground. Again I closed the entrance, and then I went home. It did not take long before I discovered that I could do much more than just predict the number of points that would come up after throwing a die. Vic, I was just an ordinary man. A man with a wife and a son. I had a job in the bakery of Alfonse Lanois and loved searching the neighborhood as an amateur archaeologist. But now I began to dream. And I do not mean dreaming the way everyone does—and probably also not the way a Neanderthal man did. I began to dream like a modern human being who had been given something from Neanderthals who had died from long, long ago. I will also tell you all about the world I built up in my dreams; slowly but surely I have become afraid to go to sleep and step into that world. I have found out things no one else could know, Vic. A month after I had left the cave, I contracted a loan at a bank in Les Eyzies. With that money I began to speculate. Three months later I bought the bakery from old Alfonse Lanois, who immediately retired. Three years later all the houses in that street were mine. I was on my way to becoming extremely rich. My marriage never had been much and became worse by the day. I felt the need to be alone. I wanted to sleep alone and dream. A divorce was unavoidable. I bought a house for your grandmother and your father and arranged a generous monthly allowance. Well, I am sorry now that I hardly took care of my son and that I never visited him later in America. The news about death of your parents was a great shock. Please believe me, Vic. It is something I cannot put right. Now I have nothing left to wish for. If I could only live long enough, I would finally possess the entire world. However, I have no friends. In Saint-Milles they say that my partners live in the Golden Street. How right they are. There they have their big villas and offices. They bow for me and they always agree with me. I am their guru and lead them to financial paradise. There is much I have shared with them. My businesses are too big to deal with all by myself. Do you understand? Someone wants to worm my secret out of me. Someone put a knife to my throat..."

He touched his neck.

"Many men would like to become my successor—the big man that can speculate with my inexhaustible capitals, after I'm dead and gone. Everyone hopes that I will invite him to the castle one day for an important interview during which I will tell him that he is the chosen one who is allowed to take my place. But that's not the way it will be, Vic. I am sick and tired of them. I have lost my interest in money. Your wishes are of much more importance than mine ever were. The quest for a beautiful melody, for a beautiful text . . . no, the most beautiful melody and the most beautiful text! A true musical enchantment. Vic, you are my heir! What I want to give you is not just real estate and money. Unfortunately I will also ask certain things of you that are not without danger. Yes, I wish you to go into the cave and be awash with the mysterious powers from the past. For they are still there, deep down there under the ground. It will change your life, and you will rather dream than be awake. But before you make a decision, I will tell you about my own dream world. You know already that it begins to frighten me more and more. I have begun to see shadows and shapes not of my own making. How I wish that you would give it a try..."

He fell silent and slowly shook his head.

"What is it you want to say?" urged Vic.

"Maybe I ask too much of you. I wish that you would work together with me. It is all about an experiment. The Neanderthals came together in their dreams. I have a feeling that someone is trying to penetrate my dreams. Before it comes to the moment that I meet someone in my sleep who is going to do terrible things with me—"

Again he fell silent. Vic asked:

"Have you always been alone in your dreams, up till now?"

"Yes. I assumed it would always be like that. For I was the only one who had entered the cave. You'll understand that I bought Ricard as soon as I had the money for it. That way I was able to keep the entrance of the cave hidden forever."

"Please tell me what you expect from me."

"An experiment, Vic, an important experiment. After you have been deep down in the cave and have returned again, I hope you will use your powers to find the perfect song text and will not, like me, change into a money-grubber."

"The experiment, Grandfather," urged Vic.

"I wish you would try to break into my dream world, while I myself try to step into yours. My God, Vic, I have built something special. Not here, in Saint-Milles, but in my dream world! It is my biggest wish to walk together with you through the streets of my town—the town that exists in my head! Please, don't think I talk double Dutch. I tell you the truth."

"I know that, Grandfather."

"If you only knew how grateful I am for that. If I told this all to someone else, I would be called a fool. No doubt about that. If my partners knew my secret, they would recommend me to the best psychiatrist in France."

He heaved a sigh and sprawled in his chair.

"Enough for today, Vic. Think about everything I have told you. I feel greatly relieved now that I have been able to share my secret with you. You are very dear to me. What I never could have said to your father, I will say now to you: I love you!"

The silence that followed took too long. Vic searched for words in vain.

Finally he said:

"*Bar-er* . . . the hibernation of the cave bear. It is interesting indeed to think about what the world would be if the Neanderthals had managed to survive..."

10

Early in the morning Vic sat down at the breakfast table with his grandfather. They ate, drank coffee, and talked about informal things. Only after they had gone to the library together and closed the door behind them did they become confidential. Vic had hardly gotten any sleep that night, spending most of the night thinking about the things Jacques had told him. He had wondered if Jacques had lost contact with reality and had begun to believe in his own dreams. Now, even at this early point in time, he decided that it all had to be true. He had made a decision for himself, too. He looked at the sorcerer of Les Trois Frères and shivered at the thought that the entrance to the cave was right there, hidden behind the books.

"I will go down into the cave. I am prepared to go after you have told me everything about your special dreams. But there is something I would like to suggest..."

"First let me tell you how extremely happy I am with your decision. Great! You can hardly imagine how glad I am that you don't think I'm a fool. No doubt you turned the matter over in your mind last night. Let me hear your suggestion."

"First, I solemnly promise you that I will not talk with anyone about the things we discuss and do. But I would like to implicate a third person in this."

"Your American friend Mike Brewer."

"You guessed it. He is reliable through and through and really my best friend. Besides, he is strong and he approaches subjects with an open mind. Or did you already inform someone else about your doings as well?"

"Nobody. If you say that Mike Brewer is reliable, then I believe you. Do you only want to inform him, or do you want him to go with you into the cave?"

"I want him to join me."

"Don't think I agree with this hastily and without consideration. I never do things hastily and without consideration. You have to understand that I want to hand over my power to you. Yes, my power, my money, everything. Which means that I will have to accept your decisions as long as I don't see any risks. Mike Brewer. The third man. It is all right with me."

"I will have to get used to all this. With a stable friend like Mike at my side I will feel much stronger."

"I will make up my will in your favor. All my partners will be crestfallen when they hear they missed the boat. All I did in my life, Vic, was make a huge mountain of money. I did it with a wicked pleasure. Now I will use my last days by helping you on your way on your search for something of spiritual value beyond everything that has to do with wild fantasies. I suggest that we meet again this evening, at dinner, in the same room as yesterday. Or would you like to come with me to the partners?"

"Tonight is all right. First I will go to the office of the

newspaper to see how Nadine Aron is doing—I hear she is out of the hospital and back at work. After that I will carefully start a conversation with Mike."

"Do you realize what is going to happen, Vic? You must not do things hastily and without consideration either."

"If life itself is a challenge for everyone, Grandfather, then that must go for me in particular, don't you think? You already guessed it, I did not get a wink of sleep last night. Everything is not only new to me, it is also the most fantastic thing I have ever heard. Being an artist I am used to special ideas, but this really beats everything. I won't let this opportunity slip by. Please forgive me for not reacting more enthusiastically to the news that I will be your heir. You possess so much that I am hardly able to grasp it. This is too—"

He fell silent and shrugged his shoulders.

"You will get used to riches, Vic. Believe me. You will get the best advisors, people you can depend on. Let's not talk about that anymore for the time being. If your friend Mike will not join us, he will have to be as silent as the grave about what you have told him. If he's on, you must take him with you tonight for dinner. Then he can hear as well what I have to explain to you about the miraculous contents of my dreams."

Vic walked up to the door.

"Wait a moment," said Jacques. "Tell Nadine that I will pay her a visit soon as well. Give her my kind regards and wish her a speedy recovery. I will send a present for her along with you."

Vic left the park of Ricard in a brand-new Italian sports car. He drove trough Saint-Milles and parked in front of the building of the newspaper. Not much later he found himself in the office of Nadine Aron. She was sitting behind her desk and drinking coffee from a big cup.

"Hello Vic," she said. "If you'd come one minute earlier, you might have met Inspector Legrand. The police do not take kindly to this affair, and Legrand was here yesterday as well. They want to find the offender as soon as possible. Who on earth is so mean and evil that he ..."

She put her cup on the desktop, pushed her chair backwards, and gave it a quarter turn. Then she stretched her legs. She was wearing a miniskirt, and she was in plaster from her toes halfway up her calves.

"I live on painkillers and strong coffee," she said. "The only positive thing about that is that it doesn't make you fat."

"What have they done to you ..." stammered Vic. "Who could have something like that on his conscience?"

Nadine shrugged her shoulders.

"That's difficult to say, of course. I just talked with Legrand about that and we have come to the conclusion that almost all the partners from the Golden Street are fanatical golf players. Which makes the number of suspects very large..."

Vic walked up to her, came standing behind her, and rolled her chair to the window.

"Hey! What are you doing?" she cried.

"You'll have to recover quickly. Just look outside. Do

you see that red Maserati?"

Her mouth fell open.

"Is that yours?"

He dropped the keys in her lap.

"No. Yours. A present from my grandfather. It has hardly been driven. In fact it's brand-new. My grandfather hopes you will get well soon, and he is intending to pay you a visit."

Nadine burst out in tears. Carefully he pushed her chair back to the desk. She took a packet of tissues from a drawer.

"Jacques Poiron is the hero of Saint-Milles," she said, after having dried her tears and blown her nose. "We owe all our prosperity and wealth to him and him only. Without him everything would be so different. The newspaper was set up with his help—I sit here in this beautiful building because he has taken care of that. Why are people so cruel? First Jacques was almost killed, and now they have almost crushed both my feet."

Vic sat down opposite to her and waited for her to calm down.

"What exactly happened?" he asked.

Slowly she shook her head.

"First let me try to deal with the fact that I have suddenly become the owner of such a splendid car," she said. "Believe me, you begin to feel a lot better with a present like that. Well then, Vic, here I sit with three broken toes. I had been in Les Eyzies for the paper. Nothing special. An interview with the coach of a sports club. On my way back I saw a car standing at the side of the road. A man was walking up to the middle of the road and waving with his hands and I was forced to stop. I am sure that he was already wearing a hat, but had not yet covered his face with a scarf. But that was undoubtedly the case when I opened the door, intending to step out. I don't know either where that golf club came from all of a sudden. Maybe he had laid it on the ground next to his car. He kicked my door open wider and held the golf club in both hands, ready to strike. I already had my feet out of the car, touching the ground. He was a tall, slender man and wore a dark suit, a white shirt, and a black necktie with white stripes. He started to talk. His voice sounded strangled behind the scarf. He said I had to answer his questions, or he would crush my knees!

"I couldn't count on any help coming along. You probably know that it is seldom busy on the roads round Saint-Milles. I nodded and said that I would cooperate. It was all about your grandfather. Jacques Poiron must have developed a special method for make profits over and over again. I, being the owner and editor-in-chief of *Le Journal de Saint-Milles,* should know more about that. I shrugged my shoulders in despair and believe me, my eyes bugged with fear as I watched the golf club coming down. Fortunately he spared my knees. I screamed when he hit my foot. The question was repeated. Again I had no answer. And so the second blow followed. My other foot was hit. My goodness, Vic, I simply didn't know the answer. Here in Saint-Milles we all know that your grandfather can do things no one can, and we all are well aware of the fact that his talent brings us wealth. No one has ever dared to ask him how he manages to do so—I think we're scared he would get annoyed and move to somewhere else! And then there was that idiot who threatened him with a knife and almost drowned him in the river . . . the same idiot who hit my foot one more time, and again, and again..."

She leaned forward, her elbows resting on the desktop, and hid her face behind her hands. For the second time she started to cry. Her husband Maurice entered and swore full out when he saw her sitting there like that.

"Damn! This is fucking unbelievable!" he said, as he walked up to her and put his hand gently on her head. "When Martin Legrand has found the offender and brings him to trial, I will keep myself calm. As long as he is in prison, he is safe. On the day he is a free man again, I will wait for him with a golf club in my hands, and I will break him from his toes up to his fucking crown."

He turned his head and glared at Vic.

"Do you understand what I mean? When I'm through with him, they will have to pick him up, for he will never again be able to take a single step."

For the first time in a long while Vic took his sunglasses from the inside pocket of his jacket and put them on.

He remained silent and watched Maurice comfort Nadine. After a while she managed to produce a smile again, and then she showed her man the keys of the sports car. Maurice turned up his nose at it.

"No one can make this all right again, no one can make us forget what they have done to you, Nadine. Not even Jacques Poiron with all his goddamned money."

"Let it go, Maurice," she said. "It's all bad enough. I don't want to think about it any more. Vic is here, and you can show him his pictures. Please let's pretend that everything is just all right again. If I can do so, with these painful feet of mine, than you can do it as well."

"Yeah, you're probably right," he sighed. Then he turned to Vic again. "But there is one more thing I would like to say. I think about it over and over again, that I was just a little too late to see her attacker. I would have chased him in my car and pushed him from the road, straight into the ravine." He looked over his shoulder to his wife. "What kind of car was he driving, Nadine?"

"That is what Legrand wanted to know, too. I don't remember exactly. But I do know that it was an old one. Yes, an old car. A Fiat, a Renault, a Japanese . . . no idea. How strange that you see quite other things in situations like that. It struck me that there was a dent in the door. Oh, and the color was green. Dark green. I forgot to tell that to Legrand, I will call him immediately."

As she started to dial the number, Maurice said to Vic:

"You see? An old car. I could have caught up with it and . . . Oh well, Nadine is right. I have to let it go. Come with me. There's another office here where I keep your photos."

Vic stood up and followed him.

In Maurice's office they looked at the pictures.

"We're going to work together with Disque Dragon," said Maurice. "I think your friend Mike Brewer is a nice fellow. As long as you are here in Saint-Milles, I am your only photographer and there is much demand for your pictures, all over the world. Can you imagine, Vic, that I am still trembling with anger?"

"I can understand that, yes," responded Vic. "Who does something like that . . . to a woman!"

"Go ask that question in the Golden Street," said Maurice. "There must be someone there who is able to give you the answer."

Then he started to swear wholeheartedly.

Vic looked at the pictures closely and tried to think of a way you get out of there as soon as possible.

11

On an early Sunday morning Jacques Poiron had closed the door between the rooms of Tobias and Julia Poiron and the rest of the castle. With that he prevented them from discovering anything about the experiment that would be executed presently. Then he went to the kitchen where Vic and Mike sat at the table drinking coffee.

"This is the day, my friends. Are you both still determined to go?"

Vic blew on his coffee and nodded silently without looking up. He looked pale. The bearded giant opposite to him grinned. "You bet, Mr. Poiron," said Mike. He did not call him, as suggested, by his first name. "It is an incredible challenge. I've worked together with your grandson for a long time, and we have become close friends. Our worlds have interwoven. Perhaps the same will go for our dream worlds presently! Wouldn't that be simply great?"

"Aren't you afraid?"

"I never quite understood what someone meant when he told me that his curiosity had conquered his fear. Now I know."

He grinned, took a sip from his coffee, licked his moustache, and continued:

"Actually, I am a free man in every way. I mean, there has never been someone who was waiting for me. First I followed Vic to France. Now I will follow him into the great unknown."

"Do you both realize that this can change your life completely?"

"We have discussed that several times before, Grandfather," remarked Vic.

He was right. Two weeks had gone by since Vic had paid a visit to Nadine Aron. That same day he had told Mike everything about the discussions he'd had with his grandfather. Mike had been enthusiastic from the very start. Together they had several meetings with Jacques.

In the meantime Vic's new album was released. He recorded some new numbers in the Disque Dragon studio, performed exclusively for Jacques's partners, gave interviews, and wrote more new songs. Every day the friends talked about entering the cave. Vic told Mike all he knew about Cro-Magnons and Neanderthals and showed him books and pictures. Still they had postponed the moment they would go several times. Only after Jacques had told them that he was beginning to feel more and more angry in his own dream world where grotesque shadows threatened him, did they set a firm date.

The coffee cups were empty. Silently the three men rose to their feet, left the kitchen, walked through the corridor, and entered the library. On the table lay two sets of red overalls and two helmets with built-in battery-operated lamps, and two flashlights. Vic and Mike put on the overalls and the helmets, and each fastened a flashlight to his belt. The sorcerer of Les Trois Frères was pushed aside, and the panel behind him was opened. Cold air came streaming in. Jacques shook hands with both of them. There were tears in his eyes. He was the first one to say something.

"I will wait for you here. No mater how long it takes, I will not leave the library. Lots of success. If I wasn't too old for it, I would come along with you, for in fact we do not know what will happen when someone reaches the bottom of the cave for the second time."

"We'll come back as soon as possible," said Vic. "Don't you worry about a thing."

He turned around and stepped into the darkness.

"I realize how unique my situation is," said Mike to the old man. "Everything seems to be so unreal. But it won't be long till I find out if everything you told me is actually true. No, no, I do not doubt. It is just—just too fantastic to accept it just like that. Do you understand what I mean?"

"Yes, I understand. I am glad that Vic does not have to go all by himself."

Mike grinned.

"Well, I better hurry then, for I don't believe he is waiting for me."

He also went inside. Jacques left the panel open. Dizzy with emotion, he stumbled to the table. He sat down and stared up at the cave paintings. Fear came over him. For the first time in years, he decided not to go to sleep this afternoon. And he would prevent himself from dozing off while he remained sitting here at the table— too many shadows slid through the streets of his magical dream town.

"You promised me, Vic," he whispered. "You will return as fast as possible. I need your help."

Vic went down the stone steps. In the cellar he waited for Mike. They stood opposite to each other and then turned away their heads when they blinded each other with the lamps on their helmets. Their laughter sounded hollow and nervous.

"Thank you," said Vic.

"For what?"

"For coming along with me."

Vic walked on carefully. With his hands he touched the chilly walls. He bumped his head on the ceiling and continued on in a stooped position. After some time he even had to go on all fours. He wondered if the giant behind him should be able to wriggle through the narrow passages.

He lost his feeling for time.

He had no idea for how long he had been walking and crawling now.

Suddenly he heard Mike's voice.

"We're not alone here. Do you feel that, too? I just can't describe it. The presence of someone else . . . an entity. I know that sounds vague, but I think your grandfather said it the same way."

"I know exactly what you mean," Vic said, without stopping or looking back. "Perhaps it isn't explainable.

We are not alone. I can feel that just as well as you. And now there is that pressure on my ears my grandfather warned me about."

"As if you are deep down under water. He said that several times."

Now they had trouble not slipping. The tunnel curved down abruptly. The friends fell silent. They went on all fours, and sometimes they crawled like earthworms over the bottom. Vic reached out his arms. He began to slide. Behind him Mike gave a shout.

"We'll be smashed!"

"Keep it up!" shouted Vic. "There! The light!"

Faster and faster he slid over the smooth bottom of the tunnel, toward a bright white light.

It was impossible to stop.

Suddenly he was surrounded by light, and he had the feeling as if he was floating.

"It was as if my body was made out of tin," Mike would say to him later. "A tin body, repelled by strong magnets. My head was empty, and I began to feel terribly cold."

Vic himself had experienced it in another way:

"As if I had landed in the center of a cold star..."

Although they were floating in the cave together, they did not seem to be able to communicate. Each of them had his personal experience of the bitter cold of a remote ice age, where they joined wandering Neanderthals and let themselves be carried along to a smoky cavern. They curled up near the fire and started to dream.

Bar-er, the hibernation of the cave bear. The world began to color up. Something had lodged in their minds and would never disappear again. Neanderthal brains worked so very differently than theirs. From that moment on a power of fabulous origin housed in their head. They both had received a key that gave entrance to the infinite kingdom of dreams.

In the moment that they came back to reality and found themselves crawling back through the narrow cave, they knew that the land of dreams was just as endless as the universe. Silent, too tired to speak, too full of their own thoughts, they moved on upwards. Only after they had arrived in the cellar and had sat down there with their backs against the wall, their lanterns switched off, were they were able to talk again.

"That power, where does it come from?" said Vic. "I mean, how can it still be there after all these thousands of years?"

He looked up along the stone staircase and saw light burning in the library. From the place where he sat he could only see a small patch of the cave paintings.

"The white light obstructed the view," said Mike, gasping for breath. "Maybe there is an altar, or something that has saved thoughts through the ages like a battery holds energy...I can swear to it, Vic, that something crept into my head."

". . . And something of that energy in the cave comes loose as soon as someone is in the neighborhood," whispered Vic. "I really need some time to come to terms with all this..."

They had gone down into the depths of the cave and come back again, and now the steps of the stairs to the warmth of the library seemed an impossible obstacle.

Jacques Poiron, who had heard their voices, appeared like a ghost in the opening and stared down into the darkness.

"Vic? Is that you?"

"Yes."

"Is everything all right?"

"I guess so."

"Is Mike there with you?"

"Yes. We'll come up in a little while. We need some time to come to our senses."

"I understand. You must be exhausted. I'm so happy that you have returned."

One hour later they found themselves in the big kitchen of Castle Ricard again. It turned out to be late in the afternoon. Vic realized he must have floated in the white light for a long time. Mike had taken a bottle of beer from the fridge and after he had opened it and taken a few swigs, he started to look for food. Vic and his grandfather sat down at the table.

"Do you regret going there?" asked Jacques.

Vic leaned with his elbows on the tabletop with his chin on his hands and rubbed his closed eyes with his fingertips.

"No, absolutely not. It has been a marvelous experience, and I am still astonished about what has happened."

He began to tell about his experiences. In the meantime Mike had begun to prepare a great meal, and a delicious smell filled the kitchen. Jacques listened in silence and with close attention to his grandson's story.

He did answer a phone call from Tobias Dupont, who checked at set times to see if everything was all right with him. After Vic had told him everything, Jacques took a big white die from his pocket, showed it in his open hand, and said:

"I will roll it towards you. It will stop with the six up."

He threw the die. It bounced over the tabletop and came to a halt right in front of one of Vic's elbows.

"You see? Six. Your turn. Name a number of eyes. You will see that it is always good."

Vic picked up the die and rolled it between thumb and forefinger.

"Two," he said and at the same moment he dropped the cube.

The die rolled to the middle of the table. It stopped and the upper side showed two black spots. Mike bent over the table and with a grin he snatched away the die.

"Five," he said and then he threw it.

The die rolled along the length if the tabletop and stopped right at the edge.

"Unbelievable," he sighed. "Five it is..."

"You can repeat it as often as you wish," said Jacques. "You will always succeed. You can only ask yourself two things where this is concerned: is it you who knows the future, or is it you who makes the future?"

"What is the answer?" Vic wanted to know.

"I hope to find that out together with you. For I have not wondered too much about it myself. I have only made use of my new capabilities. My way. I did great business. Everything I initiated became a success."

Mike put the food on the table. He opened a bottle of Bergerac for Jacques and two bottles of beer for Vic and himself. Then he sat down, too.

"Enjoy your meal, friends," he said. "I am as famished as a Neanderthal man who has returned without a catch from a long hunt through a frozen land."

He tried to produce a smile, but tightened his lips when he saw how the others gave him a serious look and nodded.

"Yes," said Jacques. "All three of us have been able to feel for a short while how it was to live in that time, so very long ago. Not like a Cro-Magnon—no, like a Neanderthal! It is an experience we can share with each other. And with no one else ..."

12

For the first time Vic and Mike entered the tower of the castle. They stared their eyes out in the big, round reception hall. They too appeared to be able to distinguish the divine spark in every stone in the wall. Each both described this new experience in his own way.

"A stone remains a stone," said Mike. "The consciousness of a stone can not be compared with that of an animal, not to mention that of a human being. Still, I am able to perceive, feel, and see something that I can only describe as consciousness. I never knew this...This emerald, for instance, gives me a good feeling." He touched it with his fingers. "The marble radiates pride, power, and beauty. And this here gives me a vision of endless patience and eternal darkness..."

"It is a meteorite," explained the old man.

"There is no measuring equipment to register this," said Vic. "However, I know that my experiences of this moment are real. Our definition of consciousness is wrong. Everything has a . . . a soul? Is that the way the Neanderthals saw it, Grandfather? Did everything have a soul in their eyes?"

"Don't forget," said Jacques, "that we are no

Neanderthals! They have given us something, a valuable present from far-off days. Thanks to them magic has come into our lives, and now we are able to see things that remain invisible to all other people. What seems to be something like elusive sorcery to someone else appears to be tangible to us, visible and understandable. The experiences the Neanderthals had must have been different from those of the three of us. Just take the fact that we are discussing this, with so many words...They were not able to do that. But an understanding—a deep, almost holy understanding—definitely was one of their most important qualities."

"They saw with different eyes," remarked Vic.

"That is it!" said his grandfather. "That is the expression I have searched for myself in vain for such a long time. And you, being a true poet, were able to come up with it spontaneously. Yes, they saw with different eyes..."

They went up along the winding staircase.

The library in the tower was much bigger than the one where the sorcerer of Les Trois Frères stood. The round wall was filled with books from floor to ceiling. The shelves were of walnut, the vertical supporting beams provided with the most beautiful wood carving.

"Everything we know about dreams, psychology, and archaeology is collected here," said Jacques. "Well, of course that is exaggerated, but on the other hand there are books here that you will not find anywhere else. Unique exemplars that have cost me fortunes."

Vic and Mike walked along past the books. Every now and then they squatted down to read the title of a book on the undermost shelves. They heard the old man chuckle.

"Human wisdom," he said. "Our wisdom. About what we see with our very eyes, Vic. I begin to find your remark more and more interesting. Seen through the eyes of a fly, a mouse, a cat, or a dog, everything looks totally different. The Neanderthal man, *Homo sapiens* like we and still so different from us, saw his own world. And we were allowed to catch a glimpse of that."

Vic and Mike sat down opposite to him.

"We have to make a vow," said Jacques. "We must promise to each other that we will keep this all to ourselves."

"We have discussed that often before, Grandfather."

"That is true. But perhaps a vow is not enough. Taking an oath will better. And because this is something very special, I suggest that we also make a special ritual of it."

"What do you have in mind?"

"Someone was trying to get a secret out of me. I could have been killed. You run the same risk. Especially if it leaks out that you have the same knowledge I do. For us there is much to win or to lose. Be on the alert, don't let yourself be surprised by someone who will do everything possible to get you talking. Come. Vic, Mike, put your hand on mine."

They did so and Jacques said in a solemn voice:

"We see our world with different eyes. Only the three of us. We will meet in our dreams. Our talents will remain a secret to outsiders. Therefore we swear an oath of allegiance to ourselves and each other and will never betray our secrets. Yes, so I promise..."

He had closed his eyes while he was talking. Now he looked at the two others.

"So I promise," said Vic.

"So I promise," said Mike also.

* * *

Vic rolled on his side and pulled up his legs. He shivered with cold under his blanket. After all the events of the day, he had believed that it would be hard to fall asleep, but right after he went to bed he knew that he would succeed. A strong desire came over him to enter the land of dreams. Shivering like a Neanderthal near the fire, he lay there. And then, suddenly, his body relaxed. A smile passed over his face. He found himself in an empty, white world. It was quiet there. He started to experiment. First he wanted to see his hands. They appeared immediately. Using only the power of his thoughts he colored his fingers red, green, and purple. His nails grew black and then red like carbuncles. All of a sudden there were smooth golden rings around all his fingers. He started to decorate the gold with loops, curls, letters, and other imaginative marks. He concentrated on a ring on his right forefinger while he brought his hand closer to his face. It was as if he were looking through a strong microscope; the grooves in the gold seemed like deep ravines. Five more rings appeared in front of him. He strung them together with the gold rings and flung them through his white world, high above his head. He let the chain grow bigger and revolve on an imaginary axis. Now he himself turned around and around and, pointing with his finger, he made the horizon appear. He colored the sky dark blue. His rings moved along like five golden suns and five silver moons. Spontaneously he had started the building of his personal dream world, and he had great fun! After these first experiments he decided that he should not do things overhastily. He wanted to know if everything he made appear was his to do with as he pleased. A gravel walk came into existence and stretched out to the far horizon. With a simple gesture of his hand he let the path fade away again. He looked up and took a silver and a golden link from the rotating chain. Then he placed them back again. It was obvious that he was lord and master of his own world. The sky turned black. The suns and moons radiated. He raised his hands. With thumbs up and forefingers pointed he fired imaginary bullets into the darkness, and twinkling stars appeared all around. When he lowered his hands, he suddenly realized that this was not a real Neanderthal dream world. Neanderthals had never known of revolvers; they had never even progressed to the invention of the bow and arrow. They had never seen gold or silver. He was able to make use of an innate Neanderthal quality, and now he could build his own dream world. Was he able to predict the future as his grandfather did? Looking up to the rotating chain of rings, he asked aloud:

"For how long will I live?"

His voice sounded familiar to his ears. It remained quiet. There came no answer, and his mind was not filled with impressions concerning his future.

"Music!" he cried out.

Slowly he sank down on his knees in the transparent, endless white. He was able to hear different instruments. The rings were jingling as they moved in a curve through the sky. They went from east to west and disappeared behind the horizon. The sound faded away and swelled again as they came up again in the east. He heard violins and flutes. He hammered with his fist in the air, and there was the sound of drums and cymbals. Musical ideas filled his brain and were pressed into his dream world on the stream of his thoughts. But soon he had to stop. Smiling, he shook his head; so many beautiful tones he had never heard before, and now he needed some rest to come to his senses again. But he could not remain at rest for long.

He jumped up and started to dance around.

He stretched his arms and waved his hands.

"Big concert halls with unknown acoustics!" he shouted full of enthusiasm. "I have to get cracking. A town full of music. A song at every corner, an orchestra in every building!"

He realized that he was perfectly happy. Now he had the time to bring music to perfection. He was convinced that he was able now to make the perfect song. It did not matter how many nights he needed. He knew he would do the trick. The music swelled. Vic Emmett still danced. Filled with this novel happiness, he made up new variations over and over again for the invisible instruments that sounded from the white world and the dark sky. He went into ecstasies. Not for a single moment did it cross his mind that all this was happening in a dream.

To him this was reality, and he never thought about the fact that he lay on his side in a bed in Castle Ricard, fast asleep.

His body and mind were in two totally different dimensions.

13

Right before he awakened, Vic felt a sensation of floating. With his arms spread, he flew up high into the dark sky. Beneath him he made grassland and forests appear. He conjured fantastic rocks, lakes, rivers, and a sea. He plunged down and split the grassland, went through the earth, and came up again in a jungle. At full speed he flew right through the rocks, dived into the waves of the sea, and disappeared under the surface. In the next moment he went straight to the horizon. His world appeared to be endless; there were no bounds.

Then he noticed he was on the verge of waking up. In spite of all impressions of the dream, he knew that he would feel relaxed and rested when he opened his eyes. This was all he had to do to step from his dream world into reality: open his eyes. . . .

It is a riddle of the mind how easily someone can come back from a dream into reality. While he had a good stretch, Vic thought of the wonders he had seen. Then he opened his eyes and started when he saw his grandfather seated in a chair in front of him like a life-sized, futuristic view of himself.

Vic smiled sleepily at his grandfather. "Unbelievable,"

he sighed. "When am I dealing with reality—when I am asleep, or when I am awake? Good morning, Grandfather. Did you come in to ask me about my experiences? I believe I just gave you the answer."

He was wide awake. Jacques jumped up from the chair, and only now was Vic able to read fear in the eyes of the old man.

"Vic! Couldn't you find my world? I was so scared, so very scared! Grotesque, dark shadows slid through my streets, shades moved behind my windows!"

Vic searched for words.

"Well, I . . . I didn't try. That was obviously not in the order of things yet. First I have to discover my own world. Explore it, build it up . . . I am so sorry. Was it that bad again?"

"It has never been worse. Can someone suffer from a persecution complex during his sleep? Is this something unique for what men like you, Mike, and I have come to be? Or are there actually certain entities that have found the way to my dream world? It is exhausting me; my nerves are all to pieces. I fear the moment that I will be confronted with someone in my dreams who will threaten me. The shadows are begin to take a definite shape. They have become human figures, and I have a feeling that they will become recognizable soon."

Vic got up, walked past his grandfather, and went into the bathroom. He left the door slightly ajar.

"I am sorry!" he shouted, while he took a shower. "It just didn't cross my mind to look for you."

"You are right!" Jacques shouted back. "It was not the

time for it. I just had hoped for it, because I need your help so badly. Yours and Mike's."

Vic heard from his voice that Jacques had come standing closer to the door.

"By the way, it wasn't my intention to scare you. I shouldn't have entered your room just like that."

"No problem."

"You know . . . the Neanderthal dreams are a blessing. Only you can't switch them off. It is not possible to go to sleep without letting the dreams come. You will have to deal with that. I never expected the shadows to appear. And you have no idea how fear can strike when you start to see something which is not a part of your own dreams!"

"I will do my very best to reach you, I promise," Vic shouted over the sound of the shower. "I'll make a definite attempt to find you tonight."

After a while he came into the bedroom again. He had wrapped a towel around his waist. He saw that Jacques was still standing near the door, staring at the floor downheartedly.

"Grandfather, I've been living here for quite a while now and I would like to have some more rooms for my own use."

Jacques looked up in fright.

"Do you say so because I was in your bedroom when you woke up?"

Vic came standing in front of him and put his hands on his shoulders.

"Of course not! Don't you worry about that. There is much I have to tell you about my dreams. Heavenly sounds came to my ears. Now I feel the urgent need to get myself some instruments and work certain things out. I need recording equipment, so that I don't have to run to Mike's studio every time I have an inspiration. There are also many personal belongings from America that I want to unpack."

"I see. Well, besides the rooms of Tobias and Julia Dupont and my tower, you can have any rooms you want. And don't forget that one day Ricard will be your property..."

After Vic had dressed, they went to the kitchen. There they talked about common things as long as Tobias and Julia were there and discussed Vic's experiences as soon as they were alone again.

"I have the disposal of my own will," said Vic. "Which is very special in dreams. Or, said in another way, that distinguishes Neanderthal dreams from normal dreams."

"I've made a penetrating study of everything concerning dreams," said Jacques. "There are people who have taught themselves to remember everything that has gone through their head at night. They are able to manipulate their dreams and can, in a certain way, determine what is going to happen. It is undoubtedly a very interesting and exciting occupation, but it has nothing to do with what we are experiencing. I can show you a pile of books on the subject."

Then Jacques asked his grandson if he wanted to come along with him to the partners. He had important things to say during a meeting and would feel very supported by Vic's presence. And so it happened that they left Ricard around half past ten and walked through the grounds to the Golden Street. This time the meeting was not held in Armand and Claire Laurin's house, but in a four-storied office building that accommodated the companies belonging to Bertrand Collin and Antoine Chevalier. Vic had never met Antoine. He was six feet tall, and with his broad shoulders he looked more like an athlete than a businessman. He had half-length curly hair and a moustache and wore corduroy trousers and a sweater. The partners sat together at a table in a big meeting room.

Antoine showed Vic to a place between Régine Moret and Tessa Collin.

Jacques sat down at the head of the table and waited until everyone was quiet. All eyes were focused on him now.

"Friends," he said, "from today on, some things will change. I do not think, in view of my advanced age, that it is like a bolt from the blue to you when I say that I would like to take things a bit easier."

No one reacted. It seemed wiser to the partners to wait for what more the old man had to say.

"It is even my intention to retire from business entirely in the course of time," said Jacques, and now a murmur went up.

"What do you mean by 'course of time,' Jacques?" Antoine wanted to know.

The old man shrugged his narrow shoulders.

"I don't know. Preferably as soon as possible. My health is falling off by leaps and bounds. My intuition has begun to let me down. Today, for instance, I have no special suggestions for you. It is getting rather empty here..."

He tapped his head with his fingers.

Suddenly he began to smile.

"Don't look so downcast. Please don't act like this takes you by surprise and that I have frightened you. You are all very well able to go on without me. Dear friends, together we have made incredible fortunes. If there is anyone here who does not want to go on after my retirement, he can start throwing money about for the rest of his life, and there still will be enough left to let his children and grandchildren roll in wealth."

Someone started to laugh. Someone else laughed along with him.

Régine looked at him with tears in her eyes and said:

"We understand, Jacques. You need rest. If you only knew how much we are in your debt; for you have brought us all where we are right now."

She started to clap her hands. The partners followed her example. They all rose to their feet. Jacques remained sitting and stared at the tabletop. As soon as the applause had died down, he continued:

"There is something else of great importance you have to know about. One of the most important things in my life was the arrival of my grandson Vic. Being my only descendant, he will inherit all my capital and property. At an early date I will make my will. Vic Emmett will be the new lord of Castle Ricard and the owner of the premises in Saint-Milles. I hope to live long enough to gather a group of experts round him who can assist him by word and deed."

Again there was applause. And again it was Régine who began to speak:

"Congratulations, Vic. Terrific! I am so happy for you. And as far as you are concerned, Jacques, I hope you are intending to live longer than the time you need to call a number of bankers, lawyers, and other advisers together. A man of your reputation can do a thing like that within two or three days..."

The partners burst out in laughter. Jacques laughed along with them and nodded enthusiastically.

"Yes, Régine, you are right. It is not my intention to step out that soon. Life is far too beautiful, especially now that my grandson is with me all the time."

Another partner began to speak. It was Sergio Paladino, a man of Italian origin with straight, dark hair, a sharp nose, and thick eyebrows.

"Dear Jacques, I am very sure that I talk on behalf of everyone when I tell you that we are so proud of you. Proud, and above all grateful. You have molded us, you have made us the persons we are right now. It is true— there is nothing to worry about, and the generations to come will also lead a life of luxury. Please allow us to organize a party for you in the nearby future, so that we have the chance to thank you properly. At that same party we will strike up a close friendship with Vic and see to it that he will feel at home forever in our midst. It would be great if he was willing to make music for us that day. We would love to see him perform."

After him other partners also got up to speak. Soon they were indulging in reminiscences, and Jacques was praised again and again as the inspiring leader who had laid the foundations of countless profitable enterprises. Régine offered act as one of Vic's advisers, and thereupon various other partners did the same. Vic felt like an heir to a throne, surrounded by old advisers who did their utmost to keep their privileges and secure their positions, and it did not make him feel comfortable. He took his sunglasses from his inside pocket. From behind the dark glasses he looked around the table and wondered in silence who of the partners had given orders to put a knife on his grandfather's throat and hit the feet of Nadine Aron with a golf club.

* * *

Mike Brewer looked as if he had seen ghosts. He sat on a leather chair in the dark studio. There was dead silence in the room. He clutched the armrests as if he were afraid to fall and compressed his lips. He stared out in front of him, with his eyes wide open. That was how Vic had found him here, and it seemed that Mike hadn't noticed him at all.

"Mike ..." said Vic in a soft voice.

The reaction of the giant was bewildering. Heavily frightened, he let go of the armrests and hid his face behind his hands. He pushed off with his feet, and the chair rolled backwards on its little wheels. The back of the chair bumped against the mixing unit. Mike lowered his hands and took a deep rasping breath.

"Vic—Vic—" he said hastily. "I will never ever sleep again! Do you hear what I say? Never again!"

Vic took a chair and sat down opposite to his friend.

"What has happened?"

Mike panted, licked his upper lip and moustache, swallowed several times, and forced himself to calm down.

"This is worse than a bad trip," he said. "Believe me, I know what I'm talking about, for there have been times I could hardly deal with hallucinogenic stuff."

"I know Mike, I know. You couldn't stand it. While others had fun, you became downhearted. Finally it scared you so much that you kicked the habit spontaneously. And what has happened now?"

Mike reacted with a number of counter-questions:

"How the hell can I get rid of this? Why didn't I take this into account? Is there no way back? How long can someone stay awake, how long can someone keep on walking round because he is too scared to fall asleep?"

He nervously ran his fingers through his hair and he began to pluck at his beard.

"My God," sighed Vic. "This comes so unexpectedly. So I am the only one of us with positive experiences. My grandfather is hunted by shadows, and you . . . Please quiet down and tell me all about it."

Mike rose to his feet and left the studio with uncertain steps. He came back with an opened bottle of Bergerac. As soon as he sat down again he placed the neck between moustache and beard and started to drink. After the bottle was half empty he took a moment to take a deep breath. Then he emptied it completely.

"That will not make your dreams more pleasant," warned Vic. "I hope this will not make you loose tongued either. Don't forget we have sworn an oath."

"No, I will not forget. Damn, Vic, I went to bed full of hope. I expected so much from this. Slowly I rolled on my side and turned up my knees. Sleep came over me almost immediately. It became ice cold. A biting wind seemed to go right through me. My body froze. I could see my hands. They seemed to be made of glass. Suddenly they burst, and the fragments fell down around me. Everything turned white. I felt a screaming pain. It felt as if I was being stabbed by sharp knives of ice. I got lost in that white world and couldn't tell if I was standing still, walking, or running. My hands had disappeared for good. I couldn't see my feet either. I had become invisible, I had been dissolved in the white. All that remained was that stinging pain. Finally it was the growing fear that woke me up. Numb with cold, I lay on my bed. Then the warmth came back. What remained was that fear. And I'm still afraid. It is my wish now to stay awake forever!"

"You know as well as I that such a thing is impossible. Sooner or later you will fall asleep. Let us hope you will be able to overcome your fear."

Vic told about his own experiences. Mike listened attentively and seemed to forget about his own misery for a while. Then Vic went to the other side of the studio and sat down at a piano. He tried to remember what he had heard in his dreams and began to play. At first his fingers searched for the right tones. Then his playing became more self-confident, and soon he went into a trance. His head moved up and down to the rhythm.

All at once he felt two strong hands around his wrists, forcing him to stop playing. He looked up in surprise. All the lights in the studio were on now.

Mike was standing next to him and looked at him with tired, bloodshot eyes; tears ran down his cheeks and disappeared in his beard.

"Stop it, Vic! Please stop!"

"Mike! What are you crying for?"

"It is so beautiful, so incredibly beautiful...I recorded the most of it. You've just surpassed yourself."

"Then why do you make me stop?"

"You'll get too tired. You've already been playing for four hours straight!"

"Impossible! I feeling like I've only just begun."

But a look on his watch told him that the giant was right.

He heaved a big sigh.

"I imagine, Mike ..." he said, "that we both will go insane before long. Raving mad!"

He burst out in laughter. Mike wiped away his tears and laughed along with him.

Together they went back to the part of the studio where the recording equipment stood. Before Mike started the music he went for a second bottle of Bergerac. This time he took little sips. Then he sat down at the controls.

The piano music began.

Dark, unearthly music filled the room. Bizarre chords alternated and suggested a horrible thunderstorm nearing; amidst the thunder sharp, high tones came down like flashes of lightning. This was not anything like the music Vic remembered hearing in his dreams. Neither could he recall that he had played this himself;

sitting at the piano he had lost himself immediately.

Vic and Mike were not the only people present here. Disque Dragon was in operation. Michelle Ferrer, who had been hired to run Vic's management, had left her office and entered the studio, where she had listened to the music with increasing amazement. Then she had left to tell others that she had heard something horrible that she could not place at all. Soon the studio was filled with curious people. They listened to the odd composition, and every now and then some of them pressed their hands against their ears. Michelle gave a scream when high notes suddenly gave her a stinging headache. At that moment Mike looked up. He put the bottle of wine, which was already almost empty, on the floor and abruptly shut off the music. Vic blinked his eyes. Michelle, whose headache immediately disappeared when the music stopped, asked with a trembling voice:

"What was that?"

Vic made an indifferent gesture.

"Nothing special. A little joke. Brought it with me from America. It is an artist who claims he can do anything he wants with an instrument."

"That music comes straight from hell, if you ask me," said Michelle. "I hope you are not considering releasing something like that by Disque Dragon."

"Don't you worry about that," said Vic; he looked at her and smiled. "I don't think there is a record company in the world who would give a chance to someone like that."

Michelle smiled back at him.

"Then we are in agreement, Vic," she said.

She left the studio, and the others followed her.

"From this day forward we have to watch what we are doing," whispered Vic to Mike. "As long as we don't know ourselves what is happening, we have to keep all our actions secret from the outside world."

Mike heaved a deep sigh.

"You're right," he said. "I will destroy this recording. I will do it immediately..."

14

Mike Brewer found himself in the bar of a fancy hotel in Paris, staring out glassily at his umpteenth glass of whiskey. Saint-Milles had begun to weigh down on him, and he had jumped at the invitation from some of the partners to come along with them. Sergio Paladino and Antoine Chevalier had taken care of him, and together they visited exclusive restaurants and nightclubs. It struck them that he looked even worse in the morning than the night before, but thought it had to do with the fact that he didn't allow himself a moment's rest with the girls in his bedroom. Mike was accustomed to the night life in the States, from New York to Las Vegas, but then he was still a producer who worked for Greg Albin's MultiRec. Now he was a well-to-do man himself, being fêted by two fabulously rich men; Sergio was, for instance, the owner of the nightclub they just had visited, and the hotel was owned by Antoine.

Dark-haired Sergio, a man of small stature, sat to Mike's left, and the blond Antoine, just as big as himself, sat to his right. There were no other visitors left on this late hour. Mike had a strong will. He was drunk, but not far enough gone to forget that he had to remain silent about certain things. Just as on every night before each man retired to his own room, the partners began to ask questions.

Sergio had taken an advertising brochure from a pile on the corner of the bar, unfolded it, and turned it around. It showed a tourist street map of Paris. He nudged Mike with his elbow and pointed with a finger at Boulevard Saint-Germain.

"Look, Mike, we are here right now. If I made this walk ..." he let his finger slide along the boulevard, flicked his thumb over Pont de la Concorde and slid it from the north side of the Seine along Champs Élysées up to Place Charles de Gaulle, where the Arc de Triomphe stood " . . . I would pass so many buildings owned by the partners that I would lose count."

He ticked so many times with the tip of his finger on different spots on the map that it made Mike dizzy. It was obvious that Sergio'd had too much to drink as well. "Here, here, and here . . . you'll find our buildings everywhere, in all districts of the town. I am just mentioning Paris, my friend—and believe me, France is a big country. And who do we have to thank for that?"

"Jacques Poiron," answered Mike.

He emptied his glass and placed it on the bar. The barman hurried to refill it.

"That's right," said Sergio. "He is a visionary. Predicts the future, where business is concerned, with faultless precision. No one can match that. Now he's going to take things easier, and he wants to spend time with his grandson. Do you know what we think about that?"

"No idea" was Mike's reaction; in spite of his

drunkenness he stayed on the alert. He preferred to sit here listening to the partners rather than lie in bed, where sleep would catch him and carry him along to ice-cold dreams.

"We are happy for him. Everyone hopes he will have a pleasant time." Suddenly he banged his fist on the bar. "Damn! We are men of means, we have reached an improbably high level. We should be as invulnerable as the gods! And still it is possible that a mere nobody like that policeman Martin Legrand can come troubling us time after time. The fatso bumps in everywhere, asking stupid questions. As if one of us should have threatened the old man. Do you understand anything about that?"

Now Mike only shrugged his shoulders. Now the big man to his right began to speak.

"What Sergio means is that this is a straight insult to us. Not one of us would ever bother Jacques. What Legrand does not understand is that we would derive no benefit at all by knowing how the old man does his tricks. Do you have any idea what this hotel is worth? I am not just the majority shareholder, I am the one and only owner. If I sold all my other properties, I could fill all the rooms of this hotel from floor to ceiling with money! Making money is a disease. It would be better for many of us to follow Jacques's example. We are young, we have an entire life ahead of us. It would be smart if we finally started to enjoy it. But what is your impression of Jacques? He never met his grandson before, and all of a sudden they seem to be inseparable."

"I think his grandfather only did business all his life,"

said Mike. "Maybe money was some kind of a disease for him as well. One says that men become more gentle when they grow old. Now he has reached a point at which his emotions prevail above his stinginess."

After having said so much he needed another shot of whiskey.

Antoine grinned.

"You're an honest man, Mike. I agree with you. Come, it's time to turn in. Shall I send a nice girl to your room again?"

"No, no, thanks. I'll get me another drink. I prefer to stay here for another while."

Antoine and Sergio left the bar. Mike ordered another glass of whiskey. He took one swig too many. Suddenly he felt sick and dizzy. Still he managed to control himself.

Slowly he got up, thanked the barman, turned on his heels, and walked away with short strides. He could not find the lift and took the stairs. Step after step he stumbled his way up, and every second he began to feel more miserable. He had never felt so bad before. It was a miracle that he was able to find his room on the fourth story. Instead of lying down on the bed immediately, he sat down on the floor and opened the minibar. He drank small bottles of liquor, washed down his burning throat with beer. With great difficulty he managed to get up again and stretched his length on the bed.

"Demons of the ice-cold plain, just come and get me now," he sighed. "And please see to it that my soul freezes over and I never wake up again!"

* * *

Every time Vic tried to get to sleep, he made up his mind to search for his grandfather in his dream. He had moved into other rooms, where all his personal belongings from America had a new place. During the day he was very busy. He had performed on a television show and after that given interviews. He had worked on new songs and together with Michelle Ferrer of Disque Dragon had selected musicians to accompany him at the party that was being organized to honor Jacques Poiron. He had phoned Mike in Paris several times and had begun to worry about him; his voice never sounded sober.

When he went to bed, he was tired.

"I will do my very best to reach you, Grandfather," he would think, before he rolled himself on his side and closed his eyes.

But as soon as he had started dreaming he had forgotten about this promise. Full of energy, he had started to build his own town. He made mountains appear and cut big stones out of it with his bare hands. He threw them on a heap until it had become higher than the highest mountain.

When he wanted to have granite, he colored the stones deep black with the power of his thoughts. When he wanted to have marble, he made colorful flames in white blocks. The first building arose in a place that he considered from that moment on as the center of his town. It became an enormous concert hall with a domed roof. He succeeded in giving form to everything he had in mind. He worked with the utmost concentration and had an eye for details. The outside of the building was freakishly formed, with high doors and a flight of steps. Inside he made balconies and chandeliers hang down from the dome on golden chains. He covered the chairs with plush. But when he wanted to fill the hall with an audience, he was faced with a unsolvable problem. It turned out to be impossible to conjure up people. Only with the utmost exertion did he manage to create a large number of motionless shadows, whom he provided with clothes and trinkets. Seen from the stage, where he had placed a grand piano, they looked like men and women of flesh and blood. He only had to think of applause, and it sounded through the hall. Here he played a spontaneously composed number, and never before had an instrument sounded that beautiful and clear. Afterwards he rose to his feet, made a deep bow, and let the ovation last for a long time. He decorated the inside of the dome now with beautiful, colorful paintings. There was no limit to his creativity. Outside he laid out a huge park around the building and populated the trees with birds. Without any difficulty he made trees, plants, and animals appear. Everything he wished for himself he called to mind, and a moment later it was actually there. Night after night he went on. He played in the concert hall, roamed through the park, constructed roads, and built beautiful houses. Soon there were canals and lakes. He couldn't get enough of playing around with materials and forms. Until he had built a house in a new dream that was totally to his liking. It counted twenty rooms, and he had decorated them all carefully. He sat down in an easy chair, leaned back, and looked around with satisfaction. Suddenly his face fell. He felt lonely here. He was a man who could easily be all by himself for a long time, but there were also moments that he longed for some company. The chirping birds on the windowsill didn't cheer him up. The motionless shades he could create were no solution either. He got up and began to walk up and down the room. Only after a long time did he stand still. A vague thought had crossed his mind. Desperately he tried to find out what it was that stayed right under the surface of his dream consciousness. Then he knew it.

"Grandfather!" he whispered.

With large strides he left the room, went through the corridor, and swung the front door open. He looked outside and frowned. He had hoped to find the old man standing on the doorstep by projecting him there in thought. No one was there. Vic Emmett found himself all alone in his beautiful dream world.

In the meantime Jacques Poiron's health was getting worse. Every morning he asked Vic if he had tried to search for him yet. Now, finally, Vic say yes, even though the result had been negative.

"Keep on trying—please, keep on trying," pleaded Jacques. "If you only knew how afraid I am during the night ..."

"I have to succeed," replied Vic. "I know for sure that the Neanderthals could step from their own dream worlds into those of others without difficulty. You built yourself a town and started to do business with the future. I am working on mine and want to compose heavenly music there, I want to find the ultimate song there. Now, being wide awake, I see the building of a town as something symbolic. We are no Neanderthals, that is what we have to keep in mind. What would they have built in their dreams?"

"I really wouldn't know," said Jacques with a sigh. He made a weak and nervous gesture.

"Perhaps they kept each other warm in their dreams," mused Vic. "They fled from the cold and entered a sunny paradise full of flowers and plants. They created a world that was much more pleasant than the white, frozen reality. Slowly but surely I begin to understand why they were so different from us. They had found their own, unique way to escape from the hard, miserable existence in long-lasting ice ages."

"Help me, Vic," urged his grandfather. "Do your utmost to find me. My dreams have become nightmares, and I know that I can't stand them much longer..."

* * *

Mike Brewer lay on his belly on the hotel bed, still dressed. Fuddled with drink, he had fallen asleep immediately. The cold cut right through his soul. His spirit remained calm and resigned. If death was intending to come and get him, he was welcome. He gave himself up to fate. And that became his salvation. Deep asleep, he breathed more quietly. His dream grew clear as glass. Actually the cold was not all that unpleasant. It was as if drunkenness were a tangible phenomenon instead of a physical condition. And that tangible thing froze over and then broke into shivers; it burst into tiny pieces of ice, and he began to sober up. The first things he saw were his hands. They were stiff and red with cold. He moved his fingers. Then he saw his feet, and at the same time he started to move them through his white world. With his arms spread he let himself float away. He thought of warmth, and felt the temperature rise. A soft wind blew in his face.

"Heaven! Earth!" he cried out, and a merry, relieved laughter followed when he heard his own voice clearly.

Everything above him became blue; beneath him it became green. In the distance both colors were separated by a long, straight, black line. It looked all very much like a children's drawing. Still roaring with laughter, he had to admit to himself that he was not as sober as he had thought. He loved floating. He dived several times, and then he made his big body turn somersaults through the air. Only after a long time did he land in the green. He managed to let grass and bushes grow and plant trees as high as the highest skyscrapers of New York. Still he roared with laughter. The trees grew thicker and even higher. The ground was covered with ripe fruit in all possible forms and colors. He picked one up and tasted it. It tasted good. As he ate, he let himself rise slowly along the trunk of a huge tree. He sat down on one of the upper branches. The view was breathtaking. He let himself fall and zipped down. Right before he touched the ground he slackened his speed and landed softly on his toes. Leaning his back against a tree he tried to order his thoughts. Who was he? Mike Brewer. Where did he live? Above the studio of Disque Dragon in Saint-Milles, a small town in France. Where was his body at this very moment? In a hotel room in Paris. Where was he right now? In a world he could only reach during sleep, but that was far more realistic than all the others he had ever dreamt. Where would he prefer to be?

"Here ..." he sighed, "for here is my paradise..."

* * *

Antoine Chevalier and Sergio Paladino had breakfast in the restaurant of the hotel that morning. They had ordered orange juice with vodka to chase away their hangovers and hardly touched the food. The first joke Antoine made was about Mike.

"Just take a look at ourselves. And then imagine what the American will look like if he shows up in a while. Bloodshot eyes, as sick as a dog, a splitting headache . . . I hope I won't burst out laughing."

"Toothpaste in his beard and the worst breath of entire Paris," supplied Sergio. "He has gone too far. He can't stand liquor at all, and still he keeps on drinking."

But they looked up in surprise when they saw Mike step into the restaurant. He wore clean trousers and a shirt and walked boldly upright toward the table. His hair was still wet. His eyes looked bright. After he had sat down with them, he rubbed his hands, well contented.

"A good morning to you, my friends," he said in a merry voice. "I see you are not very hungry. Never mind, for I am starving. Whoever doesn't believe I can wolf down everything that's here on the table can make a bet with me."

He poured himself a cup of coffee and began to breakfast. Both other men turned their faces away and took small sips from their orange juice and vodka.

"We still have some more days to make fun," said Mike with his mouth full. "And then we'll have to go back to Saint-Milles. We mustn't miss the big party."

"That's right," said Sergio. "All the partners will be present, so we will be there, too. Where did you get all that energy from, so all of a sudden?"

Mike looked as him, and his eyes narrowed when he started to chuckle.

"I believe that just happens of itself when you finally have decided to sleep alone for just one night," he answered.

15

The party was organized by the partners and lasted an entire week. They spared neither trouble nor expense to make it a success. All hotels in the villages and little towns in the neighborhood were full up, a large field was filled with luxury trailers, and the partners had opened their own doors for the most important guests. On the parking lots in Saint-Milles stood the most impressive limousines. It was busy in the decorated streets, and the restaurants and pubs did good business. Jacques Poiron himself hardly ever showed up these days. He looked tired and pale, as if a gigantic leech had quenched its thirst with him. His clothes had become a size too big for him. Doctor Jean-Louis Gilbert had visited him already several times and finally had referred him to the hospital for a searching examination. Charlotte Laffont, the matron, had been present for that. She suspected that his suffering was mainly mental, and was having a disastrous effect on his physical condition.

"A serious lack of sleep can undermine a person's strength," she had said to him. "I can give you pills. You should eat good meals. I can also supply extra vitamins and minerals. The truth is, Monsieur Poiron, that you are not getting any younger."

He refused to take sleeping pills.

"Then maybe you want to talk with someone about your worries. It would be no problem to send for the best psychiatrist in Paris. He will be here as soon as possible."

"I have no worries at all," Jacques reacted stubbornly. "And if I did, I would prefer to discuss them with Régine Moret. She knows me through and through, and I know that I can trust her. I don't want to have anything to do with strange psychiatrists."

"As you please," said the matron, knowing it was useless to argue.

Ill or not, he was still the big boss.

He was administered oxygen and left the hospital in a wheelchair. The man who had always danced through the park every day around noon on his way to his bench at the riverside was no longer able to stand on his feet for too long. Vic was constantly with him. He pushed the wheelchair and sat together with Jacques in the backseat when Tobias Dupont drove them around. From behind the closed windows of the car they looked at the festivities. But soon the old man became bored. He tapped Tobias on the shoulder and asked him to drive back to Ricard.

Mike Brewer had the week of his life. Festivals were organized on big fields around Saint-Milles and different artists performed there, all hoping to land a contract with Disque Dragon. Mike worked there as the sound engineer, and also judged everyone who got on stage. Michelle Ferrer, Vic's manager, worked together with

Mike to draw up a report about artists who could possibly mean something to his new company. Mike was smiling all day. He had a good time, and as soon as he was back in his apartment he went to bed. He did not build towns in his dreams. He roamed through the big forests he had made appear, floated between the trunks and high above the tops, and felt even more happy than during the day.

"Do you do your utmost to find me?" asked Jacques time after time, when he was alone with Vic and Mike. "Don't you understand that I am slowly going downhill?"

Vic said that he had tried and tried. Mike had to admit that he had not thought about it at all in his dreams.

"My own world is so special. I only have an eye for the scenery I've created myself. Believe me—every time I go to sleep, I solemnly make up my mind to use all my time to search for you. And then I step into that beautiful, quiet, green world, and all I want to do is float..."

Jacques could not run away from all the festivities. In the park of Ricard everything had been made ready for the guests to meet him. Over a thousand guests were invited. Most of them came by boat from Saint-Milles. From the river they had a beautiful view of the castle and its surroundings. They were mainly business friends who owed Jacques much. They came from all parts of the world. In droves they walked past the tables full of food and drink; tens of cooks worked in the open air at big grills and cookers, and the air was filled with delicious smells. Music sounded everywhere. Tents were set up, and anyone preferred to get out of the sun during the day could sit down under one of the countless umbrellas.

At night the park was lit by many-colored Chinese lanterns.

Vic opened a door of the castle and pushed his grandfather outside in his wheelchair. Now the music fell silent, and everyone looked up. Vic led the old man through the park. Again and again he had to stop to allow people to congratulate Jacques. Many of the visitors were seized with the unpleasant feeling that they had come to say goodbye to a dying man. They all thought they would never see him again. Jacques made constant use of an oxygen mask that was connected with a plastic tube to a storage tank under the seat. Several times he gestured with both hands that he needed more space, after which Vic pushed him on.

When grand fireworks were let off at the bank of the river, the old man watched them from behind one of the windows of the white tower. Then several partners made speeches. Jacques sat straight up in bed, shivering with fear, fighting sleep.

"Please stay with me, Vic," he asked with a trembling voice. "I don't think I can stand a new dream. Talk to me, see to it that I stay awake as long as possible."

Nothing could be heard of the sound of revelry outside. The walls of the tower were thick and had double-glazed windows.

"Please believe me, I do my utmost to reach you. There must be a way to find you. But you must try to understand that it is useless to be afraid of shadows…"

"Here and now no shadow could intimidate me," said Jacques. "But you know as well as I that in that other world, in our sleep, everything is completely different. How would you react if all of a sudden something popped up in your dream which was not created by yourself?"

"I must admit that it would frighten me, too."

The old man shook his head slowly.

"Charlotte Laffont has told me that I am not getting younger. What she tried to make clear to me was that I have to take into account that death is already waiting for me. I hope it is not my time yet, for there is so much I want to find out. Imagine that I could die, right in the middle of our experiment!"

It was already early in the morning when Jacques rolled himself on his side, pulled up his knees, and closed his eyes. Vic had stayed awake the whole time, and now he remained watching by his grandfather.

After just one hour the old man woke up again. There was fear in his eyes.

He had hardly moved during his sleep, and his breathing had been quiet. Now he started to pant, and sweat dripped down his temples.

"How terrible it was," he said. "Horrible! I could clearly feel someone's presence. And I also heard voices. Unintelligible jabbering it was, but nevertheless voices! I began to feel sick and dizzy. There was that vague scent...Vic, I feel so tired, so very, very tired..."

"Maybe it had been wiser for you to ask Doctor Gilbert for a sleeping pill. Do you want me to drive you to the hospital, so that you can have a talk with Charlotte Laffont?"

"Certainly not! You don't know by half what an effect that stuff has on your dreams. Never ever take sleeping pills in this situation. It will make your nightmare compete! No, I would like to go for a drive in one of the cars this morning—drive around quietly and enjoy the surroundings. It has been a long time since I have been out of Saint-Milles. Will you come along with me and sit at the wheel?"

"Sure," said Vic, suppressing a yawn.

After having breakfast Vic picked out a car. He chose a little, sporty Renault. His grandfather stepped in with great difficulty. The wheelchair was left behind in the garage. Vic drove up to the gate, which was opened by a security guard. In his mirror he could see that it was not immediately closed again. Another car loomed up behind them. It was the big Mercedes in which Mike and he had been brought here from Paris.

"Our guardian angel is following us," he remarked.

Jacques did not take the trouble to look behind him, responding:

"I know I can always count on a man like Tobias Dupont."

After a short time they left Saint-Milles behind them. After they passed the hospital, Jacques showed Vic a road that led to a high, rocky plateau.

"Let me show you a cave with the most beautiful Cro-Magnon paintings," he said. "It is closed to everybody, but I know someone who will be happy to open the iron gate for me which is placed in front of the entrance. This ride is doing me a world of good, can you imagine that? It is such a beautiful morning, and I have always loved this country. Do you also see the world with different eyes than before you started dreaming?"

"Oh yes, absolutely. Everything moves, everything lives..."

"Right. Everything is alive. But death lies in wait, Vic. For me. Are you afraid of death, Vic?"

Vic understood why he was asking this. It had been clear for some time that Jacques knew he had not much longer to live. Vic decided to give an honest answer.

"Death already showed his cruel grin when I was still a kid and my parents had that accident. Then it was Rita Cianello's turn, my girlfriend..."

"I know, I know. Together with a member of your band. An overdose."

"Kenneth. Kenneth Kenning. The events made me gloomy and introverted. I do not fear death, although I prefer to keep him at a distance as long as possible."

They drove along a long, winding road that led through a rocky territory with a forest in the distance. There was no oncoming traffic. Vic turned up the speed. He had opened his window, and the wind made his hair fly.

Suddenly a shot rang out. Immediately he looked in the mirror. He saw the Mercedes swerving wildly.

"What was that?" cried Jacques.

The Mercedes went off the road. Its left front wheel bumped up against a boulder. The car spun and almost turned over. Vic lessened speed quickly.

"Tobias. He needs help!"

A big, rusty Fiat, which had been hidden behind the Mercedes, came up to Vic at a high speed. A second shot rang out. A bullet hit the bumper of the Renault. Looking in the mirror he could see that the driver of the Fiat held a revolver outside the window. Immediately he stepped on the gas. Jacques had turned half in his seat and recognized the danger.

"Go, Vic, go! Ride like the devil! Someone wants to kill me!"

A third shot rang out. This time it missed the car. The road was full of curves. The Renault accelerated, and the wind roared inside through the open window. Vic divided his attention between driving the car and watching his fast-nearing pursuer in the rearview mirror. Strangely enough, he did not think for a minute about the danger that threatened for him and his grandfather; he only worried about the situation of Tobias Dupont. What had happened to him? Was he injured?

"Faster!" cried Jacques.

There was much spirit in the little Renault, and Vic managed to enlarge the distance between himself and the rusty Fiat. He drove as if all the demons of the underworld were chasing him. Following the winding road, he reached the forest. The morning sun had only just climbed above the plateau. Among the deciduous trees it suddenly became dim and full of shadows. The long-drawn warning sound of a motor horn was heard, and he saw headlights flash. A truck neared at full speed. Reflexively, Vic turned the wheel to the right. The car went off the road and the tires plowed through the friable soil. The truck narrowly missed him, the sound of its horn reaching a crescendo and then fading. With much effort he managed to bring the Renault onto the road again. He looked over his shoulder. The truck had stopped at the edge of the forest. It sat bathed in sunlight. The Fiat had swerved to the right, too, and come to a standstill against a tree. The hood had burst open, and the windshield was broken. Flames shot out from the motor. Vic slowed down, stopped, made a U-turn, and drove back. Carefully he approached the burning wreck. The driver of the truck, a tall man in blue overalls, ran up to it, too, a fire extinguisher in his hands.

Vic stopped and got out.

"Didn't you see me, you idiot?" shouted the truck driver at him, as he spouted foam over the motor. "You were driving far too fast; you came on to me like a madman!"

Vic did not answer. He noticed that the left door of the rusty car stood wide open. The man who had fired at him had disappeared. He looked around in despair.

"We'll have to call the police," said the truck driver. "Do you have a cell phone?"

"No," said Vic, still bewildered. "Do you?"

The fire was extinguished. Vic saw a car nearing. It drove past the truck and then entered the forest.

"Tobias!" he sighed. "Thank goodness!"

The Mercedes rocked to the side of the road. The left tire was flat, and the wheel was out of position. Tobias stepped out and limped to the Fiat.

"The police are needed here," said the trucker. He pointed at Vic. "He drove far too fast, and I believe that the driver of this wreck has fled in panic into the forest."

"I've already informed them," said Tobias. "A police car is already on its way from Saint-Milles. How is your grandfather, Vic?"

Together they went to the Renault. The truck driver stared at them with a frown.

"So you know each other," he said, but the two were out of hearing range.

Tobias opened the door.

"Monsieur Poiron!" he cried out. "Monsieur Poiron!"

Jacques sat there sprawled in his seat, leaned heavily backward. His chin rested on his tiny chest, and his mouth was open. Every time he breathed, a rasping sound came from his throat. Tobias took his cell phone from a pocket of his jacket.

"An ambulance," he said, more to himself than to Vic. "An ambulance . . . as quick as possible!"

As soon as he had made his call, he bent over the old man and opened the collar of his shirt.

"Can you hear me? No panic. Please try to keep calm. An ambulance will be here in a couple of minutes."

Jacques stared out in front of him with his eyes wide open and did not react to Tobias's voice.

Vic sat down at the edge of the road. To him everything suddenly looked threatening. It was as if the trees had eyes and looked down on him while they raised their branches like bony fingers. The leaves whispered unintelligible words. The ground beneath him seemed to tremble. He remained sitting there for a long time and saw all kinds of things happen without actually registering them; withdrawn into himself, he was not involved in what was going on around him. The police arrived. Inspector Martin Legrand sent a number of policemen into the forest to search for the driver of the gutted car. The ambulance was there not much later. Two male nurses examined the old man. They administered him oxygen and put him on a stretcher. A few minutes later the ambulance drove back. The truck left now, too. The driver would go to Saint-Milles to deliver his goods and then go to the police station. A garage in Saint-Milles would send a tow truck to pick up the Fiat and then return for the Mercedes. Legrand remained in the forest to wait for the return of his men. Tobias sat down at the wheel of the Renault.

"Let's go, Vic!" he shouted.

Vic rose to his feet, still looking benumbed.

"I'll see you in my office later," Legrand said to him, as he got into his car.

Vic nodded, sat down, and closed the door.

The Renault drove back.

"I hope it will come right with your grandfather," said Tobias.

Finally Vic opened his mouth.

"What can be the matter with him?"

"He does not react to anything. It might be shock. But one of the men from the ambulance was talking about quite something else. He said he was convinced that Monsieur Poiron had lapsed into a coma."

This brought Vic back to reality.

"Into a coma ..." he repeated. "If only he comes out of it soon ..."

A shiver ran down his spine when he pictured to himself Jacques Poiron lying motionless in a hospital bed with a hollow, motionless face, pale as death. No one could imagine that the spirit of that same man was doomed to roam about in a continual nightmare, hunted by shadows.

Tobias drove fast and self-confidently.

"First we'll go to the hospital. The police station comes later. I'll have to leave this car behind there. They want to take a good look at that bullet hole. This is the third attack in a row. Again the offender managed to get away. He shot at the Mercedes, too. In both cases he tried to hit the tires. He missed and hit the back. The reason is clear to me. First he wanted to force me to stop. After that he would concentrate on you. If he had managed to get you ..."

He fell silent. Vic looked at him.

". . . then he probably would have knocked you out and tortured your grandfather till he gave away his secret."

In the hospital they had to wait for a while before they were allowed to see Jacques. He had a room for himself and was lying there exactly as Vic had imagined.

"Now look at him," whispered Tobias. "That poor man. There he lies. In his own hospital. Almost everything in the whole neighborhood belongs to him. Wealth cannot save him; only a straight miracle can pull him through."

"He must come out of his coma," said Vic. "Tobias, see to it that this room is guarded. Both day and night!"

"Understood, Vic," responded Tobias. "You can count on that."

He did not realize that he was taking orders from the

grandson automatically, now the grandfather was out of circulation for the time being.

16

There was no change in the condition of Jacques Poiron. He lay there motionless on the bed in the hospital, and his eyes remained closed. A stomach tube supplied him with artificial feeding. No one could tell if he would ever wake up again.

It struck everyone how calmly Vic behaved following all these events. He himself was the only one who knew the reason for that. For years on end he had been troubled by evil dreams. In dark nights he was confronted time after time with the appearance of Rita Cianello and had witnessed her death again and again. He had seen her die in a thousand different ways. But from the day he had gone down into the cave he had no longer suffered from nightmares, and as soon as he fell asleep he slipped into a world where he felt at ease. In those marvelous surroundings, where he felt present both spiritually and mentally, he found a certain rest, and during the day he felt more relaxed than he had in years.

Every day he sat at his grandfather's bedside. He read different newspapers to him and talked to him. When he was convinced that no one could hear him, he made him the same promise over and over again:

"I will come to you. In your dreams."

This time he had only just entered Jacques's room, when a second visitor showed up. It was Sergio Paladino, who shook hands with Vic and them came and stood right in front of the bed. For a long time he looked at the motionless old man in silence. Then he turned toward Vic and said:

"Charlotte Laffont has sent for many specialists. They come from all over the country and from abroad. All they say is that there is nothing they can do for Jacques. If a miracle takes place, he will come out of his coma one day. If it fails to occur, this will be the first days of his eternal sleep..."

Vic nodded. He sat right in front of the bed. Sergio pushed a chair next to his and sat down with a sigh. When the man folded his hands in his lap, Vic noticed that he wore a gaudy golden watch with diamonds around his right wrist and a thin golden bracelet around his left wrist. Because Vic had not reacted to what he had said, Sergio continued:

"Yes, eternal sleep. Maybe it is for the better that he never returns to reality again. A man of his age could wake up with serious brain damage, and that is the last thing I would wish for him."

Vic still remained silent, and Sergio changed the subject.

"I heard you sing for the first time at your grandfather's celebration. Your voice, your compositions, and your lyrics have made a deep impression on me. The grandson of our beloved Jacques Poiron turns out to be a great artist."

"Thank you," was all Vic said now.

"You are talented enough to survive forever. You are very well able to provide for yourself. And I heard from Régine that you received a nice sum of money from your grandfather."

"What are you driving at?" Vic wanted to know.

Sergio Paladino turned around one of his many rings and stared fixedly at the motionless face of the old man on the bed.

"You know that everything in Saint-Milles is about money. Much, very much money. It is money that keeps the partners together. It would be a great disaster for you if Jacques died without coming to his senses first, but believe me, for us everything is not arranged either."

"Please explain yourself," said Vic, feeling irritated.

"Well, as far as you are concerned . . . you are probably counting on a big legacy. I don't think that Jacques has yet made a will to your credit. When you go to claim your rights and call the partners to account, everyone will tell his own personal version of what Jacques ever promised to you. Do you understand me? That can get rather problematical. In the least worst case it will slacken things down, in the most extreme case it will take years of legal procedures to get what you believe is yours."

Vic looked up at him with big eyes.

"Don't get me wrong, Vic. I'm only telling you what I think. There are partners who are convinced that they will be one of Jacques's heirs."

"You and Antoine Chevalier took Mike Brewer with

you to Paris. From him I heard that you are so rich that you never ever have to worry about a thing. Doesn't that go for most of the partners?"

"That is true. But what will fall to your share is such a fabulous wealth, that even the richest persons in this world will be jealous of you. Don't you forget either that everyone here would like to pull the strings. Saint-Milles is like a huge jewel and a little kingdom as well. Ricard is the castle from where every partner would love to rule…"

"I understand," said Vic, hoping that the man would hold his tongue from now on.

But Sergio continued:

"We all have our own businesses here. But all the interests are closely knit. We are connected to each other via the threads of an invisible web. Your grandfather has always been the spider in that web. Even after he retired from business, he continued to arrange one thing and another with us. His signature is of incalculable value, Vic. Only after countless contracts have been signed or canceled by him, can he—"

"Quietly die," Vic supplied.

"Those are your words. But that's how it is. Anyway, I am happy to learn that this room is guarded both day and night. Well done. When Jacques Poiron comes out of his coma, I will give a party bigger than all the festivities of the last time together. Charlotte should send for more and more specialists!"

He rose to his feet and made the old man a bow.

"Please don't let us down, Jacques," he said. "Now we need you more than ever."

He patted Vic on the back and left the room without

saying another word.

Before he went to sleep that night, Vic concentrated on his mission: finding Jacques Poiron's dream world. He managed to banish all other thoughts. As he sat down on his bed, his spirit slid through the twilight zone between waking and sleeping. Then he rolled on his side and pulled up his knees. He shivered with cold. But the thought of his grandfather had already almost faded away when he entered his dream world and energetically set to work. He moved his hands like a conductor, and everywhere the contours of new buildings loomed up. Boulders came rolling toward him and heaped together. Vic quickly gave a form to everything that came up in his fantasy. Only when he wanted to relax, and stopped working and began to float high above his town, did it occur to him that he had made up his mind to something. Then he remembered.

"Grandfather!" he cried out. "Where are you?"

He did not expect to receive an answer. He was all alone in this world. He flew along at great speed, seeking the borders of his town. It was a long journey. Finally, beneath him there was nothing to see anymore. He began to wonder if he was still moving. He wished that he was back above his town, and immediately he could see the well-known buildings in the depths below.

"I cannot reach the borders of my world by flying," he thought. "Maybe I would travel on forever, like an astronaut lost among the stars."

He slowly descended on the metal dome of a concert hall. He sat down and looked out on his town.

"Now I must try to think clearly," he said aloud.

He came into a state of inner calm. He knocked on the roof with the knuckles of his right hand. A vibration spread through the dome, and what he heard was a clear sound. He knocked harder and felt pain in his fingers. Sound. Pain. He could see, float, fly, feel, smell, build, compose; he could make decisions, effect changes, create plants and animals. Everything here was real, but in a different way than during the time he was awake, and also differently than in a normal dream. This world, no matter how strange, was tangible, visible, and real. The only thing that made him shiver every now and then was the feeling of loneliness.

No one had ever suspected the existence of this dimension.

"I have influence on my surroundings," he said to himself. "If I want to reach the borders of my world, all I should have to do is think about it. I want to be there right now..."

Immediately he felt himself rising up from the dome. At a dizzying speed he tumbled through the air, bridging enormous distances in seconds. Everything around him had turned white. Then, as his speed slackened, he saw a wall rising up in front of him. It was a transparent wall, like glass, and behind it grotesque shadows moved to and fro.

"This is fine," he sighed. "Now it becomes interesting..."

* * *

Mike Brewer had drunk French cognac, and after that he had used cocaine. Early that evening he had already given up his intention to leave the alcohol alone. Later he had not declined the offer to take a good sniff. He lay stretched out on his bed in his apartment. While he listened to Vic Emmett music he enjoyed the sweet attentions of the woman who had rung the doorbell unexpectedly and asked if she was allowed to come in. He knew her. She was married. He knew her man as well.

"No need for you to go all the way to Paris to have a good time, like you did not long ago," she had said to him. "Here in Saint-Milles you can get everything you need. And what is not here yet, can be delivered right away. You will find no other place with so much money swept together into a heap, and rich people know how to spoil themselves. Believe me, I know all about it."

Later she started to ask him questions. About Vic and his grandfather. He gave vague answers. He knew that there were certain things that had to remain a dead secret. After his first climax he drank again, and also used some of the coke. His second climax was sensational.

"Take another drink," she said. "The party isn't over yet."

There were new questions, and his answers were mostly short:

"I don't know. I have no idea..."

When he got sleepy, he began to feel afraid. Mortally afraid. With so much mess in his body he did not dare to visit his dream world. He could not form an idea of how he would feel when he roamed through his self-created forests in this condition. It seemed horrible to him to be all by himself soon. He began to think of bare trees of rotten wood, covered with evil-smelling fungus.

"You have to keep me awake," he said to her. "I don't want to fall asleep."

"Oh, but you're not going to sleep at all," she laughed. "The night is still long."

"I really mean it. As soon as you see me close my eyes, you have to shake me awake. Please, help me."

He looked at her with the trusting eyes of a dog. She brought a glass to his lips. He kept his lips tightly closed, and the cognac dripped into his beard.

"What is the matter with you?"

"Nothing. Just see to it that I stay awake."

"You really are frightened, aren't you?"

"Yes."

All of a sudden she had the idea that there was more going on here than she had ever dared to think. She had come to him to pump him for details about the old man and his grandson, but now she realized that she was on to quite something else.

"Some more coke. That will keep you wide awake."

"I want my body clean again as soon as possible. Otherwise I don't dare to go to sleep."

She smiled at him.

"Sure. One last sniff. It makes you think better. It gives you fresh courage."

"Vic would forbid me!" he sighed. "Vic used to do this shit. Thanks to that he lost his girlfriend and his best friend."

"Exactly. One more sniff, and then you stop."

"Well, all right then."

Fear struck harder. He sat up and looked around with dilated eyes. She wrapped her arms around his big body and began to rock him softly to and fro.

"Give me one reason why you should not fall asleep right now. Only when I know what is troubling you, will I be able to help you."

In that moment it sounded very logical. Mike nodded. He pushed her away and sank down on his back. He folded his hands behind his head and stared up to the white ceiling. Suddenly he burst out in laughter, and she laughed along with him.

"Is it so funny?"

"Funny?" he roared. "It's too crazy for words!"

And then he started to talk. It was as if he were telling it all to that empty ceiling. At the beginning the woman had no idea what he was talking about. Too afraid that he would stop, she did not interrupt him a single time. Mike mixed up the events, and in thought she tried to put everything in the right order. Slowly but surely she succeeded, and when she did, she had a story that seemed too fantastic to be true. After some time he started to rave. His sentences became shorter and shorter, and finally he was only jabbering unintelligible words. He closed his eyes. He was asleep. Slowly she stood up from the bed and walked with unsteady steps to the living room of the apartment to collect her clothes.

Mike did not hear her leave.

She closed the door softly behind her and took the stairs down to the ground level.

In his dream world he tumbled through the jungle.

This was no longer his paradise. The branches were lashing out at him, and he could not evade them. He felt pain. He tried to escape by going up, but the trees grew higher and higher at the same speed. With a loud crack he broke thick branches, and then he fell downwards. He was no longer able to change his direction. Like a bomb from a plane he whizzed to the ground to destroy everything and especially himself.

"No!" he cried. "No! I don't want to die!"

Right before his heavy body touched the ground, he remained hanging in the air.

"I cannot see a thing!" he shouted. "Am I blind?"

He felt around with his hands. His fingers touched wet wood. Branches pushed him down, pressed him onto the ground between the roots.

"I'm choking!"

He wildly lashed around. Every branch he got hold of broke off. It seemed as if the earth wanted to swallow him up. With his hand he grabbed the roots of a tree, and he began to work his way up.

"I am the king of my own world," he sighed.

He was able to see again. The trees changed form. They had leaves and fruits again, and everything began to look once more like his splendid paradise.

Mike woke up. The sun was blazing down behind the curtains. He realized that he had slept for a long time. A screaming headache lay in wait, ready to strike as soon as he moved. He remained lying there motionless, and in fright he asked himself what had happened the night before.

17

Vic had paid a visit to the hospital, and now he was on his way back to Ricard. It was a long walk, and he had decided to take a rest in the center of Saint-Milles, at Chez Marcus. A guard followed him at a short distance. There was always someone in the neighborhood who could protect him when something happened.

An old Citroën bumped with its right wheels against the sidewalk and stopped with screeching brakes. The driver bent to the right and opened the door.

"Vic, please step in for a while."

Vic sat down on a threadbare seat with broken springs.

"Inspector Legrand. How are you doing?"

"I'm fine. I have found out one thing and another, and I want to inform you about it. But your grandfather goes first. Have you seen him? You're a loyal visitor."

"Yes, I was with him just a while ago. The situation remains the same. He is asleep..."

"Everyone in Saint-Milles prays for him. You have to know that. We owe all the prosperity in this neighborhood to him and to no one else."

The inspector started to chuckle.

"Imagine, Vic; even the police station is owned by your grandfather! He rents the building to us for a nominal amount. We have so much space there that some of the offices are still empty. And there are so many cells that arrested men from other districts often get locked up here with us. Jacques Poiron has made something very special out of Saint-Milles."

"I hope that he will wake up again some day and then will be able to enjoy life once more for quite some time," said Vic.

"That's what we all hope. Now listen. We found out where that big, rusty Fiat of your pursuer came from. There is a filling station belonging to George Roulland along the road to Les Eyzies. He also has a garage and sells secondhand cars. Someone bought a car from him and traded in the Fiat. George said that the Fiat was so rusted through and the motor was in such bad shape that it could only make one last ride—to the scrap yard. He hadn't even bothered to take the key from the ignition. The spare keys were still in the glove compartment. A policeman from our station went to have a talk with him, and he said that the Fiat should still be there. But when he went looking for it behind his garage, he realized that someone had stolen the car. He joked about it, saying he was only too glad to be rid of it so easily."

"When someone attacked Nadine Aron with a golf club, there was also talk of an old car," said Vic. "Could it have been the same one?"

"No," answered Legrand. "That was a dark green car. Nadine remembered the color. Now we think it must have been a Renault that was stolen from George

Roulland earlier. It was a worthless wreck as well. He hadn't even taken the trouble to report the theft. We have never found the Renault."

"And not a trace of the perpetrator ..."

"As you know my men have combed the forest where the burning Fiat stood. They found nothing. No one spotted the fleeing man. Nevertheless, we have come a step further. The simple fact that both cars were stolen in the neighborhood tells us that we have to look for the perpetrator right here in Saint-Milles."

"Do you have any suspicions?"

Legrand shrugged his shoulders.

"You know how it is in small towns: everyone knows everyone. As far as that is concerned, Saint-Milles is no exception. I know all the natives by sight. But everything here began to change from the day that Jacques Poiron bought old Alfonse Lanois's bakery, where he had worked. You grandfather did splendid business, bought the whole town, and began to look for collaborators. A new district came into being, filled with villas and offices..."

"The Golden Street."

"That's what we call it, yes. And it is lesser-known territory for the police. We've never had anything to do there. I hardly know the people who live and work there. Until these attacks started, I had never even been in Castle Ricard before and never met your legendary, mighty grandfather. These days I visit the Golden Street often, and I make appointments with different people there. Time after time I am dumbfounded when I see all that wealth there. I have the impression that there are more paintings of old masters handing on the walls of those villas than in the Louvre in Paris! It is a world in itself. The Golden Street is the richest little piece of France."

"Are you looking for the offender there?"

"The offender. Or the principal. Yes, I take into account that we may well find him there, some day…"

Outside sounded the fast swelling sound of a helicopter. Martin leaned forward and looked up through the windshield. Vic did the same. High above the houses they saw the machine fly over.

"There's a place behind the Golden Street where choppers can take off and land. What is delivered here, Vic? Employees for the offices? Champagne and caviar for a huge party? Drugs? Tell me that! That is why I repeat—it is a world on itself. Everything there happens without our knowledge. I cannot raid every building just like that or search each and every chopper that lands."

Martin leaned back again.

"Shall I take you back to Ricard, Vic?"

Vic forgot about his intention to buy himself a drink. He did not feel like going back to the castle either.

"I want to go to the studio," he said. "Work out some ideas together with Mike. I have quite a few numbers in my head. It is not so far, I can walk…"

Mike started the Citroën.

"I'll drop you there. No problem."

They drove away. Vic opened the window and shouted to his guard that Inspector Legrand was driving him to the studio.

Mike was working in a small studio, together with French musicians who were there under contract through Michelle Ferrer. Vic himself went to the biggest studio and sat down at the piano. He began to play. Soon he noticed the lights going on behind the broad window, in the part of the studio where the recording equipment stood. Mike knew that Vic always came first and had left the others behind when someone had told him that his friend had arrived.

"Vic ..." Mike's voice sounded through the loudspeakers. "Hello. What are you doing?"

"I want to try a couple of numbers. Piano and vocals."

"I was working with a band."

"Do you prefer to go on with them?"

"No, but maybe you would like them to accompany you."

"That might be a good idea."

He played along. The musicians entered the studio and plugged in their instruments. They had never made music with the famous American before. In silence they waited until he looked up at them and nodded. Guitars, bass, and drums joined in, one shortly after the other. In the beginning they had to search for the chords and the right rhythm. Then it sounded like a solid whole. At that moment Vic started anew, and Mike recorded it. Everyone played passionately and with inspiration. Before going into each new number, Vic first played the musicians a sample. When the others understood what he was driving at, he stopped and signed to the drummer. The latter tapped off, and then everyone started together. The compositions had a magical beauty. It seemed as if an invisible power pushed the musicians in a certain direction. They had a feeling that they had never played so well before; it was a strange experience to rise above themselves. After six numbers Vic thought it was enough. He stood up and went to Mike. The musicians stayed behind, lost in wonder.

Mike sat in his big leather chair at the controls and did not look up when Vic came standing next to him.

"Is there something the matter, Mike. Didn't it turn out well? Never mind, they were only tryouts."

"It sounded perfect. I have recorded it all."

"Mike?" asked Vic.

Make stared through the window at the musicians, who were standing close to each other and talking about their experience. Then he slowly turned his head. It gave Vic a shock when he saw his tired face. There was fear in the big brown eyes of the producer.

"What is the matter with you? Has it anything to do with your dreams?"

"It's nothing. Don't you worry about it."

"We've know each other too long for me to shrug this off. I can tell that something is bothering you."

"I'll tell you about it later," said Mike with a sigh. "Is that all right with you?"

The musicians had started to play again. Mike turned down the sound.

"Listen, Mike. There's something we have to settle. Are you still in search of my grandfather in you dreams?"

"Of course," answered Mike, without looking up.

"Tonight we have to try something else. I just said

that we've known each other for such a long time. We are best friends. Maybe our spirits are attuned better to one another than to my grandfather's. Let's try to meet in our dreams. Do your utmost to reach me. Go out to the boundary of your world. You will get there by thinking of it with all your might. You will see a transparent wall. That is the place where you must start looking for me. Together we will be stronger. Together we can find out what our possibilities are and go searching for Jacques. You really got to try, Mike!"

"I promise."

Mike looked at him again, and Vic knew that he meant what he said.

"All right then. This effort has to succeed. I'm going to Ricard now. We'll meet tonight, Mike. We will find a way to find each other."

Mike nodded.

"You can count on me."

Vic left the studio. The guard came outside through the same door and followed him. Vic did not know what to think of Mike. Never before he had seen such terror in his eyes. If he did not succeed in making contact with him this night, he would go back to the studio the next day to have a quiet conversation with him.

Now he tried to concentrate on something else. His compositions got better every time. He was convinced that this had to do with his dreams. He indulged his passions in the concert halls of his mind, and when he woke up he could still remember parts of the music and the lyrics. In thought he kept on working on it, and in that way the interpretation of a work came into being that had its origin in a mysterious source. More than often it happened that his own playing scared him when he sat down at the piano and concentrated to the utmost, trying to repeat what he had composed in his dreams. Sometimes it evoked feelings of panic, sometimes it made his flesh creep when he produced tones that called up hellish visions.

He was living in two worlds, and there were big differences between them. . . .

18

Once again it became obvious that Vic was leading two lives, after he had gone to bed and rolled on his side. He had made a mental note to think only of Mike after he had arrived in his town, but as soon as he found himself there, he entered his favorite concert hall and sat down at a black piano. He was shivering with cold, and his fingers felt stiff.

Between day and night was the frozen white landscape of Neanderthal thoughts from a long-forgotten ice age.

His spirit defrosted and his hands warmed while he played.

Clear tones went up and turned around under the huge dome of the hall.

He made fanciful butterflies appear around him, with many-colored wings and coal black eyes. Soundless, as if they would not disturb the music, they flew above his head. He was awash with a feeling of boundless happiness. He played fast and with virtuosity, and all of a sudden he ended with a bizarre-sounding chord and got up from his music stool. In the midst of a cloud of butterflies he reached the dome and went right through it. The echo of the last piano chord faded away beneath him. High in the sky, floating with his arms stretched, he enjoyed his feeling of happiness for a long time. Then two names came to his mind: Jacques Poiron and Mike Brewer. He remembered what he had promised to himself on the other side of the frozen land, where the normal lives of men were being enacted. To find his grandfather, he had to search for Mike first. Together they could make plans and discover the boundaries of their dreamlands. He hummed the composition he had created just a moment ago and wished that he could reach the transparent wall where he had been once before.

Behind him the fanciful butterflies burst apart. He bumped with his face and chest against the wall and bounced back. Soon he managed to recover himself and began to shout, to the rhythm of the music that was still in his mind:

"Mike...Mike...Mike!"

It gave him a shock when an impressive forest appeared behind the high wall. It was a jungle of trunks, branches, leaves, creepers, bushes, and elusive shapes.

"Mike...Mike...Mike!"

Vic's heart beat fiercely in his chest. He felt something was bound to happen. The wall trembled. This could be the big breakthrough!

"Mike...Mike...Mike!"

He banged his hands against the wall. It felt like cold, hard glass. The jungle on the other side was of impressive beauty. The branches and leaves moved to and fro. There was a strong wind. Vic floated along the wall in a horizontal direction. His fingertips touched the surface.

Suddenly he saw Mike. The giant was floating between the branches of the trees. There was a bewildered expression in his eyes. His hair and beard were wet with perspiration.

"Mike! I'm over here!"

Vic beat with both fists on the transparent wall.

Soon he understood that Mike could not hear him. He had to try something else.

While he kept a close eye on his friend, he concentrated, and in thought he started to repeat the same words over and over again:

"Look at me, Mike, look at me, Mike, look ..."

Mike turned somersaults between the branches, flailing about with his arms, kicking his feet. He neared the transparent wall. He bumped against it with his head and bounced back in fright. He looked toward the wall, and in a flash he saw and recognized Vic. Immediately he moved up to the wall again. His red, sweaty face was like a grotesque, terrifying mask. Slowly his lips began to form words, and Vic understood him.

"Hell. Green hell!"

"We have found each other!" shouted Vic. His heart thrilled.

Mike pushed his hands against the wall. Again his lips moved:

"I'm so sorry..."

The next moment he had disappeared.

"Mike!"

Vic remained hanging motionless in the air and stared through the wall at the jungle. Mike did not come back. And then all the trees, bushes, and plants wilted and finally vanished into thin air. Mike's world was no more.

. . .

Vic floated back to the center of his town and tried to think. Only after he had gone back to the concert hall and his fingers had touched the keys of the piano was he able to find an explanation for what he had seen.

His heart skipped a beat, and now he was seized by panic.

When Mike disappeared, he had been woken up in his bed in the apartment above the studio. Then his world was wiped out. . . .

Vic wanted to open his eyes, but it was difficult to wake up from his deep sleep. Only after some time did he succeed. He sat up and turned on the light. The sweat bit in his eyes. He stood up and got dressed. He knelt down and put on his shoes. In the dark corridor he threw his jacket on. He was so at home in the castle now that he was able to find his way in the dark. He reached a side door and took his keys out of his pocket, feeling with his fingers which one he needed. He ran through the park and reached the fence.

There a guard stepped up to him.

"Vic, where are you going to? Do you have any idea what time it is?"

"After midnight, I guess," said Vic.

"Half past one, to be exact."

Vic thought it best not to inform the man about his uncomfortable feelings.

"When I have an inspiration, I don't give a damn about the time," he said. "I have to go to the studio to get something recorded. Maybe you don't understand that, but Mike Brewer does. We have to get to work."

The guard nodded.

"No problem," he said. "I'm at your service both day and night. Just wait a minute, then I'll come along with you."

He took a cell phone from his pocket and called someone inside the castle. After that he opened the gate and let Vic go first.

"Shouldn't I get us a car?" he asked. "We'll be there faster."

Vic was far too nervous to remain standing here and wait until the man had gotten out a car. Besides, the studio was not far away from here.

"No, thank you. I prefer to walk. Then I will be able to think things over for a while."

"All right, then I will not bother you any longer," said the guard, and kept a few steps away from him from that moment.

Behind the villas of the hilly Golden Street were the dark office blocks. But in the building of the studio there was light behind the windows of most apartments. In front of the central entrance a big group of occupants had gathered. Two police cars had parked not far away from there. More to the right stood an ambulance, and in the shining of the headlights men in white were busy putting up a screen in order to hide something from the sight of gapers.

Now the guard came walking next to Vic.

"What's going on here?" he asked in a soft voice. "I didn't hear any sirens. And there are no flashing lights either."

Vic gave no answer and began to walk faster. He saw Inspector Martin Legrand walking up and down, giving orders to policemen. Martin caught sight of him too and immediately came toward him. He took Vic by the arm and guided him to a street lamp.

"Vic, what are you doing here so late?" he asked, surprised.

It was the guard who supplied the answer.

"He's an artist, he has an inspiration. I'm accompanying him to the studio."

The inspector raised a hand.

"I'll talk to you later. Please leave us alone for a moment."

In the meantime Vic began to feel dizzy. Only with great effort did he succeed in remaining standing on his feet. He put up a stony face.

"To the studio?" Martin repeated the last words of the guard.

"There's this song in my head. All the tones and words, all the details are clear to me. Now I need Mike to make a recording."

"Does he know that you were on your way?"

"What do you mean?"

"Did you call him to tell him you were coming around?"

"Well, no, I have the keys to the building's via main entrance and to the studio. I was intending to give him a call when I got there."

Martin gave him a piercing look.

"What the hell is going on here?" asked Vic.

"Talking about your friend...he jumped out of a window. Right through the pane. It woke up everyone. I am sorry, Vic, but he is dead!"

Again he took him by the arm.

"If you want to take a look at him ..."

Vic put a hand on the shoulder of the policeman and leaned heavily on him.

"It is dreadful," said Martin. "It looks very much like suicide, although I don't want to jump to conclusions. Are you all right, Vic?"

"I don't think I have the guts to look at him. Is he lying there, behind that screen near the ambulance?"

"Yes. He came down flat on his face and chest. Killed on the spot. You'd better come along to one of the police cars. You can sit down inside. No one is allowed to enter Mike's apartment. I will be busy for the time being. But I also want to have a talk with you this very night. Is that possible?"

"I could not sleep a wink anyway," said Vic.

The door of one of the police cars was held open for him. He sunk down sideways on the backseat, with his feet on the ground outside and his forearms on his thighs. Suddenly the tears rolled down his face.

"Someone will bring you some coffee. For the rest, there is little that we can do for you," said Martin. "You only have to tell me if you prefer to go home. Then I will drop by later."

Vic nodded. He looked out through his tear-filled eyes. Cars drove past. A police officer gave him a plastic cup of coffee. His hand trembled so much that he spilled hot coffee on his trousers. His guard had come up to him and leaned his arm on the open door.

"Give the cup to me. I will give you a little sip every now and then," he said. "I just heard what happened to Mike. This is dreadful!"

Vic tried to smile. His lips were trembling.

"I don't even know your name, and you would protect me with your life..."

"Louis Lanois. A celebrity like you does not have to know all names. And everyone knows yours..."

Vic saw Martin Legrand circulating among the people at the entrance of the building. He talked to everyone, gestured, and made use of a pen and a notebook.

Vic's head was empty. He just sat there, with his legs outside of the car, drank coffee, gave free rein to his tears, and sobbed softly. He had never taken into account that one day Mike Brewer would no longer be there. It had always been a matter of course that they should grow old together. Mike was the friend with whom he one day would have reminisced about the good old days.

Now his body lay on the street, behind a screen, and Vic was too scared to go and take a look at him.

19

"Are you all right?" asked Martin.

Vic had pulled his legs into the car, and Martin slid in next to Vic.

Vic shrugged his shoulders almost imperceptibly and stared out in front of him.

The ambulance had taken away Mike's dead body. The people had gone. It had become dark behind the windows of the big building.

"His apartment is locked up. No one can go in there without permission. For the time being we'll assume that it was suicide. Can you think of a reason why your friend would decide to jump out a window?"

Vic shook his head.

"Something must have happened, Vic. You knew him the best. You came here from America together. You have been sitting here all by yourself in the car for over an hour. Did nothing cross your mind during that time that could be an explanation for what has happened?"

"Nothing."

"Too bad. I had hoped you could give me a clue. My people and I have had a talk with almost everyone who lives in that building. We came away none the wiser."

A police officer opened the front door and sat down behind the wheel. Louis Lanois got in on the passenger side. The motor started, and the car pulled away slowly. Martin went on asking him question after question. He answered none of them. The car stopped in front of the castle gate.

"Tomorrow we'll have another talk," said Martin. And to Louis he said: "You watch him carefully, you hear? He is totally confused. If I had understood that he was in such an emotional shock, I would never have let him wait for me for that long in the car."

Back in his room, Vic fell asleep immediately. He played the grand piano in the big concert hall of his dream town and felt perfectly happy. *Bar-er* . . . the winter sleep of the cave bear. To Vic Emmett the night had become infinitely more pleasant than the day. Not a second of that night did he think about his grandfather.

He hid his tear-filled eyes behind his sunglasses when he walked about aimlessly through Ricard the next morning. Régine visited; she managed to calm him down a bit and promised to arrange everything for Mike's funeral.

"You just take good care of yourself and leave everything to me," she said. "And you're always welcome to unburden your heart with me. Being a psychologist, I have learned to listen. You can always count on me, and you know that you can trust me."

She promised to come with him when he got permission to enter Mike's apartment.

The next day, later in the afternoon, Tobias Dupont came up to him to tell him that he was expected at the police station.

"Shall I take you there?"

"All right," said Vic.

He felt stronger than yesterday. Long talks with Régine had done him good.

A quarter of an hour later Tobias parked the big Mercedes in front of the police station.

Vic got out and went inside. He had never been here before. Martin Legrand had not exaggerated when he had said there was plenty of room here. The immense hall was provided with a marble floor. The desk in the middle was like a lonely island in a calm sea. It was there that Martin came to meet him. He took Vic with him to the second story, where his office was.

"Sit down, Vic. Now tell me: was Mike Brewer an alcoholic?"

"I would not call him that. As a matter of fact, liquor did not agree with him. After a few glasses he was already drunk. When he worked, he preferred mineral water."

"Régine Moret told me how he fell asleep in Las Vegas while he sat with you at a table in a restaurant. Antoine Chevalier and Sergio Paladino took him with them to Paris, and both of them have told me that he wasn't sober for a minute. It seems that he drank unimaginable amounts of whiskey there."

"There have been moments in his life that it was difficult for him to leave the bottle alone," admitted Vic. "Still, I do not understand why Mike ..."

He did not finish his sentence. The death of his friend had hurt him deeply.

At the same time a feeling of indifference had come over him; all he wanted to do was make it through the day so that he could lead his other life at night.

"How about drugs?" he heard Martin say.

His eyebrows popped up above the brim of his sunglasses.

"What do you mean by that?"

"Mike had drunk cognac and sniffed cocaine. Enough to make a giant stagger. And who knows—maybe it was also enough to make a man think he was able to fly!"

Vic sat up with a jerk, frightened. In his thoughts he saw his friend floating right in front of him in his jungle, his lips forming the words: "Hell. Green hell!" And then: "I'm so sorry..."

Seeing Vic's reaction, Martin said, "Believe me, I don't like to bring this up. I have heard what happened to your girlfriend and someone from your band. I understand you have never used hard drugs yourself..."

Painful memories came back. Something within Vic broke. His shoulders began to shake. His head sunk to his chest. Martin understood that he needed some time to gather himself again and remained silent.

Slowly the feeling of sorrow became more bearable again. Vic managed to calm down and made use of the silence to think and marshal the facts. His grandfather was in a coma, and there was a good chance that he would never wake up again. Mike was dead. Of the three men who had gone down into the cave, he was the only one left who was able to tell about it. He decided to put his cards on the table. He did not count on the inspector believing him; he just thought it best to tell him the truth from the very beginning. But maybe it was not wise to go into details. He knew one thing for sure: it would be a great relief to talk with someone about this.

"Martin, there are certain things you should know about. Being a policeman, you cannot keep everything to yourself and you have to draw up reports. What I have to tell you, however, is something one should not make public."

"Some things never leave my office. And not everyone is allowed to take a look in my reports, be assured of that."

"I know for sure you will think that I am just a storyteller."

"Try me..."

"About my grandfather's talents. No one understands how he made his fortune and how he built up his empire. He makes use of a gift. You know as well as I that there are people who are trying to get that secret out of him."

"Of course!"

"I am an initiate, Martin. I know where his talent comes from. Besides me there was someone else who knew all about it."

"Your friend Mike Brewer."

"Well guessed. It is as if a curse rests on that knowledge..."

Martin grinned and shifted to the edge of his chair.

"Go on. I'm not someone who can be easily scared."

"There is this cave right under Ricard. A long, narrow tunnel leads to a room where a glaring light is shining. Whoever manages to reach that room will be immersed in that light. Soon after having returned from the cave, there will be a change in the way of thinking. Every dream becomes a special experience. You are able to build up your own dream world in which you can make optimal use of your capabilities. My grandfather reached that subterranean room, and after his return he seemed to have at his disposal a talent for predicting. He could see the financial circumstances of companies in the near and faraway future. In that way he managed to make his fortune. At first Mike was afraid of his own dreams. Later he created a beautiful jungle, and he enjoyed floating around in it. I myself give concerts in my dreams, and I make the most beautiful compositions."

Martin looked at him in a dazed sort of way. He searched for words, opened his mouth a few times, and then pressed his lips together without saying anything.

"Vic ..." he finally brought out. "Are you serious about this?"

Vic nodded.

"And do you expect me to believe it?"

"I can only hope so."

"You do understand that this is easy for me to check, don't you? Is it still possible to enter that cave you were talking about?"

"From the library on the ground floor."

"What you tell me sounds to me very much like the visions of a drug addict," said Martin in a sharp voice. "At least, that is the first thing that comes to my mind. I am sorry that I have to tell this to someone like you. Please, Vic, don't expect me to take this seriously. This is the most absurd explanation you could have given me. I am willing to forget it entirely, if you tell me something else now quickly. Be realistic, and don't come up with rambling stories. Your friend is dead!"

"As long as you do not believe me, I hope you will keep everything to yourself," said Vic. "Don't talk about it with anyone. I have told you the truth, Martin, nothing but the truth."

"What has it to do with Mike's suicide?"

"That is not clear to me either."

Vic had his suspicions, but he did feel like bringing them up.

"Sometimes a junkie becomes so terrified that he wants to put an end to all his misery," said Martin. "When you see monsters coming at you to tear you apart and you don't realize that it's only a dream, then there is only one way to escape....Would you come along with me to the hospital?"

"To pay a visit to my grandfather?"

"No. To get you examined. I want to know if you have used drugs lately."

"Believe me on my word..."

"How can I believe you when you make such curious statements?"

Vic rose to his feet.

"Well, let's go then. Right now. My chauffeur is waiting for me outside. He can drive us to the hospital."

Martin got up, too, and walked to the door of his office.

"Tobias? I will send him back home. We'll go in a police car. After the examination we'll come back here.

We are not finished, you and I. Or do you already have other appointments for today?"

"No. And I no specific plans either."

"There is also another reason I want to take you to the hospital. You knew Mike Brewer best. You will have to identify him. The doctors have done their utmost, and he does not look as horrible now as when he was lying there on the street last night..."

* * *

Vic sat down at his grandfather's bedside. A doctor had examined him thoroughly when he had arrived with the inspector. His blood was being tested in the hospital lab. The results would be available soon.

Jacques Poiron lay motionless on his back. He looked as if he were dead.

Somewhere in this same hospital lay the inanimate body of Mike Brewer.

Vic shivered. He had seen Mike. Now he desperately tried to think of other things.

He did not succeed in that. He was still thinking of Mike when the door opened and Martin came in. The inspector came standing in front of the bed and made a bow to the old man. Then he put his hand on Vic's shoulder. He said in a soft voice:

"Believe me, Vic, I sympathize with you. I know what goes through you when you have to identify a dear one. But damn you, why do you tell me such odd stories? Come with me. You look pale. There is a coffee machine at the end of the hall."

After Vic had touched Jacques Poiron's forehead with his fingertips, by way of saying goodbye, he went along with the policeman. He greeted the guard who stood at the door and went down the corridor.

"How do you like your coffee?" asked Martin, when they stood in front of the machine.

"Black. Without sugar."

"You are clean. Entirely. You have never ever used drugs. The doctor also looked at your pupils, didn't she?"

"Yes."

"Do you know what she said? That you have beautiful eyes."

He grinned. Vic did not react.

"Was it hard to look at Mike?"

Vic nodded. He had taken a plastic cup from Martin and as he blew on the hot coffee his sunglasses steamed up.

"And then there is the desperate situation of your grandfather. Please, Vic, tell me that I have to forget that story about the cave. Then we'll start a brand-new conversation. You don't have to worry about a thing. I don't suspect you of anything."

"I told you the truth. In a very brief way. I would only make it worse if I started to dwell on it."

"It all sounds too fantastic."

"Still, it is the truth. I only tried to give you some insight into the situation. All three of us have had to deal with the phenomenon."

"Well, all right then. Let's drink our coffee and then go to Ricard. I want to see that cave with my own eyes."

"Yes, let's do that. Martin, I was tottering on the brink of collapse when I was in your office. I just had to inform you about the facts. The fact that you don't believe a thing of it is of less importance to me."

In the castle Vic took the inspector with him to the library. Martin looked around in surprise. He was deeply impressed by the paintings. Vic wasted no time. He rolled the sorcerer of Les Trois Frères to the left, pushed aside some books, and pushed the buttons on the little panel.

"Grandfather has given me the code. I know I betray his confidence right now, but I want to do this."

The wall came forward and then slid to the right to reveal the empty space behind it. The rock bottom was visible, and within it the hole with the staircase leading down. Martin had brought a flashlight with him from the police car. He walked inside and stared down along the stairs, then put on the light. With careful steps he went down the stairs and reached the cellar. There he sank down on his knees and stared into the tunnel. He moved the flashlight searchingly up and down.

"It is rather narrow down there," he remarked.

"You have to go on all fours most of the time," said Vic. "I think you may be too fat to pass the most narrow parts."

Martin turned around and went upstairs again with fast leaps. When Vic had also returned to the library, he saw how the inspector's face shone with perspiration. Martin raised his hands in despair. Then he wiped his forehead with his arm.

"I was born and bred in a part of the country where it is full of caves," he sighed. "Still I have hardly ever entered one. Obviously I am liable to fits of claustrophobia. And right here it seems to be worse. Just taking a look inside, I began to feel dizzy. That surprises me. What is lying in wait deep down there?"

Vic shrugged his shoulders.

"There are different names for it."

"Such as?" urged the inspector.

"A forcing power, a combination of prehistoric thoughts, the echo of a spell, a white flash that goes right through you and provides your brain with new, unknown possibilities ..."

20

The cemetery was too small for the crowd that had come to pay their last respects to Mike Brewer. No one in Saint-Milles had stayed at home. They stood queued up along the outer fence and on the paths. It was extremely hot that afternoon. There was heavy weather on the way. The first clouds loomed up in the far distance. But the sun stood still right above the grave. Vic had sung a song and played the piano in the auditorium. With a trembling voice he had given a farewell speech. Because Mike had no family, it had been Vic who was the first man walking behind the bearers who brought the coffin outside. The people bowed for the coffin wherein the man lay whom they had hardly known. Right after that they also bowed for Vic Emmett, whom they considered the new lord of the castle and owner of the countless properties in and around Saint-Milles.

Felix Baudin said a few words on behalf of all the partners. Michelle Ferrer, who had worked closely with Mike in the studio, burst out crying halfway through her eulogy. At the end of the ceremony, Vic was no longer able to speak. He let himself be carried along by Régine, who resolutely brought him to her car.

"Tonight you'll sleep at my place," she said. "I already told Tobias Dupont. No one is expecting you in the castle."

It started to rain as they drove away. After the last visitors had walked past the grave, a storm had risen. Thunderclaps sounded like salutes for the giant who rested in the soaked earth.

That evening a helicopter rose from the plateau behind the Golden Street. The machine flew in a wide curve around the villas and came dangerously near the protruding rocks behind the castle. Then it skimmed high above the park and quickly descended above the roofs of Castle Ricard. The sound of the motor and the rotors was lost in the howling of the storm. The rain sheeted down continuously. The chopper hung right above a flat roof, swung to and fro by treacherous blasts of wind. The left side was open. A man dressed in black jumped outside and landed with soft soles on the roof. He was long and slender. After him jumped two other men who were appreciably less lithe. They stumbled and fell. Immediately the helicopter swung away, descended, and flew in a wide circle back to the plateau. Together, the three men crawled away from the edge of the roof. Their woolen balaclavas were soaked. They wore leather overalls and gloves. The slender man moved away on all fours. He was the only one with a rucksack. After some time he came back again to the two others and said:

"We'll have to climb down to another roof. There's a small window there. I don't think it is connected to the security system. Let's take a chance on it. Follow me."

Staggering in the roaring storm, they went to the edge of the roof and climbed down. When they reached the window, the man put down his rucksack and took out some tools. As he tried to wrench open the window, he said:

"Here we are far away from the white tower of Jacques. The rooms of Tobias and Julia Dupont are at the other side of the castle. Let's hope no one else is present. When we are inside, we will go down the staircases to the ground floor. No more talking as soon as we are in. Is that clear?"

"Yes," answered the two others.

The window was open. He took a long rope from the rucksack and tied it around a narrow stone chimney nearby.

"I go first. You follow immediately."

He let himself down through the window, grabbed the rope, and climbed down. The others had trouble wriggling themselves through the opening and holding the rope, but finally all three of them stood on the floor of a huge attic. The blazing beam of a flashlight swung to and fro, long enough to give the men an impression of the layout. A hand screened the light, and now only a part of the floor remained visible. Carefully the men began to walk. The ray of light slid along in front of them. Almost all the steps of the antique wooden staircase creaked as they descended. Lamps were burning in the corridors on the ground floor. The wind knocked the windows. After having opened several doors, the man in front found the library. He beckoned to the others. Then he closed the door behind them and searched for the light switch. The lamps went on high above in the dome. The men looked up in amazement at the paintings. If not for the bookcases, they could easily have imagined that they found themselves in a cave decorated with real Cro-Magnon paintings. The slender man rolled the sorcerer of Les Trois Frères aside and began to take books from the shelves and put them back again. Then he found the panel with push buttons, put down his rucksack for the second time, and searched for tools.

"It is all right to whisper here. This is the most important part. If I am not able to push that bookcase aside, everything has been in vain, and we'll have to go back immediately."

He turned his back to the others and began to dislodge the little panel with a screwdriver. It came loose easily, and now the wires lay bare. The man took off his gloves and took another tool.

"There you go," he whispered.

The bookcase slid aside.

After the men had gone down the stone stairs, they stopped in front of the narrow, dark tunnel.

They took off their soaked balaclavas. The rucksack was put down. Extra flashlights were taken out of it and small crash helmets that were actually meant for bikers. One of the men fumbled with his chin strap and then took off his gloves in annoyance and fastened the strap with his bare fingers.

"Stay right behind me," said the leader. "You are not used to crawling through narrow tunnels. No matter what happens, don't panic. Once we're on our way, we cannot go back again. Probably there will only be enough space to turn round after we reach the bottom of the cave. Talk as little as possible, try to save your energy. Prepare for mental shocks. What is going to happen to us could be terrible. Can we go on?"

"Yes, we're ready," said one of the men, and the other nodded in the light of his lamp.

They started their journey through the darkness. Walking, stooping, crawling. Staggering, falling, bumping. An indefinable feeling of fear came over them and grew as they penetrated deeper into the cave. Soon they gasped for breath in the narrow tunnel and sucked in the stale air. Lack of oxygen benumbed their mind. They completely lost their sense of time. Then they slid down abruptly, toward the glaring white light. They screamed, made flailing movements, held up their heads to avoid bumping their chins on the floor.

Surrounded by the light they lay motionless. Each felt a biting cold and for a long time felt connected with a deep, marvelous past—they saw images from Neanderthal lives and caught a glimpse of a new phenomenon: *Bar-er*, the sleep of the cave bear. Feelings they had never experienced before now took possession of them. They saw something of the dream world that would become so familiar to them later.

Their way back was a long and hard one. They had the feeling that their muscles and bones were frozen, and every foot they went up cost them a lot of energy. Halfway, the panic struck. Panting, they tried to crawl up faster. In places where there was enough space to run on their feet, in a stooped position, they tried to pass each other. The long, slender man was pushed aside. He shook off the other and kicked behind him. They all pushed each other and lashed out. Soon the three man were in an insane fight. A flashlight fell on the rock bottom and bounced down; the beam of light turned around and around and finally disappeared into the depths.

"Control yourselves!" shouted the long man.

But he himself was both furious and afraid as well. When someone caught hold of him again and tried to push him away, he gave a knock with his elbow. A scream sounded. The man behind him bumped up against the wall. Then he tumbled backwards and fell on his back in a side corridor of the cave. He scrambled to his feet and felt about in the darkness. The last man crawled along with a flashlight in his hand.

"Wait for me! Don't leave me alone!" cried the man from the side corridor.

He tried to get up, bumped against the wall for the second time, and fell.

Something began to move, something came loose under his cold fingers. The grinding sound of tumbling stones was rising. The two others turned around and looked at what was happening in the light of their lamps. They saw how the man came crawling in their direction, panting, his eyes wide open with fear. Right behind him big stones rolled down from the side corridor into the main tunnel with a thundering noise. Still under the influence of their shocking experiences in the white light, they were hardly able to cope with the feelings that were forced on them now; it seemed to them that the stones had come into movement by an invisible but plainly perceptible power.

The stones dashed together in a narrow part of the tunnel and became stuck. The stones that followed could not get further and filled the hole like a cork in a bottleneck.

"Away from here!" shouted the long man.

They went up higher and higher, until they finally reached the cellar. There they sat down and gasped for breath as if they just had come up from the depths of the sea. They took off their helmets and searched for the balaclavas, which were still wet from the rain. The long man was the first one who rose to his feet again. He picked up his rucksack, switched off his flashlight, and went up the stairs to the library. After the others had passed him in silence, he shoved back the bookcase and pushed the panel into place. He put back the books and rolled back the sorcerer. The men left the library. The light was shut off. Through dark corridors and along creaking stairs they went back up to the attic. The long man grabbed the rope, climbed up lithely, and slipped through the window. He helped the others by pulling up the rope. It was still night. They had to bend down to keep themselves from getting blown away by the storm. The rain beat in their faces.

The leader took a cell phone from his pocket and held a short conversation. Ten minutes later the chopper appeared. The pilot had to do his utmost to keep the machine right above the roof. It swung to and fro frightfully. After the three men had climbed in with great difficulty, it flew away on the storm like a giant dragonfly.

21

Vic stayed for a week in Regine's big villa. Except for her he wanted to see nobody. While the storm spent itself outside, he stayed inside and tried to come to his senses. He made music, swam a few lengths in the indoor swimming pool, and sat down for hours at the fireplace. Régine, who worked together with different partners doing big business, always left early in the morning for meetings at Armand and Claire Laurin's place. In the afternoon she worked in her own offices. She owned countless enterprises, of which an investment trust and an estate agency were the most important. She tried to be back home as early as possible.

Her talents as a psychologist came in handy when she tried to calm Vic down. She listened to him when he wanted to unburden his heart and remained silent when he did not feel like talking. At night, in bed, she was one of the most passionate women he had ever met.

One day, when the sun was shining again and the temperature was rising, Vic returned to Ricard. It was not by his own choice that he went back to the castle. Inspector Martin Legrand wanted to meet him there and had asked if Régine would come along with him.

Martin was already there, together with another policeman, whom he introduced as René Bougard.

"René is a famous amateur speleologist. He wants to explore the cave and tell us about his experiences. Do you give him permission to enter the cave?"

"Well . . . yes," said Vic, fairly overwhelmed.

They went to the library. Vic shoved away the sorcerer and opened the bookcase. René Boullard was wearing overalls, strong boots, and a helmet provided with a lamp. He did not seem to care about anything. Régine stared after him as he went down into the darkness. Martin had brought some chairs from another room into the library and placed them around the desk. He sat down, and Vic and Régine followed his example.

Immediately Martin began talking.

"Régine, I have asked you to be here because, first, you are one of Jacques Poiron's closest fellow workers and, second, because you have the capability as a psychologist to fathom someone's personal world of experience. You know the old man through and through, and I believe you know Vic as well by now..."

He fixed his gaze on her. She did not lower her eyes.

"That is right."

"Did Vic talk with you about the origin of his grandfather's talents?"

"No, he hasn't said a word about that."

"Will you allow me to fill her in, Vic? I have already told the speleologist what he can expect in the cave, according to your explanation to me. Hope you understand that I had to do that. For the time being I want to involve only Régine in these affairs. Everything seems too fantastic to me to talk about it with other people at the police station."

"It is all right with me for you to inform Régine," said Vic.

"You guys are making me curious," said Régine.

Martin began to tell her what he had learned from Vic. He sketched the situation in clear, short sentences. Régine sprawled in her chair, and with her hands folded behind her neck she stared up at the splendid cave paintings. Then Martin ended his story. It became very quiet. Cold air streamed into the library from the opening to the cave.

Régine was the first to speak.

"Just suppose that this is all true..." She started to shiver. "That could mean that René Bougard will come back out of that cave before long as a totally different man..."

Vic nodded.

"What is down there, Vic? What kind of powers hide there in the darkness?"

"He has never made that exactly clear to me," said Martin. "He only spoke in vague terms. He called it a forcing power, a combination of prehistoric thoughts, the echo of a spell, a white flash that goes right through you and provides your brain with new, unknown possibilities. Yes, I did remember it all very well, but I just don't know it all means..."

"Please, Vic," said Régine. "Explain this to us. Take your time. I'm listening..."

"We think that we know our history, but by no means

do we know everything," started Vic. "Allow me to give you insight into my grandfather's way of thinking—ideas that were adopted by my father and later by me....Let me give you some examples. When someone tells us that the imprint of the sole of a shoe has been found in two-million year old stone, we don't immediately say that is impossible. When someone says that human footprints have been found next to those of dinosaurs, both a hundred million years old, then we think that a searching inquiry is needed. Everywhere, all over the world, we find impressive buildings constructed with stones weighing twenty tons and more, that often had to be brought to the building site from distances of many hundreds of miles. How that could ever happen is still a mystery. And many smaller objects are a mystery as well; in Egypt they've found alabaster jars, perfectly hollowed out. How did one ever manage to do that?"

"What is it you're trying to say with all this, Vic?" asked Régine.

"I am talking about the Mystery Human Being," answered Vic. "It has always exercised me. Now we come to a subject closer in time. The Cro-Magnons. You know, Régine, how much my grandfather wanted that everything that has been found of them in this area was showed to me."

"I showed you round myself. And with much pleasure..."

"I all seems so obvious. Hunters with the capability of painting works of art." He pointed up, and his finger described a circle in the air. "Paint the animal, and it will be spellbound and fall prey easily to the hunter. For all the animals painted seem to be prey: horses, deer, mammoths.

"Recently a cave has been discovered in the ravine of the Ardèche river, where quite different animals were painted on the walls by Cro-Magnons! Lions and hyenas, owls, and even insects! That was the end of the theory about putting a spell on prey. My grandfather and father have said it so many times: 'Get yourself a big piece of alabaster and try to hollow it by yourself. Go to France and make those colors all by yourself—red and yellow ochre and black manganese oxide, and make a painting on a rock wall. You might as well stay home, for you won't succeed.' The past is as deep and dark as the cave behind the bookcase."

All three of them looked at the open bookcase and shivered.

"This all is nothing compared to what I am about to tell you now," continued Vic. "The Neanderthals, who shared their space with the Cro-Magnons for some time, were a special sort of human being. They were very much like us, but nevertheless the differences were enormous. Their brains worked in quite a different way."

"How do you know that?" asked Régine. "I would say that this is typically something we will never find out."

Again Vic stared at the opening.

"We found the solution down there. The Neanderthals survived the bitter cold of the ice age by drawing themselves back into a world of dreams. They lived in another way than we did. Their night was of more importance than their day. Their dream world of experience has nothing to do with our own dreams. They closed their eyes and stepped into another dimension."

"Vic," whispered Régine. "You cannot expect me to take this seriously, can you?"

"That's not what I expect of you. All I am doing is informing you in all honesty about what happened to us. We reached the bottom of the cave, got overwhelmed by a white light, and then things were shown to us no one else has ever seen before, and we were blessed with the talent to move around freely in our own powerful dreams. The way of living of the Neanderthals was revealed to us. It happened to Mike Brewer, it happened to me....My grandfather went before us. He was the pioneer who first entered his special world of dreams. There he developed his talents, learned to see into the future, and predicted exactly what was going to happen to certain enterprises. That way he was able to buy and sell at the right time..."

"Amazing!" said Régine. "I don't have to tell you how often I have witnessed that during meetings. Jacques Poiron was the well we all could draw from. He showed the way to the big money. But I refuse to believe that it has anything to do with the Neanderthals. Go on, Vic, tell us more about it."

And Vic told them all he knew.

They rose to their feet, went into the kitchen to get a big thermal coffee server, and then walked back to the library again.

"*Bar-er,* the sleep of the cave bear," said Vic. "Maybe Mike became so afraid of all the possibilities that he could not cope with it. I have seen him fly in his dream world. Maybe he was awake and thought that he still was able to fly round and fell right through that window."

"I think it has more to do with the fatal combination of alcohol and drugs," said Martin. "And you, Vic, are a highly talented composer, blessed with a huge dose of fantasy. Sometimes, when you are talking, you even make me doubt. Still I prefer to have my feet firmly on the ground."

"Are you able now to predict the same things as your grandfather?" Régine wanted to know.

"Absolutely not. It seems that you can only develop the qualities you already have possession of. I give concerts in my own world. My music becomes more beautiful time after time. I have started my quest for the most beautiful piece of music..."

Martin raised his hand.

"Wait a minute! I have been to the studio several times this week and have talked with almost everyone there. I heard that you and Mike were listening to awful-sounding piano music once. It even gave a headache to Michelle Ferrer; she said that music had come straight from hell. At the time you said that it was a recording of an American artist. Could it have been you yourself, Vic?"

"Yes, I can admit that now. It was me who played that. It sounded so beautiful in my dreams, but it scared Mike and me as well when we listened to the recording."

Martin raised his eyebrows.

"Drugs," he said. "Oh, I know how you hate drugs. We have already discussed that together. But when I hear things like this—"

"No matter what you think about it," said Régine, "it still remains a fact that Jacques Poiron was never wrong with his predictions. In all these years he never made a single mistake. He behaved like an eccentric. If he had wanted so, he could have collected all the money in the world! No other businessman has ever been able to hold a candle to him. I have great difficulty with everything you have told me, Vic. Still, I can't help but think of all the miracles I have seen performed by Jacques Poiron."

Again there was a silence. All three of them stared at the opening in the wall. And again it was Régine who finally spoke.

"I cannot figure this out," she said. "No matter how I think about it, I hesitate between two opinions. Nonsense at the one side, the proof in the person of Jacques Poiron at the other. Dreams....In fact we still do not know what the function of dreams is. At first it was thought that everything an individual dreamt had to do with personal experiences and the working out of that. Later there was also talk of common primal ideas, passed through generation after generation. And the sleeping individual might be susceptible to special influences that he would not be subject to when he was awake. But none of this provides an explanation of your assertions. There actually are people who have learned to control their dreams—the so-called lucid dream, in which the sleeper is aware of himself and is able to decide which fantastic adventures he wishes to go through."

"You are talking about our dreams," said Vic. "Those of the Neanderthals are different. There is a difference between ordinary dreams and *Bar-er*."

There was a sound as if a stone bounced down and hit a rock bottom somewhere. There was something happening inside the cave. Vic and the others fell silent, watching the opening in the wall. When nothing else happened, Régine began to speak again. Her voice sounded nervous and hurried, and she kept an eye on the dark opening.

"When I come to think about it, I remember that Jacques often told stories about Neanderthals. He was just as interested in them as he was in Cro-Magnons. He told about squat figures, heavily built humans with a brain volume equal to ours or sometimes even bigger. Low forehead, beetle-browed...Sometimes, when meetings lasted too long for him, he even drew Neanderthals. And what he drew was very realistic indeed. They would have been rather primitive and hardly able to express themselves verbally."

"In their dreams they were able to do everything," said Vic. "But I am sure that my *Bar-er* is very different from that of the Neanderthals. It is the radiation of that prehistoric power that has a special effect on my modern brain. Maybe that is the best way to describe it. The pure magic takes place in the dream—"

A beam of light moved to and fro in the darkness of the opening. Footsteps sounded on the stone stairs. René Bougard appeared. He took off his helmet and turned off the light. His face was streaming with perspiration. His overalls was torn in different places. He sat down on a chair and raised both hands.

"Please give me some time to rest," he panted. "Can I

have a cup of coffee?"

Martin poured it out for him. The speleologist took a sip and then rose to his feet to take off his overalls. Under it he wore trousers and a T-shirt.

"Don't keep us in suspense for too long, René," said Martin.

"You don't need special training for this expedition. A bit of stamina will do. And you must not suffer from claustrophobia."

Martin felt a shiver running down his spine.

"Most of the time you have to go on all fours, and here and there you have to wriggle yourself through narrow holes. You have to concentrate and must control yourself and hope you won't panic. You have to squirm through like a snake. And then, unexpectedly, the tunnel ends! I managed to dislodge a few stones, but behind them everything was completely jammed. No room, no glaring white light...This was the end of the journey. So I had to turn back. Believe me, even I was afraid now. That was terrifying! It was too narrow there to turn around. I pushed off with both hands and slowly worked myself up through that sheer tunnel. It ate up my energy. I broke out in a cold sweat. Time after time I hurt my feet by kicking against protruding rocks. It is extremely difficult to climb backwards through such a narrow, winding tunnel! I began to see ghosts in the light of my lamp. It was a real nightmare. You can hardly believe how glad I was when I finally reached a side passage where I could get up and turn round. For a long time I just stood there panting. Finally I regained enough power and courage to go on. What I have discovered, Martin, is a dead-end tunnel."

"What is your conclusion?"

René looked meaningfully at Régine.

"Well, I am not the psychologist here. Otherwise I would probably say that people who have hardly any experience in the exploring of caves, will have panicked completely when they had to free themselves from desperate straits. I don't know what mortal fear can do with the human mind, but I can make a few guesses..."

Martin nodded.

Then he asked himself a question:

"Can someone have such a fright that his spirit clings to wild fantasies that he will never lose again and finally will consider as plain truths?"

He looked at Régine first and then at Vic.

They both remained silent.

22

Martin Legrand had to make sure. The next day he sent the speleologist back into the cave to explore the side passage. When René Bougard had come back again, he said that the passage went up sheerly and ended in a low, broad room full of stones. Further on, this room narrowed again and formed a passage that came to a dead end.

"No room with a white light," concluded Martin. "Not there either."

"We can say that for sure now," said René. "But there is a sinister atmosphere down there. It is hard to describe. In fact you have the constant feeling that you are not alone there."

The inspector raised his eyebrows.

"I cannot make it more clear, sorry for that," said René.

They left the library and walked through the corridor to the big hall, where Vic sat at the piano. Vic stopped his playing when he saw them enter and let himself be informed briefly by the inspector.

He made no comment.

After he had seen both men to the door, he went to

the library, closed the door, shoved back the bookcase, and put the sorcerer in his place.

He sat down at the desk and tried to relax. Just like his grandfather had done for so many years on end, he felt an urge to sleep and dream around noon.

For several minutes he stared in the glass eyes of the sorcerer.

He habitually slept well during the night. Régine had told him that his breathing was always quiet and that he lay on his side with his knees pulled up.

"Do you want to talk with me about what has happened to you?" she had asked him the other day.

"I have already told more than enough," he had answered. "I have informed the police in the most honest way. If there are no further questions from their side, I prefer to let the matter rest."

"But you must realize that you have made me very curious."

"I count on it that you will remain silent about this to all the partners. To everyone ..."

"That goes without saying. Don't forget that I have always been loyal to your grandfather. He has a special place in my heart. And I have fallen in love with you. When you decide that you want to talk about it, I will be happy to listen to you."

During the week that he had spent his nights with her, he had given concerts in his dreams for the lifeless audience in his favorite hall.

Now he felt calm and strong enough to go on searching for Jacques Poiron again. He closed his eyes and sprawled in his chair.

A moment later his spirit entered another world. Floating above his town he felt attracted to the big concert hall, and he was already going down to it when he remembered he had a mission to fulfill. The dressed shades could wait endlessly for his performance.

"I must try to find him," he thought.

Immediately he felt himself rising. Without much effort he managed to reach the boundaries of his town. At the other side of the transparent wall everything was white. He floated past it in a horizontal direction. He slid his fingertips along the surface. It felt cold. In the meantime he concentrated on Jacques Poiron and tried to form an idea of his grandfather's town. Every now and then different colors popped up in the white. His own town was no more than a spot in the distance, and every now and then he could not see anything at all. He quickened his speed. The flight along the transparent wall seemed endless to him.

"Maybe I should concentrate on something else," he muttered. "Maybe would help to think of neutral things or try to think about nothing at all."

But that did not work. While he did that he flew further and further as well, and nothing special happened.

"A town, another town—no matter who built it," he thought then. "Or another world, a jungle like that of Mike, a desert, a village, a mountain range, an ocean ..."

More color appeared behind the wall. Red broke through the white like fast-growing veins with countless branching capillaries. Yellow bolts of lightning drove holes in the same white, and behind them it was dark. Vic's speed slackened. He floated higher, up to one of the dark holes, and kicked into it. His foot went right through the transparent wall.

"An opening!"

Without hesitation he slipped through it. He had the unpleasant feeling that he was moving himself through the blood vessels in someone's brains.

"As if I'm penetrating into a head," he thought.

It became light. Vic was floating high in the sky. Beneath him he saw a town of gray cubes. The cubes stood at equal distances and formed long, straight streets. There were no ponds, no parks, no trees, no bushes. Vic understood immediately that these unimaginative buildings were not made by his grandfather. He was on the alert. Whose world had he entered? He looked back. He could still see the hole through which he had made his appearance. Carefully he went down, looking around all the time. The streets were empty. The windows in the buildings were square and black. Vic landed on his feet and began to walk. Now he looked up. He searched for the dark hole. It was gone.

"I must not forget where I came down," he thought.

But after having walked through different streets for a while, he had lost all sense of direction. Peering from one building to another, from window to window, he went on. Suddenly he saw a light burning behind a window in a cube that was bigger than all the others. Panic struck; he was not able to make another step. He wondered how he had ever dared to float down to this gloomy town and why he hadn't changed his mind and gone back to the safety of his own dream world. He was convinced that he would grow numb with fear and would remain standing there forever if a face should pop up in the lighted window. To his own surprise he found that he could envision someone finding his dead body in the library of Ricard, sprawled on his chair.

It seemed to take ages before he was able again to move himself. He ran to the wall of the big cube and pressed himself against it. No one should be able to see him now from that window. Step after step he went to the right, until he reached a door. Carefully he pushed his shoulder against it. It swung open without a sound. He entered an empty hall. The floor and the walls were gray. Everything seemed to be made of smooth concrete. Along the right wall was a staircase.

"It would be foolish to go back now. I have come so far," he thought. "Now I must venture on."

He went to the staircase and looked up. He set a foot on the first step. After having waited for a while, he went up another step. Holding his breath, he listened. The second story was exactly like the ground floor. He went up the second staircase, and this time he dared to move faster. All he found there was another staircase. He listened again, and now he could hear a voice. And immediately he knew that he had heard that voice before, although he could not placed where or when. He went some stories higher until he could see a doorway with light shining out of it. He could hear the voice loudly now, clear and hollow in the lighted room. Vic crept up to the next stair, kneeled on it, and peered inside the room. A man sat on a chair at a gray desk, with his back turned towards him. He made pompous gestures with his arms. Vic did not have to see his face. He recognized the voice now and knew who the man was. With amazement he listened to what the man said aloud:

"Please, give me the power to see read the future. I ask the questions—let me hear the answers. Whisper them in my ears or put them directly into my brain. Give me the key to the door which gives entrance to the day of tomorrow..."

It was Sergio Paladino.

Surprised, shocked, and totally confused, Vic turned around and ran down the stairs as fast as he could. As soon as he was outside, he did a forward somersault and flew down the street, rose up, and left the town of cubes. High in the sky, he looked around. He could not find the dark hole. He forced himself to stay calm, concentrated on the wall, and went on. Everything around him turned white. His stretched fingers touched something. Later he was hardly able to describe what happened to him next. It was as if something gulped him down and directly spat him out again, and when he looked down he saw the transparent wall. He whizzed away from it at great speed and reached his own town. There he landed, entered the concert hall, sat down on the music stool at the grand piano, and wished that he would wake up soon.

He opened his eyes. He took a deep breath of relief when he saw the cave paintings. He was back in the library. The next moment panic struck again.

"Sergio Paladino!" he whispered.

He always had found the silence in Ricard pleasant. Now it annoyed him. He rose to his feet, left the library, and walked through the corridor. In a cupboard were the overalls, helmets, and flashlights Mike and he had used when they went down into the cave. Although his heart was beating heavily with fear, he took out one of the flashlights and ran back to the library. There he kicked against the sorcerer, who rolled aside wobbling. He smashed a number of books onto the floor and keyed in the code on the panel.

"What is going on down there?" he shouted with a cracking voice.

His eyes were big, his face white. He went down the stone staircase to the cellar and switched on the flashlight. The harsh beam of light pierced the darkness of the tunnel.

"The tunnel comes to a dead end. That is what René Bougard says—an experienced speleologist, a policeman! What is going on?"

He began to swear wholeheartedly. He stamped his feet on the ground and remained looking into the tunnel as if he expected that a fabulous creature could jump out at any time that felt the need to explain everything to him in great detail.

A cold stream of air touched his cheeks.

That calmed him down a bit. His fury had spent itself.

He sat down on the cold floor. The panic faded away. He searched around with the flashlight. Not far away from him he saw a little sparkling object lying on the ground. Quickly he crawled toward it and picked it up. It was a thin golden bracelet.

"Sergio Paladino wore this when he came to me in the hospital," whispered Vic. "I was sitting at my grandfather's bed when he entered. He wore this bracelet round his left wrist, I am sure of that."

He stood up and let the bracelet slip into his pocket. With a few leaps he was back in the library. He shoved back the bookcase but did not bother to replace the sorcerer. After he had put the flashlight back into the cupboard, he went outside. The watchdogs came up to him barking. Louis Lanois followed them.

Vic's face lit up.

"Louis! Did you already had a bite to eat this afternoon?"

"Not yet. But I was just thinking about it."

Vic looked at his watch. It was one o'clock. Which meant that he had only slept for an hour, while he had a feeling as if he had dreamt for many hours at a stretch.

"Come with me, Louis. We'll drive to Chez Marcus to get something to eat and drink. We can have a good talk together. After that I want to go to the hospital for a while to take a look at my grandfather. On our way back you can drop me with Régine. A deal?"

"A deal!" said the guard enthusiastically. "I'll go and tell Tobias first."

"All right. In the meantime I'll pick out a car."

Vic put on his sunglasses and walked through the park to the big garage.

During the rest of the day he wanted to think of merry things and have light-hearted conversations. He knew his thoughts would wander off to Sergio Paladino, but he would suppress the images that came up. He would do so long enough to become more or less used to the new facts, and would try to accept them bravely.

23

A camera crew from a French television station had showed up at Saint-Milles unexpectedly, wanting to do a story on Jacques Poiron. They were denied permission to film the man in his hospital bed. Now that they were here and did not want to return to Paris with empty hands, they paid a visit to the studio. There they were more lucky. Vic was present there, and they did an interview with him. The French band that had played with him before was there, too. They accompanied him when he sang some songs. There was a magical atmosphere in the studio; everyone agreed that Vic Emmett could count himself among the great songwriters of the world. To Vic this day was a blessing, after a night of searching for Jacques's dream world and being afraid to cross the path of Sergio Paladino. He sang away his misery. Especially here in the studio his thoughts were with Mike, and in fact he sang and played for him. He did not know that Martin Legrand had entered and had listened open-mouthed. He only noticed him after he had said goodbye to the camera crew and the musicians. Martin stood near the door.

"My compliments to you, Vic. Unearthly beautiful.

That's what I heard someone say a moment ago. In fact, rather appropriate to the things you have told me..."

He began to laugh but stopped immediately when he saw Vic's face stiffen.

"Have you got a moment? I don't seem to make any progress with my investigations concerning Mike. There is something I want to discuss with you."

"We can go to the studio restaurant," suggested Vic.

"No, it might be too crowded there," said Martin, and then lowered his voice: "I don't want Michelle Ferrer to see us and come sit down with us. What I have to tell you has to do with her."

"My new manager?" Vic raised his eyebrows. "She's terrific!"

"No doubt about that," responded the inspector. "Shall we go outside and take a short walk?"

Vic nodded.

"First I'll go to the restaurant to buy me something to drink. I'm thirsty."

Not much later they walked away from the building along a rising road and talked about general things. The road led along a grassy clearing on which different helicopters stood next to each other. They walked on to the helipad and sat down in a cool spot in the shadow of the biggest machine. Vic handed Martin a can of cola.

"So what about Michelle?" he wanted to know.

"She is new here. She arrived in Saint-Milles even later than you. She was working for a big company. Régine bought her out, especially for you."

"I know that."

"So it is pretty obvious that she doesn't know many

people here. You probably also know that she lives in one of the apartments above the studio."

"Next to Mike."

"Exactly. Next to Mike. I asked her before if she had noticed anything that might relate to Mike's death. At that time she said that she could not remember anything special. One of the first people she met was Nadine Aron, who does so much for your publicity. What she did not know is that Nadine is married."

Vic opened his own can of cola and took a sip. Martin continued:

"She only found that out a couple of days ago. I happened to have another talk with her, and she told me then that Nadine had visited Mike the night before his death. It is not that the walls are very thin; her French windows were open and Mike's as well. She heard them laughing, and she is also absolutely convinced that they went to bed together. Late that night Nadine left again. Later she heard Mike's voice, and she had the feeling that something had scared him. He was screaming."

"Incredible," muttered Vic.

"Michelle heard Nadine arriving and leaving. You yourself brought her that red Maserati, that present from your grandfather. The motor has a specific sound. Nadine's feet are still troubling her, and when she drives that car she often gives it too much gas, so the motor roars like a lion. Michelle stepped out on her balcony and saw Nadine park the car, stepped out, and limp to the entrance on her crutches. Can you imagine Mike and Nadine having an affair?"

"Hardly," answered Vic. "What a strange story, Martin."

"That may be so, but of course I went back with some people to Mike's apartment. Fortunately it was not already cleared out. We found Nadine's fingerprints on a cognac glass. And some short, bleached hairs on a pillow of the bed."

"So it must be true. Then I am convinced that she was responsible for the cocaine. Believe me. There have been moments he could not keep off alcohol. But hard drugs did not go with his lifestyle."

"Or maybe he hid that from you, because he knew what you had gone through. For the sake of your friendship ..."

Vic shrugged his shoulders. He stared at the office buildings and the big villas of the Golden Street.

"Anyway," continued Martin, "when Michelle heard that Nadine was married, she found the situation strange enough to tell me about it. The next night Mike jumped out of the window. I will have to ask Nadine some questions about this. I thought it better to have a talk with you first. I hoped you knew something about her and Mike."

"If I knew anything, I would tell you right away. Do you have any idea how her man will react when he hears about this?"

"Maurice Aron is a hot-tempered man. He has been involved in more than one fight."

Vic nodded and stared out in front of him. Every now and then he took a sip from his can. All kind of thoughts went through his head, and he tried to combine them.

He heard Martin's voice without listening to what he said. All of a sudden he got an idea. He squeezed a dent in the now-empty can and raised his other hand.

"Wait a minute, Martin. Maurice is short-tempered. You mentioned fights."

"Keep that to yourself. He has been arrested by us for public drunkenness and aggressive behavior. Several times. The last time was half a year ago. He was at a street party in Les Eyzies and knocked someone down who had made clear he didn't want to have his photograph taken. And what is more—"

Vic raised his hand for the second time.

"Did he ever beat up Nadine?"

"Why do you want to know?"

"It might be important."

"Then I must repeat that you must keep this to yourself. Yes, he beaten her in the past; it is a mystery to me why she stays with him. As far as that is concerned, I find it understandable that she finally went to bed with another man. It is just so sad and puzzling that Mike looked death in the face one day later. Go on..."

"My grandfather was attacked as he sat down by the river. The offender wore a black rubber wetsuit and diving goggles and had made use of a harpoon gun to kill the dogs. Not many people in this neighborhood will own such things."

"Right."

"When I visited Nadine, I saw pictures in the office that she shares with her husband. I mean pictures made by Maurice. The are hanging on the wall behind his desk.

Some of them are made under water. In seas and lakes. Splendid photographs of fishes."

"Maurice Aron has a wetsuit..." said Martin. "I have been in that office myself. To have a talk with Nadine about what had happened to her. I know those pictures. It is a pity that I didn't take a close look at them then. It is high time that I go and pay a visit to Maurice. Why did you ask if he was also aggressive to Nadine?"

"He reacted furiously at the news that she had been beaten with a golf club. He is probably the only one in Saint-Milles with a wetsuit, but I'd wager every man in the Golden Street has a couple of golf clubs. Playing golf is popular. Now imagine that he, to divert attention from himself and the wetsuit, broken Nadine's toes himself..."

Martin, who had been leaning forward with his hands on his knees, suddenly sat up straight.

"That sounds interesting. Yes, just imagine. If he is the man who attacked your grandfather, then he is also the one who stole the old cars, the Renault and the Fiat, from George Roulland. Vic, it was a good idea to talk with you first. I'm going back to the police station to arrange some things. Then I will certainly go to *Le Journal de Saint-Mill* and look around in the offices. I'm parked in front of the studio; are you going back there?"

"No, I think I'll stay here for a while."

Martin stood up and tapped Vic on the shoulder.

"Thanks. It could very well be that your theory fits. Everyone is curious about the way Jacques Poiron was able to gather his riches. Someone wanted to force him to talk, and it is very well possible that this person is Maurice Aron. I'll keep you posted. This remains between us, right?"

"You already asked me that twice," answered Vic. "You can rely on me, just like I trust you that you won't blaze abroad what I have told you about the cave of Ricard."

Martin nodded and walked away. He stopped at the foot of the clearing and looked up.

"Your French is almost without accent now. Before long no one will be able to tell that you are from America. Then you will be one of us..."

He went on. Vic followed him with his eyes.

The sun had moved up to the west, and Vic had to slide over to make the most use of the shadow of the helicopter. He was convinced that Maurice Aron had threatened his grandfather, had crushed the toes of his wife with a golf club, and had been on Vic's tail that day when he drove with Jacques in the little, sporty Renault. Now he finally had found the courage to think about the fact that he had seen Sergio Paladino in his dreams. He understood what must have happened.

"Maurice dreamt of fabulous wealth," he thought. "To get it, he had to scare my grandfather into making him yield up his secret. The first effort failed. Nadine knows about everything that happens in Saint-Milles. Being the owner and editor-in-chief of *Le Journal de Saint-Milles*, she must also know a lot about Jacques Poiron; she has told me so herself. Maurice played a game and she had to play along with him, but things got out of hand when he took hold of the golf club. The second effort to catch Jacques also went wrong. Maurice drove his car against a tree and took flight. Jacques lapsed into a coma. I was watched by my guards. Then Maurice began to wonder if Mike knew anything about it. In any case it would be worthwhile to pump him for details. And so he sent Nadine. She went to bed with him, drank cognac with him, sniffed cocaine, and then ..." He gave a visible start. What dawned on him now was outright horrible. "Mike told her everything. I remember very well how strange he behaved the day after, in the studio. He knew that he had said too much. Mike was a kind soul, and a secret was as safe with him as in the cellars of a Swiss bank. Except for when he was stuffed with drugs and alcohol. The next evening he had been drinking again and used the drugs that were left over. I met him in my dreams. I saw his lips move: 'I am so sorry. . . .' He disappeared from his jungle. Which means that he woke up in his apartment. Then his entire dream world vanished. He had taken the leap, he had committed suicide..."

It took some time before Vic was able to come to grips with this. He had great difficulty in bringing his thoughts to completion.

"Nadine told the strange story to her husband. I don't think a man like Maurice would believe a word of it. Still, he thought it worthwhile to find out if there was any truth to it. He searched for an associate. His eye fell in Sergio Paladino. I have not the faintest idea how they managed to enter the castle. The bracelet on the floor of the cellar proves that Sergio has been there. I have seen the first buildings of his town, the gray cubes...What happened in the cave? René Bougard says that the tunnel comes to a dead end. Good heavens! Martin Legrand can arrest Maurice Aron and lock him up in a police cell. But if Maurice has gone down with Sergio in the cave, no bars can stop him when he closes his eyes and starts dreaming. What will he do if he discovers the town of Jacques Poiron before me?"

24

Martin Legrand approached the affair quietly. He went in his own car to the offices of *Le Journal de Saint-Milles*. A police officer in plain clothes followed him in another car. The police officer remained sitting at the wheel while Martin went inside alone. He found that Maurice Aron was not present.

Nadine welcomed him in her office.

He noticed that she was nervous.

"What can I do for you?" she asked.

"We must have a talk together. Where is Maurice?"

"He left for Bergerac yesterday to shoot pictures for the newspaper. I expect him back in the course of the afternoon. Do you need him?"

"Yes."

Nadine sat down at her desk.

He looked at the paintings that hung behind her at the wall. Then he turned around and saw the pictures of Maurice. His eyes searched for the photographs that were taken under water. Fishes, coral reefs, seas, and lakes. Unasked, he sat down opposite to Nadine, in her husband's chair.

"The night before Mike Brewer jumped out of the

window you paid him a visit," he said, fixing his gaze on her.

"Why should I have done that?" she reacted immediately.

"That is what I would like to hear from you."

"I did not go to him."

"I don't think it wise for you to deny it, Nadine. The apartment has been searched thoroughly. Mike had not cleared up the rooms. A cognac glass was covered with your fingerprints. I am sure that the short, bleached hairs that were found on the bed are yours. You both used cocaine. Did you bring it with you?"

She lowered her eyes.

"Well, I . . . I don't know how to respond to this," she said in a soft voice. "Please give me some time to think."

Martin nodded and kept silent. He looked at different objects on the desktop. A telephone, an antique camera, a calculator, piles of pictures, several books, and a pen tray. the tray was filled with pencils, ballpoints, a pair of scissors, and rolls of adhesive tape. All of a sudden he saw a little ignition key there as well, and he recognized the shape. The rusty Fiat that had chased Vic and his grandfather had crashed against a tree. The driver had run away, leaving the key in the ignition, and now it was kept in his office at the police station. If this was the spare key, then Maurice Aron must have been the driver. He took his cell phone from his pocket and called the police officer who was waiting outside in his car.

"Simon, please drive back to the station. In the metal cupboard next to the door, in my office, is a cardboard box. In it you will find an ignition key on an elastic band with a little card. On the card you will read a license number and the word *Fiat*. Will you get it for me and bring it to me? I am in Nadine Aron's office."

"I'm already on my way," said the policeman.

Martin let the cell phone slip back into his pocket and heaved a big sigh.

"As soon as Maurice comes back, he will be arrested. I will charge him with a number of things. Shall I also accuse him working your feet over with a golf club?"

Nadine hid her face behind her hands. She burst out crying.

"I am at a loss what to do," she sobbed out. "It will be a huge relief to have Maurice locked up! I will tell you everything..."

When Martin left her office one hour later, he knew that he really had found the spare key of the stolen Fiat. And he also knew that the suspicions of Vic Emmett had been right.

He did not find it necessary to arrest Nadine. He knew her well enough to know that she would not leave Saint-Milles. It was not difficult to imagine how afraid she was of Maurice. A man who crushed the feet of his wife with a golf club to distract attention from himself really was someone to fear. And she had been very straight about Mike Brewer:

"I had to go to him to draw him out. Maurice said that it would be easy for me to seduce him. And I had to do everything I could to make him talk. Mike was such a nice man. If Maurice only knew how I enjoyed lying in bed with someone who really paid attention to me. And I am also convinced that Mike loved being together with me."

What surprised Martin the most was that Mike had told her exactly the same story as he himself had heard from Vic.

A perceptible entity present in the cave and a big room filled with a harsh light. He did not understand it, because speleologist René Bougard had discovered nothing like that—except for the fact that he experienced an unpleasant feeling in the long tunnel. Mike had also mentioned Cro-Magnons and Neanderthals.

Bar-er, the sleep of the cave bear.

Perhaps René had been right when he came back from the cave and said that panic in narrow spaces could lead to bizarre thoughts: "I don't know what mortal fear can do with the human mind, but I can make a few guesses..."

Later that day Maurice arrived. He parked his car in front of the office of the newspaper and stepped out.

Martin walked up to him, in the company of two police officers.

"Hello, Maurice."

"Inspector Legrand. How are you doing?"

"Fine, just fine. I have a lot of questions to ask you. Will you please come with me to the police station?"

Maurice stood still. Only now did he notice the two policemen in uniform who stood behind the inspector.

"I've just come back from Bergerac, I am tired. The newspaper needs my pictures. I have to go inside."

"I have to arrest you, Maurice. Let's not make a drama

out of it—come with me quietly."

"Arrest me? For what reason?"

Martin reached out his hand and dangled two identical ignition keys in front of Maurice.

"Stealing an old car, to name one thing."

"Where did you get those keys from? They look just like one I found recently somewhere on the street."

"We will have a talk about battering your wife and about the cowardly attack on Jacques Poiron. Walk with us to the car. Nadine is in possession of the fact that I'm taking you with me. She will manage to run *Le Journal de Saint-Milles* on her own."

Maurice looked up to the window behind which was the big office. He saw Nadine standing there, staring at him.

The inspector put a hand on his shoulder.

"Quick now, Maurice. I am running out of patience."

Maurice followed him to the police car and got in.

"I don't have anything to say to you," he muttered, as the car drove away. "I don't understand a thing about all these accusations."

"Nadine has told me enough. And she is willing to repeat it in the courtroom."

Maurice Aron did not make a confession. He rigorously denied everything that Martin Legrand accused him of. He sat sprawled in a chair in Martin's office, while the inspector himself walked up and down with large steps.

"My men will take a look at your home in a little while. I have a strong feeling that they will find a wetsuit there—and a big, sharp knife."

"Of course they will. I am a photographer. In the past I mainly shot nature pictures. They will also find a waterproof camera, two or three pairs of flippers, and different diving goggles."

"No one could recognize you in that wetsuit. You crossed the river and killed the dogs of Ricard with a harpoon gun. Then you took Jacques Poiron to task. You wanted to know different things from him. But he did not divulge anything. Therefore you fled. You dived into the river and safely reached the other side.

"What utter nonsense, Martin."

"Are you also going to deny striking the feet of your wife with a golf club?"

Maurice folded his hands behind his head, stared up to the ceiling, and burst out laughing.

"I'd be the last one to claim that I never get angry— angry with anything and everyone. And no one knows as well as Nadine that I am not easy to get on with. But what you are saying now is a step too far. Even for me."

"It was Nadine herself who told this to me."

"Women who are out for a divorce often say even crazier things."

"I doubt that. This is absurd enough."

"Then it is your word against mine."

"You sat at the wheel of an old car chasing Vic Emmett and Jacques Poiron. You fired a shot at Tobias Dupont, who was following them in his Mercedes, and then took a shot at them. That game ended for you when you crashed into that tree. The windshield broke, the hood burst open, the motor caught fire. You threw the door open and ran away. The key remained in the ignition. When you stole the Fiat from behind George Roulland's garage, its key was still in the ignition as well and the spare key was in the glove compartment. That was the key that I found in the pen tray on your desk."

"That's right. I already told you that I found it on the street. Now that we finally know where that little key is from, we also know that it will never be used again. For I don't think that the car you were talking about will ever be repaired again…"

Martin stood still for a while and heaved a deep sigh. Then he started pacing up and down the office again.

"Nadine was with Mike Brewer till late at night. Together they made a hell of a party out of it with cognac and cocaine. There was enough drink and drugs left over for Mike to go on celebrating all by himself the next evening. We all know about the tragic result."

"If Nadine feels the need to get away from the house and make fun with another man, I cannot stop her. We avoid each other. I stayed in Bergerac last night. The further I am away from her, the better. What Nadine does is not my responsibility."

"She went to Mike on your request. Maybe he could give information about Jacques Poiron. You gave her a nice supply of cocaine."

"I did not give her anything."

"Then where did she get it from?"

Again Maurice burst out laughing.

"Saint-Milles is the most special little town in France. You, being a police inspector, must know that even better than I, don't you? Who of you keeps track of what is going on in all these deluxe villas on the Golden Street? What is the exact cargo of the choppers that fly over high above your head? What does the pilot bring? Nadine is virtually one of the family with all these immensely rich people on the Golden Street. Everyone there wants to shine on the show page of *Le Journal de Saint-Milles*. As far as that is concerned a deal is quickly made; a bit of cocaine from the great white mountain for Nadine and a splendid article in the newspaper for the kind giver."

Suddenly he rose to his feet.

"This has lasted long enough, Martin. I am tired; I feel sleepy. Therefore I'm going straight home now. If you want to talk to me again tomorrow, please call me only after twelve."

"You stay right here, Maurice."

"Don't make difficulties about it, Martin. Let me go."

He made to pass the inspector and walk to the door. Martin pushed the fingers of his right hand on his chest.

"Not one step more."

The photographer brusquely knocked the hand away. Martin reacted quickly. He caught hold of Maurice's arm, turned it around, and held it behind his back. With his other hand he clasped his neck.

"Simon!" he shouted.

Immediately the door of his office opened. The police officer came in.

"Take Mr. Aron downstairs. There are so many empty cells in this huge building, that he is allowed to make his own choice. As long as you see to it that you lock the door behind him."

Maurice Aron let himself be carried along by the officer, knowing that it was useless to make further resistance.

Nadine Aron had, being the editor-in-chief and owner of *Le Journal de Saint-Milles,* her own column. In it she wrote, clear, short, and to the point, about the arrest of her husband and the presumable reason for it. Further, she explained that the newspaper would do without his cooperation from now on, just as she preferred to go on with her life without him at her side. She was putting an end to a horrid period in her life and asked her readers' understanding for the fact that she did not enter into great detail. She did establish a connection between the arrest of her husband and the attack on Jacques Poiron. And she confessed that she had visited Mike Brewer the night he jumped to meet death.

Many questions remained for anyone who read her column.

And being a professional editor, she knew that this was only good for sales.

25

Vic found himself in the hospital. Late that night he had gone there with Régine. After he had spent a long time at the bed of his grandfather, who lay there motionless like a dead man, a nurse took him to another floor.

Together with Charlotte Laffont, the matron-in-chief of the hospital, Régine had prepared a room for him there. There was a single bed with a table full of equipment next to it.

After he had got himself ready for the night and lay down on the bed, electrodes that could pass information about the course of his sleep were stuck on his forehead and body.

"Do you need anything?" asked Charlotte

Vic shook his head.

"No."

"Do you think you will be able to sleep here?"

"Well, yes. I've never had any trouble falling asleep in a strange room. When I am on tour, I have a different room every night."

"Then we'll leave you alone now," said Régine. "In the

room next door we can see exactly what happens. Brain activity, breathing, blood pressure, pulsation of the heart, perspiration, even the movement of your feet and fingers...With an electroencephalograph we can register the activities of your brain. An oscilloscope will tell us everything about the way you move your eyes. We will follow all phases of your sleep. We cannot take a look into your mind, but we will record all physical reactions while you are dreaming. Hopefully we will be able to draw conclusions from this all. Charlotte and I will take turns to keep a constant eye on the equipment. We have to try and stay awake..."

"Good luck," grinned Vic.

Régine bent forward and kissed him.

A moment later he was alone.

The light was out.

He lay on his back in the dark.

It had been Régine's idea to examine his sleeping state. She was still struggling with whether she could believe his stories or not.

Before he fell asleep he thought of different things.

Nadine had confessed that she had been with Mike. Her husband was in a police cell. His grandfather was close by here and still out of reach. The only way to meet him and help him to come out of his coma was by discovering his dream world and entering it. Between Vic's world and that of Mike had only been a transparent wall. Before he entered the world of Sergio Paladino, he had the sensation as if he were finding his way through huge brains. Maybe that was so because Mike had meant so much more to him than Sergio. The reason that he still had not been able to find his grandfather could be that Jacques's spirit was barely activated. The power of his thoughts was probably not strong enough to make his town visible.

Slowly, in order to prevent the wires that went from the electrodes to the equipment from tangling up, he turned on his side. He pulled up his knees and closed his eyes. Almost immediately he floated above the concert hall in the center of his own town. He came down on the dome. Beneath him shadows slipped through the streets. This was what his grandfather had been so mortally afraid of. He remembered that Jacques had said that they had started to take on human shapes, but that he never had dared to look at them for a long time and investigate them. His grandfather had never dared to do so, but Vic had the guts. His mind was sharp. He was curious. He looked down from the dome and watched the shadows in the depths. He could imagine very well that they had scared the old man.

"Unknown movements in your own world," he thought.

He tried to make them disappear by banishing them from his thoughts.

He did not succeed.

"Something you can not control. Something from the outside..."

Now he started to shiver himself.

The shadows slid up to each other and gathered in front of the doors of the concert hall. There they slowly but surely took shape. Their forms began to look human.

It took his breath away when they all raised their heads and looked up—the eyes were red-hot spots in gray, expressionless faces. The figures were all squat. They crowded tightly together and then began to form a whole that slid inside like thick smoke.

Vic let himself slip down through the dome. He saw how the doors to the hall stood open, and the smoky mass rolled in. Vic landed on the stage. By using the power of his thoughts he made his imaginary audience disappear. This was a purely instinctive action, and immediately he could see what happened next; the gray mass split up again and took on individual human shapes. They shuffled through the hall and sat down on the vacated chairs. All the glowing eyes looked at him expectantly.

Now he began to understand why his grandfather had never seen much more than fast-moving shapes and shadows.

These miraculous entities desired nothing from Jacques Poiron.

They had probably gathered in the concert hall because they wanted to hear Vic play. He no idea who they were or where they came from. They sat there in the half-darkness and did not made a sound. The surface of each figure pulsated as if it were a thin, transparent layer that could hardly keep the smoky substance in its form. Vic walked up to the edge of the stage and made a deep bow.

"I wish to extend a warm welcome to you all," he said, after he had straightened his back again. "I am Vic Emmett, and I would like to play some numbers for you.

They are all new numbers that only existed in my head until now. So no one has ever heard them. I hope you will enjoy my music, and I wish you a pleasant evening."

He bowed again, not so deeply this time, turned around, and walked up to the piano. The black instrument quickly changed into a big, snowy-white grand piano. He sat down on the music stool. He himself enjoyed the first notes he struck. He voice was loud and steady when he started to sing. The lyrics came spontaneously, and his playing was unique. He knew that he came close to perfection. He enjoyed this. Everything was of a pure beauty, everything fitted. Soon Vic was so taken up with himself that he forgot everything around him. The concert hall with its bizarre audience no longer existed to him. That only changed again when he struck the last chord and looked up to the dome, in which his voice still echoed and the pure tones from the grand piano reverberated.

It was quiet now. He turned towards the audience. The entities rose up from their chairs, merged, and formed a growing pillar of smoke that slowly went in the direction of the doors.

In the front row still sat one smoky figure. Vic stared at him, and it flashed on him that he had the shape of a Neanderthal. Above the glowing eyes the thick brow was visible. The creature ascended from his chair and floated in his direction. The body was squat, the shoulders broad. Right in front Vic he stopped and remained hanging in the air, with his feet right above the floor of the stage.

"Who are you?" asked Vic. "What is your name? Can you hear me at all? Do you understand me?"

Threads of smoke spread when the creature moved his head up and down. He pursed his lips, and then Vic could hear clearly:

"Ssh ..."

"Is that your name?"

"Ssh ..." sounded again, while the blazing eyes looked at him.

Vic realized that he was dealing with a phenomenon that in normal life would be called an apparition. What floated there in front of him was the already almost faded form of a specific power that was originating from the brain of a Neanderthal who had lived thirty thousand years ago or even more.

An almost transparent hand motioned to him.

"Do you want me to come along with you? Must you not go and follow the other wandering ghosts?"

The eyes grew bigger. The hand motioned again.

"All right, Ssh. I will follow you."

They flew outside through the dome.

"Bring me to Jacques Poiron!" shouted Vic. "Do you hear me? Jacques Poiron. I want to enter his world. Is that where we are going to?"

There came no answer, and he wondered if Ssh was able to say more than his own name. Assuming that this actually was his name—perhaps it was only an attempt to give utterance to a frame of mind, the way a horse would snort or a dog growl.

Vic saw his town vanish beneath him and the gray cubes of Sergio Paladino appear. Ssh knew how to go from dream world to dream world; Vic regretted that he did not understand how the entity managed to do this so quickly and easily. High up in the sky Ssh turned around and came up to him. He embraced Vic and shortly he had even enclosed him. Vic began to feel cold. The reason Ssh did this was immediately clear to him, as if this knowledge could be transmitted from spirit to spirit without words. In this way he had become a part of the smoky entity, which transformed him into not much more than a shadow. They went down. Together they slipped through the roof of the biggest cube. In the darkest corner they remained hanging right under the ceiling, motionless and as good as invisible.

Sergio Paladino was there. To Vic's big surprise he was not alone. He was in the company of Antoine Chevalier and Maurice Aron. So Antoine and Maurice had been in the cave as well. The photographer must have made a deal with the two men from the Golden Street. No doubt it had come as a surprise to them that they actually were able to travel to another world. One way or another they had managed to find each other there. Such was proved by this private affair that he witnessed so unexpectedly. Soon he found out that the men had a quarrel. Sergio sat on his chair at his gray desk, and the two others paced up and down the empty room.

"Don't forget that I am the one who made it possible that you are here right now," he heard Maurice say. "As a matter of fact you owe everything to me. I was the one who managed to ferret out the secrets of Jacques Poiron, and I took you with me to the castle. Heavens above, without me you would never have been able to get in there. It is high time that you reward me. Get me out of that damned police cell and make me a multimillionaire. You will have no problems with that, I suppose. I have the right to that."

"Money is never the problem," said Sergio. "But don't think that Inspector Legrand is open to bribery. We are simply not able to get you out of that jail. And therefore we suddenly have our own problems..."

"What do you mean?"

"Martin Legrand has accused you of all kinds of deeds, and you have denied them all. Your own wife has given him all the facts on a plate. It will not be long before you start to sing. The inspector will put pressure on you. Don't you understand that? You have been out for the life of France's most important man—Jacques Poiron. The police cannot permit you to go."

"And what is your problem then? You are free; I'm the one who is locked in."

"The problem is you," Antoine joined in the discussion. "Sergio already said it: sooner or later you are going to talk, and then our names will be mentioned..."

"I will never betray you."

"We think you will," said Sergio. "It is true, Maurice, you have put us on the path, and we have come far. But we can take care of ourselves from here. Antoine and I will amaze everyone. Only imagine— before long we will have gathered so much money that the capital of Jacques Poiron will shrink into insignificance! We don't say that we will possess the entire world one day, but we are going to try it anyway!"

"As far as that is concerned I wish you success," said the photographer. "If you don't want me to pop up in your dream worlds anymore, I solemnly promise to stay away."

"It seems wiser to us to say goodbye forever, Maurice. Thanks very much for everything you did for us. The only thing we want from you now is your life."

Maurice came standing in front of Sergio's desk and raised his fist at him.

"You don't think I'd let myself be murdered by you just like that, do you? I have had to fight more than once in order to survive, and I really don't think that you are a match for me."

Sergio shook his head.

"To be honest with you, I have never been involved in a fight. You'd better watch out for Antoine."

The photographer turned around with lightning speed. Antoine stood right behind him, towering high above him, and struck hard with his right fist. Maurice staggered on his feet, leaned on the desktop for a moment, and then backwards. Antoine caught him by grasping his head with both hands. With all his strength he turned the head of Maurice around. There was the sound of a short, dry crack as he broke the photographer's neck.

He let go of the photographer.

Maurice fell on the hard floor and remained lying there motionless.

Vic's mouth fell open. He had great difficulty suppressing a scream. The entity that enwrapped him searched entrance to his mind and managed to transmit to him, via the power of his thoughts, to keep calm.

Sergio had come from behind his desk and walked up to the others. He knelt down next to the photographer and looked into the staring eyes. He leaned forward and pressed an ear on the man's the breast. Then he felt his pulse. Antoine squatted behind him and used another method to establish whether his victim was really dead. With a big hand he clasped the head and turned it to and fro like ripe fruit on a branch.

"It is done, Sergio. What are we going to do with him now?"

"We'll bring him inside one of my cubes and make the windows and doors disappear. Then he will lie in the dark forever."

Sergio took the photographer by the feet. Antoine took him by his shoulders. The head of Maurice swung to and fro when they lifted him up. They rose from the floor and flew outside through an open window.

The entity brought Vic back to his own world; after an inconceivably short period Vic found himself back again on the stage of his concert hall. Ssh was standing in front of him. He looked at Vic. His eyes flashed. He raised a smoky hand. Slowly he let himself fall backward, and then he floated above the chairs in the direction of the open doors. Right before he disappeared he changed into an oblong plume of smoke.

Vic sat down on the music stool.

He did not feel fear, and he was not going to panic. Here his mind worked quietly in a different way than when he was awake. What he wanted to do now was to compose.

Soon he was busy playing and singing. He made the shades appear again and provided them with clothes. He gave himself to his music with heart and soul. The time went by until at a certain moment he sat up and felt that he was ready to wake up in the bed in the hospital of Saint-Milles.

26

Régine was standing at his bedside when he opened his eyes. She smiled at him and then she covered her mouth with her hand to hide a yawn.

"Good morning to you," she said. "The most easy patient in the hospital. That is what Charlotte said often to me last night."

She lifted the blanket and began to remove the electrodes from his body.

"Hello," said Vic in a sleepy voice.

Slowly it dawned on him what he had done and seen in his dream world. It scared him, and he tried not to show that to her. After the last electrode had been removed, Régine switched off all the equipment.

"Have you ever heard of the REM period, Vic?" she asked, after which she leaned over to him and pressed her lips on his.

"Sure. Rapid eye movements. The eyes of a sleeping person move to and fro in a fast way, and it is said that means that he is dreaming."

"The electroencephalograph measures the electric impulses of the brain and passes them through to a piece of apparatus that maps it out. You can compare the result a bit with the deflecting lines you see on a paper roll when an earthquake gets registered."

"Was it so spectacular in my case?"

"Not at all! Last night you rolled onto your side and raised your knees. You went into a deep sleep. There was hardly anything to register, on any single piece of apparatus. You breathed regularly, your heartbeat remained constant, and your REM periods—which are clearly measurable on most people—were hardly observable. One thing is for sure, Vic, you have had a good rest, while I am ready to drop from no sleep."

Vic sat up straight.

"Conclusion?" he asked.

"You are in perfect health, the most ideal partner for me," she smiled. "But from now on I won't believe another thing you say about special dreams. Charlotte even questioned whether you had dreamed anything at all last night. You hardly moved the whole time either. I have noticed the same thing at home when you were sleeping next to me."

"*Bar-er*," thought Vic. "A motionless sleep in a frozen world."

But he didn't talk about that.

"You can go wash yourself and then get dressed," said Régine. "And then you can consider yourself officially released from this hospital..."

She turned and walked toward the door, but Vic called her back. With raised eyebrows she observed how Vic looked at her very seriously, and that there was fear in his light-brown eyes.

"Yes?"

"Maybe you think that I have told you nothing but nonsense. Believe me, you will have to change your opinion about me and prepare yourself for the fact that everything is even more complicated than I have said."

She heaved a sigh.

"Listen, Vic, I know you are mentally all right. You are different from other people, which is expressed in your creativity. I just don't dare to think that you have an aberration after all—a mental kink that you could hide even from me thanks to your intelligence. Thinking about something like that gives me the creeps. You know that I love you dearly, and I would want to help you with all my might if it was necessary to make you get rid of certain delusions. In the past you had to face the most horrible events. Your girlfriend, your parents . . . I do not know how much that has changed you. I also do not know to what extent you have come to terms with all that. But do you know what actually scares me the most?"

"Well?"

"That you may have spoken the truth after all. And now you tell me that it is even more complicated."

"Maurice Aron is dead."

He said it abruptly and curtly.

Régine looked at him incredulously.

"What are you talking about?"

"Tell it to nobody."

"Maurice Aron. As far as I know he is still in a cell in the police station."

"I think you're right. But I have seen him. In some

other man's dream world. He was murdered there. I tell this to you here and now, Régine, because I can prove to you this way that I have always spoken the truth. Charlotte and you have kept an eye on me all night long. I never left this room. That is to say, my body has been right here on this bed in a relaxed position. Maybe you will be convinced that something very special is going on when someone tells you today that Maurice is no longer alive and that he breathed his last unaccountably in a police cell. And in the meantime you should also think about an absurd but topical question..."

"Ask it to me," she said with a sigh.

"Can a judge condemn a man because he murdered another man in his dreams?"

Régine searched for words in despair. Finally she turned around and walked to the door for the second time.

"I will wait for you in the next room," she said. "Charlotte will be there, too. We will talk more about this after we both have left the hospital."

Before he left, he paid a short visit to his grandfather.

In the corridor he met Louis Lanois; it was his turn to stand guard at the door of Jacques Poiron's room.

"Never seen you here so early before," said Louis, thinking that he had spent the night with Régine and had left for the hospital from her home that morning.

Vic did not make him the wiser.

"I woke up early." And that was no lie anyway. "Keep your eyes and ears open, Louis. You are doing a great job here. The life of my grandfather is sacred to me."

"I know that, Vic. You can count on me."

Régine was waiting for him in the parking lot. She had raised her head up to the already warm morning sun, and her eyes were closed. He walked up to her and laid a hand on her shoulder. When she turned around he could tell that she had been crying.

"I had thought and hoped to be stronger," she said. "If it turns out that you are right, my entire mental world will collapse. What can I cling to if such fantastic things happen to be true? It would turn everything upside down. It would be better for the entire world if you were suffering from a serious psychosis after all."

The only thing he could come up with was:

"Let me drive, you're too nervous."

She gave him her bunch of keys. Only after they were driving slowly through the streets of Saint-Milles did she start to talk again.

"During all those years I worked closely together with Jacques, I slowly but surely got used to his very special behavior. No one could find an explanation for the never-failing luck he had in business. If something remains a puzzle long enough, you come to see it as a common fact. Now I begin to see it all differently. He always was able to get his foreknowledge from somewhere…"

"That is right," said Vic.

He parked the car in front of Chez Marcus.

"What are you up to, Vic? I have to go to a meeting, I have get to work. Bertrand and Tessa Collin are expecting me."

"Then call and cancel it. It cannot be that important.

All you do there is pile up one million on another. No one will get any poorer if you don't show up for one morning. I'm starving. Let's find us an outside table at Chez Marcus."

"I get sick just thinking about food."

"Order strong coffee. It helps to drive the sleep away."

She agreed; on their way to a table she called the Collins, and by the time she sat down she was longing for black coffee.

"Aren't you nervous at all, Vic?" she asked all of a sudden.

"I am right now. At night it is totally different. It is almost unexplainable. I can imagine that you immediately think of a split personality. With our view of the human mind we do not get any further. Believe me, your psychological education simply has shortcomings."

"Is that so?"

"What would happen if it was possible to put a Neanderthal man on a shrink's couch?"

"My God, I have no idea!"

"And what to do with the brain of a *Homo sapiens* like me, that is open to impulses strange to you and everyone else, thanks to the power of thoughts from a Neanderthal man?"

Régine drank her coffee. She held the cup in both hands and leaned with her elbows on the tabletop. She saw how he attacked his breakfast.

"I cannot give an answer to questions like that. I have to admit that. Back to Maurice Aron ..."

She whispered the name and looked around nervously around to see if anyone sat close enough to hear her. It was still quiet at this early hour of the day. "On the understanding that he is actually dead, then who is his murderer?"

"I don't dare to tell you that. That is to say—not yet. We'll have to wait and see what is going to happen. Maybe he managed to survive, and it turns out to be impossible to kill someone this way after all."

"But you don't suppose so. . . .

"I don't suppose so."

"It really scares me. Do I know the person?"

"Yes."

"Now I'm going crazy!" she shouted. Her own voice startled her, and again she looked around.

Right at that moment Vic's cell phone started to ring. He took it from his pocket and looked at the little screen.

"Louis Lanois," he said, looking up at Régine.

He saw how she suddenly turned pale and how her breath caught.

"He is in the hospital. With my grandfather. Hope nothing has—"

He did not complete his sentence and put the call through.

"This is Vic. What's up, Louis?"

It was not customary for security men to call him just like that. Régine looked fixedly at Vic and tried to get the gist from what he said. But he did never spoke more than three or four words in a row:

"Are you sure?" And: "How do you know?" Finally he said: "Thanks for calling. Thank you very much."

He let the cell phone slip into his pocket again.

Régine pressed her lips together. She should have preferred to cry out: "What's going on?" But she managed to control herself.

Vic pushed his plate aside.

"Louis."

"You already said that."

"His brother often drives the ambulance. This morning, just after we had left there, he picked up Maurice Aron's dead body and brought it to the hospital. For an autopsy. Louis thought that it would interest me that the presumed attacker of Jacques Poiron is dead."

Régine repeated what she had said a moment ago:

"Now I really am going crazy!"

27

"I bid farewell to a man who meant everything to me," said Nadine Aron.

She had ascended the pulpit in the auditorium of the Saint-Milles cemetery. It was crowded and hot. All the seats were taken, and many people had to stand.

"You turn a blind eye to the one you really love. But when cruelty crops up, love can turn to hatred. I know it. I have experienced it. Right here I don't want to say more about that. For Maurice is dead, and I want him to rest in peace."

She told about his life.

How he had traveled around the world as a photographer.

About the way she met him and their common passion for *Le Journal de Saint-Milles*.

Of course she also mentioned under which circumstances he had met his death.

"Many a time he flew in the face of danger on his journeys. No mountain was too sheer or too high for him, no sea or lake too deep. For a wild man like Maurice a police cell should have been the most safe place on earth; he could come to no harm there. Death caught him in his sleep. He stopped breathing, his heart stopped beating. He was lying on his side, his face to the wall...He was examined in the hospital. Nothing special was found. It was his time to go. Let's keep it to that."

At the end of her speech she made some confessions.

"Some things have to be mentioned here. All the property in and around Saint-Milles we owe to one person only; Jacques Poiron. Everybody knows that. Maurice wanted to find out how Jacques managed to accumulate his fabulous capital.

"He would do anything to find out.

"I have written about that in the paper.

"Everyone has read it.

"He did not shrink from using a golf club to crush my toes..."

She fell silent for a while and rubbed her eyes with her fingers.

"It is a macabre coincidence that Maurice's grave is right next to that of Mike Brewer. I had a talk with Mike. On Maurice's request. What he told me is both mysterious and puzzling to me. There is a cave right under Castle Ricard. When Jacques Poiron was still a young man and worked in Alfonse Lanois's bakery, he started to investigate the castle as an amateur archaeologist. He found the cave, entered it, and underwent, as Mike asserted, a metamorphosis. Something deep down in there changed him, and when he appeared again nothing and nobody could stop him from becoming one of richest men in the world. I told Maurice all about this. I do not know what he did with this knowledge. All I know is that he is dead now..."

She looked through the hall until her eye rested on Martin Legrand, who stood somewhere in the back.

"I have told my story to the police of Saint-Milles as well. At the request of Inspector Legrand someone went into the cave that is actually there under Ricard. It appears to be nothing more than a long, narrow tunnel that comes to a dead end deep down under the ground. Which makes everything Mike Brewer told me implausible. And maybe that is good after all. In my opinion it would be crazy if it all was true and Jacques Poiron had a miraculous experience deep down there. Although many questions have remained unanswered, I prefer to take comfort today in thinking that Maurice searched for a secret that never existed and that he fell asleep in a police cell . . . never to wake up again. The news came as a shock to me. I still have not recovered from it. Maurice, I forgive you everything. And I say farewell to you as a dear friend..."

* * *

Vic went on tour and visited a number of European cities. Michelle Ferrer had scheduled a tight agenda for him. He had to appear on different television shows wherein he was given the time to talk about his life from time he had moved from America to France and then played a couple new songs, accompanied by the French band that traveled along with him. From Paris he went to Brussels, Amsterdam, and London. From London to Rome, Madrid, and Lisbon. He took a plane back to Paris and was brought to Saint-Milles by helicopter.

He had given permission to open the doors of Ricard

to everyone during his absence. Crowds of people came to the castle. Tobias and Julia Dupont showed them around. Almost all the inhabitants of Saint-Milles took this opportunity to see the famous building from the inside. Reporters and camera crews from all over the country came to see the library with the cave paintings and to enter the cellar. Only one or two dared to enter the cave and came back again as quickly as possible, scared and shivering. Wild tales were going the rounds where Jacques Poiron was concerned. Where was he? Was he still alive? Was he really in a coma in the hospital? This man had become a legendary personality.

It was quiet again in the castle when Vic returned.

Every night, when he had turned off the light again in a strange hotel room, he had entered his dream world determined to search for his grandfather. He never caught a glimpse of him. The wandering entities did not show up in the streets of his town again.

He called for Tobias Dupont and asked him for the key to the door that gave entrance to the rooms in the tower. He got it immediately. Vic wanted to go up the winding stairs one day, to the bedroom of his grandfather. Perhaps he would be able to find him in his dream world if he went to sleep there. On the other hand he found it rather scary to enter the tower now that Jacques was in a coma. So he put it off for some time. As soon as his doubts disappeared, he would make use of the key. First he took a few days' rest. Inspector Legrand did not trouble him anymore after Maurice had died in the cell. Régine shunned any talk with him about murder in a dream.

In the mornings he walked at a leisurely pace to the studio. At those times he wanted to be all by himself, and his guard walked far behind him. He saw the world change. Everything around him suddenly looked more beautiful. There was life in every cobblestone and every rock. The grass was waving at him, the trees whispered him hello. Every now and then he made dance steps. No one was surprised at this behavior. He was known as the eccentric composer and a musician. In the studio he worked on new songs.

On occasion he also came looking for Régine when she had a meeting in one of the villas or offices on the Golden Street. No one stopped him. He would sit down next to her and listen to what the partners were talking about.

"What are you doing here?" Régine wanted to know when he entered for the first time. "You've never been interested in business, have you?"

He did not answer. Soon it became clear to him that everything on the Golden Street went on in the old way. There were no new, spectacular things happening. To him this meant that Sergio Paladino and Antoine Chevalier still had not seen a way to pull off a big coup. Every time he looked into their direction, they lowered their eyes.

One late, hot, cloudless night Armand and Claire Laurin had organized a garden party. Their garden was the largest on the Golden Street and ended near the helicopter pad behind which the high rock formations rose up. Chinese lanterns hung in the old, thick walnut trees. A huge barbecue glowed in a dark corner. The guests moved along like shadows. Sergio Paladino was there with his wife. He left her alone while she was in close conversation with someone and he went to Antoine Chevalier. Together they went looking for Vic. They found him in the company of Régine.

"Hello," said Sergio. He looked briefly at Vic and then rested his eyes on Régine. "How are you doing? Mostly we only have meetings here with the Laurins, Régine; it was about time that they were giving a party."

"Yes, I agree," smiled Régine.

They talked on. Antoine joined the conversation. Vic kept silent and looked at both men. Sergio, small, slender, dark, talked fast and much and made gestures all the time. Antoine, as big as Mike Brewer once was, talked in a calm way and thoughtfully stroked his moustache with his thumb and forefinger. While they conversed with Régine, they glanced at him regularly.

It was an unique duo; they had the most miraculous murder on their conscience that was ever committed by a *Homo sapiens*—leaving aside whatever Neanderthals had done in their dreams many thousands of years ago.

When Tessa Collin came by and asked Régine a question, Sergio beckoned to Vic.

"Can we have a quiet talk? You, Antoine, and I? Please walk along with us."

"That's all right. I'll follow you."

They went deeper into the garden, past a big swimming pool where hundreds of candles burned along the edges. All three of them took a glass of red Bergerac from a table and continued on. They stopped near a lit pond. In the middle of it stood a marble satyr spitting water.

"The longer your grandfather remains in a coma, the less people on the Golden Street still believe he will ever come out of it again," started Sergio. "I drink to him. I would do anything to be able to shake his hand one more time."

Vic nodded, raised his glass, and took a sip.

"If there was only a way to reach him," said Antoine. "If we could only find a way to penetrate into his mind, in a manner of speaking..."

His remark made Vic alert. But he gave no sign of it.

"Exactly," said Sergio. "If there was only something like ..." He stared up to the dark sky and acted as if he searched for the right words. "Something like a common dream. That way we could pay your highly gifted grandfather a visit in his sleep."

"What a nice fantasy," remarked Vic. "That could very well be a good idea for a new song."

"Some things are fantasy for one person and reality for the other," said Antoine.

"What do you mean?"

The big man shrugged his shoulders.

"I don't know...It just came to me."

"Listen, gentlemen, I came here with Régine, and actually I want to go back to her. If there is something you have to say to me . . . You wanted to have a quiet talk with me. About what? About my grandfather being in a coma?"

"Yes." The voice of Antoine sounded deep.

"I am listening."

"We thought that Nadine was very honest during her speech, when Maurice was buried," started Sergio. "But still no one knows what exactly happened. What did Maurice discover? And how is it possible that he died just like that in his cell?"

"I don't understand what you are getting at. You said you wanted to talk about my grandfather."

Antoine seemed to get impatient. He emptied his glass in one gulp.

"It does not matter who he is talking about. About Mike, about Jacques, about Maurice . . . There is something special going on and all three of these men had to do with it. Two of them are dead, one is in a coma. And there probably is a fourth man who knows about it all and who is alive and kicking. It is even possible that he is standing right in front of us at this very moment."

Vic grinned.

"A fourth man? Why then not a fifth, or even a sixth man as well?"

Suddenly there seemed to be fear in Sergio's eyes.

"Three men together," continued Vic. "Oh yes, also alive and kicking. I mean, if you speak in riddles, I will do the same."

There was a silence during which everyone feverishly tried to order his thoughts.

Then Sergio asked:

"Are you dreaming often lately, Vic?"

Antoine nodded, as if he wanted to say: "Now that's a good opening..."

"Not long ago I had a horrible nightmare."

A young woman passed by with a tray full of glasses. Again they all took a glass of Bergerac. Vic waited until she had walked, and then continued:

"On Tuesday I saw something I had never seen before. Imagine a town filled with unimaginative gray cubes…"

He noticed both men jumping out of their skin.

"I was floating right above it, dived down, and landed in a street. I entered a building and went up the stairs. Someone was sitting behind a desk there. Another person was standing in front of it, and a third one was pacing up and down the room. There was an unpleasant atmosphere. It was obvious to me that these men were having a quarrel. Then one of them was murdered. They broke his neck. When I woke up again I had the feeling that this all had really happened. It was a very scary experience."

Antoine started to swear.

Vic put his hand in his pocket. He took out the thin golden bracelet and showed it on the flat of his hand.

"This belongs to you, Sergio. You lost it."

Sergio reached out his hand.

Then he hesitated.

"Mine?"

"Just take it. I found it in the cellar behind the bookcase. Near the cave Nadine was talking about in her speech. The shackle is broken."

Up to now they had been talking about theoretical things, about immaterial phenomena like dreams. The bracelet was a visible and tangible object, and it threw Sergio off balance. He shook his head and made a fending gesture.

"I don't recognize it. It's not mine. I never lost a bracelet."

"And I don't like it," said Vic, as he turned his back to the pond. "Let me do something useful with it."

He threw the bracelet over his shoulder into the water of the pond. Fish came towards it and immediately swam away again when the determined that the object was not eatable.

"When you throw a single coin into the water, you can ask for much. I hope the wish I just made will come true."

Sergio tried to smile.

"What did you wish, Vic?"

"I cannot tell you. It is said that a wish will never come true if you talk about it with someone else. I'm going back to Régine now. No doubt we will meet again this evening. If you have something sane to tell me, I will listen to you gladly."

Vic walked away. He wished that he would find the dream world of Jacques Poiron sooner than Sergio Paladino or Antoine Chevalier. Even before he had walked past the pond, Sergio popped up next to him.

"Wait a minute, Vic. Easy!"

"What's up?"

"For convenience sake, let's say that we share certain unique experiences. Well, you know what I mean. You witnessed a murder in a dream. Not long after you had woken up you heard that someone had died. Has the combination of those two facts any consequences for the one that committed the murder in the dream?"

"Who would believe me, Sergio?"

"No one. I am convinced of that. No one at all."

"Be honest with me. About the bracelet."

"Yes, it is mine." Again he tried to produce a smile, and this time he succeeded. "Perhaps I will get it back after someone has found it. Then everyone will know that I lost it at this party when I was standing there at the pond..."

"I understand."

He saw Antoine come walking up to them. Sergio immediately informed him about what had been said.

"No doubt Vic actually saw what happened. But he understands very well that no one will believe a single word of his story. What do we do now?"

"We do nothing at all," said Antoine. "As long as we do not meet in our worlds, nothing will happen to Vic. If he bothers us there, it will end in disaster for him."

"That is a threat!" Vic cried out.

"Please, not so loud!" hissed Sergio.

"Murder," whispered Vic. "That's what we are talking about. Murder, you hear? And what happened to an unlucky photographer can happen to me as well. That is what you are trying to make clear to me. And how about my grandfather?"

"A good question. Now that we have succeeded in entering worlds that we recently did not even suspect existed, we want to make use of the unknown possibilities. We still have not been able to snatch certain information from the future, which is a technique Jacques Poiron has mastered perfectly. When we find him, he will have to explain to us how he does it. Antoine is right, Vic. Stay in your own world. Never leave it. Stay away from our worlds, and don't go searching for Jacques Poiron. As soon as we find you somewhere, you have a very big problem."

"In normal life, to call it that way, we will keep an eye on you as well," said Antoine. "Don't talk about this to anyone, and we will leave you in peace. Is that clear?"

"So many things have become clear to me," said Vic.

He walked on and went looking for Régine.

As soon as he had found her, he said:

"You stay here. I'm going back. To Ricard that is."

"Don't you like it here? Wouldn't you rather sleep with me?"

"I want to be alone. We'll see each other tomorrow."

"Is there something the matter?"

"Nothing. I am tired."

She looked at him searchingly, and then she kissed him.

"All right then," she said. "See you tomorrow..."

28

Vic went through the dark night, through the Golden Street. Louis Lanois accompanied him.

"Such a pity that you wanted to leave so soon," said Louis. "Usually parties go on till sunrise. And a simple guard like me does not often get the chance to be there."

"Then go back in a while," suggested Vic. "And pay good attention to Régine. I really would appreciate that."

"With pleasure," grinned Louis.

Vic had refused his suggestion to go back to Ricard by car. The night was beautiful, the night was alive! The twinkling of the stars in the sky was filled with energy. The stones of the big villas were vibrating. He heard high-frequency sound all around him, registered the movements of hidden insects, and had the feeling he could hear the world breathe as if it were a gigantic living creature.

Mother Earth.

Neanderthal feelings that influenced his own sense organs.

He wanted to sing but held himself in because Louis was walking next to him.

This was his night. He could feel it. This was the night

that he was going to enter the dream world of Jacques Poiron.

They had reached the gate of the castle park. Louis turned back to the Golden Street, and another guard accompanied Vic to one of the doors of the castle. As soon as Vic was inside, he went to his bedroom to get the key Tobias had given to him. Then he went to the room with the door that gave entry to the round tower. He turned the key. The heavy lock opened with a sound that echoed in the round reception hall. Vic went inside. Lamps went on and shone upon the countless stones in the wall. Now he started to sing lustily, and he went dancing along the wall. With the fingers of both hands he touched the stones and felt his spirit charged with energy. It was not known to him that his grandfather had executed the same ritual many times. It was an automatic action in which the power of attraction of so many different stones played a prominent part.

Jade, marble, granite, turquoise, agate, zircon, meteorite, emerald, ruby, topaz, gneiss . . .

He sang meaningless words in a short chorus and repeated it time after time. In a deep trance he went around, until he danced to the middle of the reception hall and started to climb the winding stairs with quick steps. In thought he was with the occupant of the tower, Jacques Poiron. The cold from an ice age in far-off days caught him and penetrated his bones. His movements slowed down. He reached the fourth story and stumbled across the floor to a marble fireplace. There he sank down on the floor, turned on his side, and pulled up his knees. He breathed in deeply and let the air escape so powerfully between his lips that the white ashes in the fireplace flew up. Not much later his breathing became more regular. He did not move any more; his spirit was too far away from his body be able to exert an influence on it.

His dream world looked even more beautiful to him than usual.

He floated high above the town and felt at home.

Self-confidently he took a dive, and with his head down and his arms stretched forward he went up to the biggest dome; he went right through it, turned around in the air, and landed on his feet on the stage.

Besides feeling self-confident he also felt grim and resolute. With a simple move of his hand he made his imaginary audience disappear. He sat down on the music stool. Now he let himself be led by intuition. He stared at his fingers smoothly touching the keys. Then he closed his eyes. He kicked on the floor with the heel of his shoe. It made a loud and deep sound, and it reverberated along with the high tones of the grand piano. The sweat ran down Vic's forehead and cheeks. It also bit his eyes when he finally opened them again. With misty eyes he looked into the hall. He could see that all the seats were taken again. The concert hall was filled with gray, smoky shapes. They clapped their hands without making a sound, and long plumes of smoke moved to and fro. Their eyes glowed from under their thick, beetling brows.

"Welcome," thought Vic, and he was convinced that his odd audience received his well-meant greeting.

He felt that they understood each other. This moment

he was as one of them, and instinctively he knew what had to happen. He led the meeting with his passionate playing.

The concert hall had become a courtroom.

The tribe had come together and was ready to inflict heavy punishment on some renegades. Banishment!

* * *

At the party in the garden of the Laurins a team of cooks tended an extensive barbecue. While most of the guests were busy filling their plates, Sergio Paladino and Antoine Chevalier walked for the second time that evening to the pond in the back of the garden. It was striking how they were reeling, as if they'd had too much to drink.

Some of the guests saw them going and nudged each other.

"We don't see that often," grinned Felix Baudin to the people who were standing there with him. "Most of the time they are the last ones who fall down..."

Only with great effort did they manage to reach the pond, and there they sank down, sighing, on a bench. Slowly they sprawled across the bench; the tall Antoine rested his head against the shoulder of the much smaller Sergio. Their eyes fell shut. They remained sitting there motionless. They were in deep sleep.

Except for the two glasses of wine they had drunk earlier that evening during their conversation with Vic, they had not touched any other alcoholic drink. They had responded to a sudden urgency to sit down and go to sleep.

In the concert hall in Vic's dream world the entities made a dark, roaring sound. Vic still played the grand piano and kicked his heel on the floor. Antoine Chevalier and Sergio Paladino appeared, slowly floating through the center aisle between the rows of chairs, right up to the front of the stage. There they turned around and remained hanging in the air, trembling all over, with their feet right above the floor. In frightened expectation they looked at the half-transparent shapes that filled the rows. The roaring became louder. No words were needed to make clear to the two men why they had been sent for. In these dream worlds there was no place for murderers.

Here, in Vic's concert hall, judgment be passed on them.

Banishment was unavoidable.

The entities made themselves clear. The two men did not belong here. They had to return to their own world under the sun and were forbidden ever to return. The creatures lifted their arms and waved their hands. The growling became more melodious. Vic drew his inspiration directly from the common power of mind of his audience. It was an interaction in which the entities fed themselves with his energy; slowly but surely it brought them into ecstasies. The blood drummed in Vic's temples. He felt his fingers grow numb, and his heel began to hurt. But he forced himself to hold on because he knew what was going to happen.

He would never be able to tell from which period the different creatures dated; it was very well possible that most of them never had met during their lives because they were from different generations and from different tribes. But now, here in Vic's dream world, they had come together as one tribe and acted as such. A concentrated magical power made the walls and the dome shake. Antoine and Sergio looked up with dilated eyes. They gradually rose. Kicking their feet in the air, they slowly vanished. Before they had reached the top of the dome they had disappeared.

Back at the party, it was growing late. Tens of people had gathered near the pond in the back of the garden and made fun of the two sleeping men. Every effort was made to wake them up. Some tipsy, bold women had kissed them. Men had given them a good shaking. Claire Laurin had asked Michelle Ferrer if she could arrange for a band to play at the party. Michelle had taken care of it. Now the drummer was dragged along to the bench at the pond. He had a drum with him, and with all his might he beat with his sticks on the drumhead. It made an ear-splitting noise. When the two sleepers did not react to that at all, their audience began to worry. Someone slapped them in the face and shouted in their ears. Doctor Jean-Louis Gilbert was present at the party. Claire Laurin went searching for him and brought him over to the two men. He was very surprised when he saw them. After feeling their pulses and listening to their breathing, he could only conclude that they were in a deep sleep. He could give no explanation for the fact that there was no way to wake them up.

"I have never seen anything like this before," he had to admit.

The drummer started to make some noise again. The bystanders laughed, yelled, clapped their hands, and all of a sudden fell silent when they saw both men move. Sergio was the first to open his eyes. He looked around in surprise. Antoine had a good stretch.

"What's up?" he asked, to no one in special.

He rose his feet. Sergio did the same.

"You were in a deep sleep," said Doctor Gilbert. "It was as if you both hypnotized. What happened? Did you drink something, did you use—"

Sergio shook his head.

"No, no. Believe me, I would tell you if I had done so, I—" He rubbed his forehead with his fingers. "All I remember is that I wanted to sit down quietly. I was tired, so tired...And then I must have fallen asleep. Yes, I have been in a deep sleep."

"That's what I told you," said the doctor with a smile.

Régine was standing not far away from them.

"Could it be that you had a dream?" she asked. "It is a strange coincidence that you both fell asleep so fast."

Antoine shrugged his shoulders.

"A dream . . . I don't remember. I don't remember anything at all."

"How strange," said Sergio. "I closed my eyes, and now I am suddenly wide awake. No, I don't remember any dreams either. For how long have we been sitting here?"

"For two hours or maybe more," said Armand Laurin. "Well, let's not talk about it anymore. I hope you feel rested enough to join the party again."

"You bet," said Sergio resolutely. "I have this strange feeling. As if a heavy load has been taken off of me. And

I'm extremely hungry and thirsty."

Together with Antoine he began to walk in the direction of the villa. The others followed and made fun of them. They ignored the heckling.

"Something like this has never happened to me before," said Sergio in a soft voice, so that only Antoine was able to hear him.

"What was that?" Antoine whispered back. "It gives me the creeps. I always remember what happened to me, even if I have been dead drunk. Now there is something like a . . . like a blind spot in my head!"

"Right. That's it. That's exactly it! A blind spot!"

They remained present at the party until late that night. In silence, wondering what had happened to them.

29

Vic rested for a while. He turned around on his stool and looked into the hall. Countless glowing eyes stared at him from under thick, beetled brows. A veil of smoke was hanging above their heads. The bodies appeared more transparent than before.

"You are tired," said Vic. "Just as exhausted as I am. We'd better stop for a while. Before you all vanish into thin air."

Time went by in silence.

A shape went up from its chair and floated up to the stage. Right in front of Vic it landed on its smoky feet.

Vic rose to his feet. "Ssh?" he asked hopefully.

"Ssh," it sounded softly.

The creature stuck out its head.

Intuitively Vic did the same. Their heads touched, and Vic was surprised that he actually felt a hard skull. He realized that every suggestion in this world could be evoked and experienced as an actually perceptible fact. Now it was possible to tap each other's stream of thoughts.

A special power of attraction, an overwhelming feeling of sympathy, bridged thousands and thousands of years. Vic's brain turned icy cold. His spirit fell into the hole of time and he reached a frozen, white world. In few seconds he had insight into the Neanderthal world. The creature, in its turn, began to feel warm and received images from Vic's world of experience.

At first they attracted each other like magnets, but now they repelled each other and shrunk back. Vic stumbled over the music stool and landed on his back on the stage. The creature floated backward and came back in a curve.

"Ssh!" it sounded loudly, and two half-transparent arms and hands gestured.

The entities came up from their chairs, floated up towards each other, and formed a giant cloud. Vic was lifted up by the cloud and together with it he flew outside through the dome.

"Up to Jacques Poiron!" he cried out.

His voice sounded happy.

Ssh had read his deepest thoughts and understood what his biggest wish was. Everything was dark as Vic whizzed along in the center of the cloud. It didn't matter. His heart was singing now that he knew he was going to reach his goal. The cloud grew thin and moved along more slowly, but he himself continued along at the same speed. Now only Shh was next to him. Shh made some gestures and swerved away.

Beneath him he saw a town. Going down quickly he saw palaces, gardens, parks. Trees with shining fruits. He felt attracted to the biggest palace in the center of the town. He reflected that he himself had built the most beautiful concert hall in the center of his town. Now he was floating right above the street and slid through a gate. Inside the building he went through a hall and a corridor and then found a stone staircase.

On the twentieth story was a big room with twenty high, arched windows. Jacques Poiron lay back in his chair, his hands crossed on his belly. His legs rested on the top of his wooden desk. The eyes of the old man were closed, the lips curved in a smile.

Different colorful birds sat on the ledges. They did not move. Everything was motionless in this dream world, because the brain of its creator was not active. Vic landed with his feet on the floor and carefully walked up to the desk. Seldom in his life had he felt more relieved. He looked at his grandfather from close quarters. It was as if he were looking at himself in a later stage of life. The chest did not move under Jacques's clothes. Did he actually breathe? The cloud floated into the big room and began to divide. Human shapes came into being. The entities gathered around the desk and reached out their arms. They waved their smoky hands with spread fingers. Deep, melodious tones sounded up.

The wonder came to pass.

Jacques Poiron opened his eyes.

Vic was in a rapture of delight. It was only with great effort that he managed to suppress a shout of joy.

The old man still lay there motionless. Only his eyes rolled to and fro. Then, when his eyes rested upon Vic, his facial muscles began to move again; Jacques smiled! And he remained smiling as he slowly awoke from his deep, deep rest. His arms slid to the side, his hands gripped the armrests of his chair. Heaving a deep sigh, he sat up straight. Immediately he saw the gathered entities and recognized their origin.

"Neanderthals!" was the first thing he said.

The shapes shoved together and intermingled. What remained was a long-drawn-out cloud that wriggled outside like a snake through one of the arched windows.

Vic went up to his grandfather, stooped, put his hands on his shoulders, and asked:

"How do you feel?"

"Fine. Very fine. What has happened, Vic?"

"We will talk about that later, grandfather. Are you strong enough to stay alert?"

"I don't know. I suppose so. Everything seems so strange to me. The Neanderthals! In my dream world . . . and you ..."

He looked at him with dilated eyes and smiled again.

"You found me! Vic, you did it!"

Vic nodded.

"We have to act quickly now. Listen to me carefully, for this is of the greatest importance for your health. You have been in the hospital of Saint-Milles for quite some time already. You are in a coma! Do you understand me? You lapsed into a coma. No one there is able to help you. The only way to recover is via your dream world, and I am the only one who was able to find you here. You are awake in your dream; now you also have to wake up in the hospital. You can only do so if you stay alert. Keep your eyes wide open, stand up, walk up und down the room...I will leave you here and go to the hospital as fast as I can. When you hear my voice there, you must open your eyes. Do you understand me?"

"Heavens above, Vic! Of course I understand you. You have come to save me. I begin to remember. We were chased. We were driving in a car and—"

The many-colored birds on the ledges spread their wings, began to make sounds, and flew up.

"That's the spirit," said Vic. "Your brain is active again. Everything in this world is coming alive again. One more time, Grandfather, do you understand what I expect from you?"

Jacques Poiron rose to his feet. He stared at his feet and carefully started to walk. In the beginning he had trouble keeping his balance. Soon he did much better.

"Believe me, Vic, I will keep on pacing up and down this room till I hear your voice. Drag me out of my dream world, boy, for I cannot do this on my own. Bring me back to reality. Vic . . . I have lost my body!"

Suddenly Vic saw panic in the eyes of his grandfather.

"Please, keep calm. It is a good idea to go walk through the room. Look out the windows and change everything you see. Make birds appear, grow trees, break down the entire town—anything, as long as you keep yourself busy."

"I'll do that, Vic. Please stay with me for another little while. First I have to come to grips with everything, and it scares me to be alone again just yet."

"You were afraid of the shadows that slid through your streets. There was no reason for that. They were the same entities that have brought me to you."

"The Neanderthals?"

"Yes."

"Still, I will never feel comfortable here again."

"Maybe in the end, the human spirit is not able to be in a dream world like this night after night."

Together they walked up to a window and looked outside. Tens of loudly chirping birds flew along the palace, went down to the park, and landed in the trees. Vic began to tell about the death of Maurice Aron and the banishment from the dream worlds of Antoine Chevalier and Sergio Paladino.

"So it was Maurice Aron," sighed the old man.

Vic understood that his grandfather was shocked by everything he had said. He had hoped for that. Now Jacques had plenty to worry about, and that would keep him awake; there was more chance that he would wake up in the hospital.

He said goodbye.

"I hope to hear your voice soon!" shouted Jacques, as Vic flew away through a window.

But to his horror, Vic realized he had no idea how to leave his grandfather's dream world. He shot up like an arrow. Soon the town was no more than a dark spot in a snowy white world.

"Ssh!" he hissed.

Immediately the entity appeared, enclosed him, led him back to his own dream world, and released him.

"I need you, Shh," said Vic. "Later. I know for sure that you understand me. We will meet again in the concert hall."

Vic woke up near the fireplace where he had fallen

asleep. He went immediately into action. He raced down the spiral stairs and ran through the reception hall. After he had locked the door behind him, he went to his own room, where he put away the key. Then he phoned the hospital to announce his arrival:

"I need help. There is a big chance that my grandfather will be coming out of his coma shortly."

He felt no need to give an explanation. Then he called Tobias Dupont. Tobias was instantly wide awake and promised to get up right away and see about a car. Vic went outside. It was still dark. The sky was covered with stars. The dogs were barking. A car started nearby. The headlights blinded him when Tobias showed up.

"Hello," said Tobias, when Vic got in. "We'll go straight to the hospital, like you asked me. Is . . . is the old man going to die?"

"Oh, no!" Vic cried out. "On the contrary! Stay with me and see for yourself how he will wake up!"

The gate was opened by a guard.

Lanterns were burning in the Golden Street. It was dark behind the windows of the villas. But at the house and the garden of the Laurins there was plenty of light.

"Stop here for a minute. I'll ask if Régine wants to come along with us," he said.

He called her, and soon the front door of the villa opened and she came running outside, followed by Louis. She stepped into the back and immediately wanted to know the same thing as Tobias:

"Did Jacques pass away?"

"No. I'm on my way to wake him up."

The car accelerated.

Louis waved at them.

"Did you receive a call from the hospital?" Régine wanted to know. "Have they diagnosed an improvement of his condition? That would be terrific!"

"I called the hospital myself. To tell them something is going to happen."

"You know how to surprise me over and over again."

"In the hospital they will be surprised as well," said Vic.

Régine asked no further questions, because she understood that Tobias should not know everything. Instead, she informed Vic about the strange behavior of Antoine Chevalier and Sergio Paladino. Again he surprised her. It made her head spin, and she leaned heavily against the back of her seat when she heard him say:

"I know. Don't forget to tell Armand or Claire Laurin that there is a golden bracelet at the bottom of their pond. It belongs to Sergio..."

She swallowed her questions.

The car stopped in the empty parking lot in front of the hospital. They stepped out and went inside. A nurse was waiting for them.

"Good evening, Mr. Emmett," she said. "You came to see your grandfather? Please come with me."

Only now did Vic realize that he, being the grandson of Jacques Poiron, had much power in Saint-Milles. This hospital was owned by his grandfather, and he could come and go as he pleased. There was a guard in the corridor who greeted him and immediately opened the door for him. There was a doctor present in the room, standing near the bed. He looked sleepy. He reached out his hand when he saw Vic approach.

"Mr. Emmett . . . my name is François Bucher, doctor on duty. What a strange time to pay a visit. I've been told that something special was going on."

"That is right. My grandfather will be coming out of his coma."

The doctor looked at him searchingly.

"His condition has not changed recently."

"I have no idea what has to be done after he has opened his eyes again," said Vic, without paying attention to the doctor's remark. "That is your work. Are you ready to take care of him when he has come out of the coma?"

"We are prepared for that. Every hour of the day. Or night ..."

"Then please step aside."

Automatically the man took a step to the left. Vic came standing near the bed. Jacques lay lifelessly in his back. He was as lean as a rake. His complexion was pale. At the other side of the bed was a trolley with equipment that registered his bodily functions. He was fed by an infusion. The needle was stuck in his right arm, which rested on top of the blanket.

Vic bent forward. His lips were close to Jacques's ear.

"It is time to wake up!" he said in a loud voice. "Open your eyes, look at me. I know that you can hear me. Wake up!"

He straightened himself again and took a step backward. François looked around the room and noticed that Régine and Tobias were no less disconcerted than himself.

A short sob sounded from the bed. The old man's Adam's apple moved. The thin lips opened, and a dry tongue licked them. Tremblingly and slowly the eyes opened.

"Vic ..." whispered Jacques Poiron.

The lips pressed together, the eyes closed.

"Stay awake!" said Vic. "Please, stay awake!"

He clapped his hands a few times. François came into action. He walked up to the door, opened it, and started to shout orders. Half a minute later there was assistance. Together with a female doctor he started to examine the old man. Nurses stood by to help. Jacques opened his eyes for the second time. He moved his arms, leaned on his elbows, and tired to sit up. Finally he succeeded. Both doctors shrank back. The eyes of Jacques were bright and lit up even more when he carefully turned his head and saw Vic. Now his bloodless lips began to smile.

"Vic..." His voice was powerful. "Here I am. I have made it."

Vic was right at his side, touching him gingerly with the tips of his stretched fingers.

"Yes," he said "Yes! You have made it indeed!"

Régine covered her face with her hands. Tears rolled down her cheeks and fingers. She was shaking all over.

"Now it's your turn," she heard Vic say to the doctors. "See to it that he stays alive. We all know how weak he is physically . . . but his spirit is strong! That will save him. He wants to live, and so he shall."

He turned around and walked to the door. He beckoned to Régine and Tobias.

"Come, let's give them some room."

30

The awakening of Jacques Poiron soon was called the Wonder of Saint-Milles and even became world news. Nadine Aron was the first one to wrote about it, in *Le Journal de Saint-Milles,* followed by the big French daily papers. After that the media circus was a fact. Radio and television stations from tens of countries sent their correspondents to Saint-Milles. The narrow streets of the little town were blocked up by the busy traffic. All the hotel rooms were taken. The fabulously rich man spoke with everybody. The gate of Ricard was wide open all day. Big mobile studios stood in line in the park.

For someone who had come out of a long coma, Jacques Poiron looked excellent. He was still too lean and was not able to stand on his feet for a long time. But there was a healthy color to his face, and sitting in an easy chair he patiently gave answer to the innumerable questions the press barraged him with.

He had become a living legend now and gladly anticipated any questions that consolidated this reputation.

A visit to him was an unforgettable experience.

First there was the imposing landscape of the

Dordogne.

Then the beauty of the little town of which he owned almost every building.

After the wealth of the Golden Street came the big park, and then there was Castle Ricard at the river. The doors were opened invitingly, and Jacques Poiron received his guests in an exuberantly decorated period room.

"The most bizarre stories about you are going the rounds, and—"

"They are all true."

At night Jacques and his grandson roamed about their dream worlds together. Despite Vic's presence, Jacques hardly dared to look around. He still did not feel at ease. The knowledge that he did not belong here grew stronger and scared him.

Even without the help of Ssh they probably would have been able to continue to find each other's world, because Jacques was able again to plunge into his dreams energetically. But Ssh was always in their neighborhood and guided them to each other. He followed them like a shadow.

"It has been enough," said Jacques one time, as they walked past his palaces. "Here I had the visions that made me able to build up my capital in Saint-Milles. I would give it all away if I could sleep again like a normal human being and dream my normal dreams. Vic, I have become too old to cope with all this. If I stay here much longer, my dream world will crumble away. I cannot bear to think of what will happen if my memory lets me down and I get stuck here. That is my greatest fright; ever since

I came out of my coma, I have feared the night that I will no longer be able to leave my dream world. Imagine, if even you couldn't get me out of here! Again, it has been enough."

"I have already foreseen that," said Vic. "It can be arranged. In cooperation with Ssh and the others."

"And you? What will you do?"

"I had the opportunity to look around in a dimension other people will never be able to reach. Together with you I wish to say goodbye to these worlds. That same night I will also try to compose the ultimate song. I want to make an attempt to reach absolute perfection. After that we will turn our backs to these worlds for good. These are not our worlds, Grandfather. We do not belong here. This is Neanderthal territory. We cannot do and think like them."

"It's a deal," said Jacques with a sigh. "I rely on you. It is my greatest wish to sleep normally again, just like any other human being…"

Régine had received an important task from the old man, and she had brought it to a good end together with a great number of fellow workers. She had drawn up a list of all his property, shares, and finances. Although she knew that everything together had to be a fabulous fortune, it took her breath clean away when she saw the result. It was far, far more than she ever thought it would be.

Her relationship with Vic was still good.

Nevertheless there were many questions she had never dared to ask him:

"How did you know that Maurice Aron had died in a police cell, while you yourself were in bed in the hospital?"

"How did you know that your grandfather would come out of his coma?"

"Are all the things you told me, and that you entrusted to Inspector Legrand, true after all?"

The capital of Jacques Poiron was too big to not believe in his supernatural talents.

Further, she understood that something must have been the matter with two respected businessmen from the Golden Street. After their strange behavior at the party at the Laurins they had made decisions no one would expect from them. Sergio Paladino gave away large sums of money to good causes and put all his possessions up for sale. He said he wanted to buy himself a piece of ground in Italy and set up a farm there.

"Agriculture. My ancestors were farmers, and I know that they were all happy. I am going to follow their example."

Antoine Chevalier wanted to retire from all his businesses as soon as possible and go on a world tour. On that journey he would take time to think about what he wanted to do in the future. He was already thinking of collecting art and financing archaeological projects. He'd had more than enough of his life on the Golden Street.

In the meantime Vic had taken the time to put on paper everything he had experienced from the day he arrived in Saint-Milles. He went into great detail and did not skip a single event. He wrote about entering the cave; about his dream world; about his grandfather, Mike

Brewer, and Maurice Aron. Altogether the manuscript counted tens of pages; he put it into an envelope and closed it with tape.

Then came the solemn moment when Jacques Poiron confirmed that Vic Emmett was his only heir. It happened in the library of Ricard. Notary Vera Perrine had arranged everything; Régine had visited her to help out as much as she could. The old man and his grandson stood not far away from the sorcerer of Les Trois Frères—the guard of secrets hidden behind the wall of books. They embraced each other and could not find the words to give expression to their feelings. The notary and Régine were present, as were several lawyers who acted as witnesses. Champagne was poured. Before Vic took a sip he looked up at the cave paintings and raised his glass to a herd of fleeing horses.

"I am home," he said then.

Not much later he gave the sealed envelope to Vera Perrine. He had written his name on it with big block letters.

"I entrust this to your keeping," he said. "I am the only person who is allowed to pick this envelope up again. I will probably never do so. After my death one of your staff is allowed to open the envelope and publish the contents. Can you arrange that for me and give me a written confirmation?"

The notary nodded and asked no questions.

"So shall it be done," she said.

That night Vic slept alone in his big bedroom in Ricard. As soon as he had rolled onto his side he felt an intense cold go right through him, and the next moment he was already floating above his town in his dream world. He sat down on his music stool at his grand piano, and immediately the hall was filled with gray entities. His grandfather was brought in by Ssh and sat down in the front row.

"We all know what we came here for," said Vic. "I want to thank you all for your kind help. It was a spectacular adventure to get insight into your special world of experience, just as it was unique to sink down so deeply into my own dream world. Now it is time to say goodbye. Please allow me to play and sing something for you..."

His fingers touched the keys. The first fragile tones rose up into the dome. He began to sing. The notes stringed together, the words came spontaneously. On his way to perfection Vic was confronted with shocking images; he saw his girlfriend Rita Cianello appear, together with his former band member, Kenneth Canning. Dying from an overdose, Rita looked at him with wide-open eyes and shouted his name. Vic played and sang. He saw himself sitting in the backseat of a car and one more time experienced the accident in which his parents died. He saw his life pass before his eyes, and it cleaned his soul. Only now did he realize fully that he was a chosen one, allowed to undergo this purification. With tear-stained eyes he looked into the hall.

Immediately he knew that the old man was having his own personal experiences as well and saw things that were meant for him only.

For the first and last time he saw the Neanderthals in their true shape!

They were beautiful, so human, so filled with powerful emotions. They reached out their arms to him and waved with their hands. A deep growling accompanied his playing.

They were all having their own personal experiences as well.

Everyone in the concert hall had the feeling that this, for a little while, was the center of the universe.

All fears, frustrations, and depressed thoughts disappeared.

Under the pressure of positive thoughts the dome burst apart, and a bright white light filled the concert hall.

Perfection had been reached.

Vic's playing and singing were of an unearthly beauty.

He went into raptures.

He went beyond perfection...

The Neanderthals got up. They took up Jacques Poiron and put him on the stage. They remained standing in front of the stage and waved their stretched fingers faster and faster. The roaring now drowned the singing voice and the music. Vic was pushed up by an invisible power. His fingers came loose from the keys. Together with Jacques he flew away, up to the source of the white light.

He woke up with a start. Staring into the darkness of his bedroom, he tried to remember what he had dreamt of a moment ago. His face was wet with tears. His heart was beating fiercely. He was full of unexplainable emotions. There were memories that, he realized, would never come. They would remain elusive forever. Strangely enough he had to think of something he once had said himself:

"Sometimes the words are on the tip of your tongue, and at the same time they are further than the mind can reach. You want to catch them, but they remain hidden forever behind the horizon."

He got up, put on his trousers, and stepped into the corridor. There was a light burning in the kitchen. There he found his grandfather, who was sitting at the table.

"Vic...What happened? Suddenly I awoke and felt an urgent need to see you. I left my tower and came down here. One way or another I was convinced that you would come here as well."

Vic sat down opposite to him.

They looked at each other and were silent for a long time.

Then Jacques asked:

"It is four o'clock in the morning. Would it be odd if I opened a bottle of Bergerac right now, so that we could empty it together?"

Vic shrugged his shoulders and smiled.

"Odd or not, what does it matter? No worry, for this is entirely between you and me..."

The Author – Koos Verkaik

Koos, a 'Dutchy' with spunk and an inexhaustible drive and fathomless imagination, is one of the most prolific authors of sci-fi and children's books in The Netherlands. His novels, All-Father and Wolf Tears, earned him the moniker, the Dutch Stephen King.

He wrote his first sci-fi novel, Adolar, in one weekend when he was 18 years old and the manuscript was published shortly thereafter.

Koos has published over 60 books, both children's books and novels, hundreds of comic scripts, and he has worked as a copywriter. He is currently working on several screenplays and new novels.

To read more about Koos and his work visit his website at www.koosverkaik.com or follow him on Facebook at https,//www.facebook.com/koos.verkaik.5

Also by Koos Verkaik

Novels in Dutch

Adolar

Terug naar het Dorp

Conflict Afrika

Mana, en Toen Brak de Hel los

Dromen   De Dans van de Nar Grapstad

De Meesterparasiet

Psycho Park

Alvader

Wolfstranen

Neanderthaler

Children's Book Series

Saladin Series

Saladin het Wonderpaard
Spookpaard

Saladin en Silver
Nottingham

Silver en het

De Nar van

Slimmetje Series

Het Konijn uit de Hoed

De Boze Beer

Schipbreuk
Walvis

De Hoge Hoed is weg
Kabouterland

Ridder Joris

De Schat van Kabouter Bollewijn

Paddestoelen

Professor in Paniek

De Tovertrein

De Verdwaalde

Sneeuwmannen in

Otto de Otter

Krimpende

Wolpertinger series

De Monsterherberg

De Onderlanden

Het Land van Franje

De Drakentuin

Roest IJzervreter

Drie Dolle Prinsen

Koning Leo Lawaai

Alex de Grote

Heros de Haas

Novels in English

The Nibelung Gold

Crash

All-Father

The Dance of the Jester

HIM, After the UFO

Heavenly Vision

Children's Book Series

Wolpertinger Series

The Monster Inn

The Downhills

Uncle Balloon

The Land of Fringe

The Dragon Garden

Rusty Iron

Three Mad Princes

Saladin Series

Saladin the Wonder Horse

Saladin and Silver

Silver and the Ghost Horse

The Jester of Nottingham

www.ingramcontent.com/pod-product-compliance
Lightning Source LLC
Chambersburg PA
CBHW020404260626
47156CB00007B/2222